Death in Dark Waters

Also by Patricia Hall

In the Ackroyd and Thackeray series

and

Death in Dark Waters

PATRICIA HALL

 St. Martin's Minotaur ❦ New York

This is a work of fiction and all characters, firms, organizations, and instants portrayed are imaginary. They are not meant to resemble any counterparts in the real world; in the unlikely event that any similarity does exist it is an unintended coincidence.

www.minotaurbooks.com

Library of Congress Cataloging-in-Publication Data

Hall, Patricia, 1940–
    Death in dark waters / Patricia Hall.—1st St. Martin's Minotaur ed.
       p. cm.
    ISBN 0-312-32155-4
  1. Thackeray, Michael (Fictitious character)—Fiction. 2. Ackroyd, Laura (Fictitious character)—Fiction. 3. Police—England—Yorkshire—Fiction. 4. Yorkshire (England)—Fiction. 5. Women journalists—Fiction. 6. Drug traffic—Fiction. I. Title.

PR6058.A46D439 2004
823'.914—dc22   2003066819

First published in Great Britain by Allison & Busby Limited

First St. Martin's Minotaur Edition: February 2004

10 9 8 7 6 5 4 3 2 1

Death in Dark Waters

Chapter One

The crowd of young people spilled out of the entrance to the Carib club into Chapel Street, where the red and green lights which shook in the strong wind scattered dancing patches of colour onto the rain-soaked tarmac. The kids were high on chemically induced adrenaline and the music which had just come to an explosive end inside, where the sweat-soaked, dreadlocked DJ had sunk into a seat close to his turntables utterly exhausted. In the narrow street outside, lined on each side by tall warehouses most of which had been recently converted into offices and shops, the dilapidated building which housed the Carib was squeezed between a mini-cab office and an indie record shop. The street was narrow here, pot-holed and puddled, although it was used as a day-time rat-run between Aysgarth Lane, the main road out of Bradfield to the north, and the university quarter half a mile away on another of the town's seven hills.

At four in the morning, it was apparently deserted until the jubilant clubbers spilled off the narrow pavement and across the road to avoid the showers of fizzy water being sprayed about by a couple of girls in mini-skirts and tops that were more strap than substance and unlikely to protect them from the wintry, rain-spattering gusts from the west. It was their shrieks of laughter which almost drowned the squeal of brakes as a taxi came fast around the bend in the road from the Aysgarth direction. Jeremy Adams never knew what hit him as the cab swerved wildly, skidding on the wet surface, missing three or four revellers by inches before it caught him from behind and tossed him like a rag-doll head-first onto the kerb.

"Man, what the hell is you doin'?" a tall black youth in combat gear cried out angrily as the vehicle slid to a halt. He pulled open the door and dragged out the driver, an Asian man little older than he was himself. From the passenger compartment shocked faces, dark eyes staring from beneath white headscarves, gazed out at the now silent crowd.

"Get an ambulance," a girl's voice cried, shrill and shaking in the silence, and half a dozen mobile phones were instantly pressed into use. A skinny blonde girl in a short black skirt and silver top knelt beside the boy who was lying absolutely still in the gutter with a pool of blood around his head. She seemed oblivious to the fact that the rain, which had been relentless for days, had resumed, soaking her hair and thin clothes within minutes. Someone passed her a coat which she tucked around the boy's body.

"Jez, Jez, come on Jez, it's all right, you're gonna be all right." Behind her, the taxi driver edged his way through the crowd and looked down for a moment at his victim before turning away, shaking, to vomit in the gutter. The tall youth who had pulled him from the cab followed him.

"You was driving too fast, man," he said loudly, his words echoed by other youngsters, black and white, who gazed in horror at the victim.

"He was right in the middle of the road," the driver muttered, wiping his face with his hand. "I got to get these women home. I drove from Manchester airport. It's late. It's very late. There's snow on the motorway. They wanted to get home quick."

Suddenly the mood of the crowd changed, like embers fanned into life by the sharp wind which funnelled down the street. Exhilaration slid perceptibly into a mutter of anger, sullen at first but menacing enough for the young driver, his face grey with shock and his dark eyes beginning to take on a hunted look, to begin to edge his way back to his cab. By now the numbers packed into the narrow defile outside the club had swelled as more sweating dancers emerged from the double doors. Murmured explanations passed on a version of events which cranked up the tension quickly amongst the teenagers who began to

10

clog the street and hem in the taxi and its occupants in spite of the downpour.

"I'll get the police," the taxi driver said, his voice high with anxiety. "Let me use my radio to get the police."

"We did 999," someone called out. "They're on their way."

"Don't let him drive off," came another shout and the crowd surged to surround the cab, pressing the driver backwards against the bonnet and rocking the vehicle until sounds of protest could be heard from the women inside.

Standing above the crowd on the steps of the club a tall dreadlocked man in a sleeveless vest under his unbuttoned Armani shirt, evidently as impervious to the chill Pennine wind as the scantily clad girls, put up a golf umbrella and glanced at his companion, standing almost as tall and as dark in the shadows except where the dim street-lights caught sallower skin and lighter eyes.

"Feel like sorting this little lot, sergeant?" the black man asked, making sure they were not overheard, and if there was a hint of irony in the courtesy his companion ignored it.

"No way," Kevin Mower said. He glanced up the street to where blue emergency lights could already be seen in the distance. "Not only am I not on duty, I'm actually on the sick. Let the plods deal. It's only an RTA."

"If one of those hyped-up little bastards hits the driver it'll be a lot more than that," his companion said. "I've seen it happen in a flash. I get the feeling that the brothers here don't like the Asians much."

Mower watched as the black man raised his voice and slipped easily into the broad accent in which he performed.

"Is you all goin' to block the street so's no ambulance can get through?" He spoke from the steps behind the crowd from under his blue and gold striped umbrella but was authoritative enough to cause many of those jammed into the narrow space to turn around. "I say they as didn't see what happened get off home now, and let the Old Bill through to sort it," went on the dreadlocked DJ, still a good head above the milling mob even as he stepped down to street level. The now urgent sound of a siren indicated that either an ambulance or the police or both were about to arrive. A collective shrug of sullen acceptance seemed to go through the assembled clubbers, most of them now thoroughly drenched and cooled down by the rain, and gradually those on the edge of the crowd, who had arrived last and seen least, began to drift away down Chapel Street in the direction of the brighter lights of Aysgarth Lane and the taxi ranks where they would find transport home.

Almost casually the DJ stepped down from his vantage point beside Mower and shouldered his way through those who remained as far as the taxi and pulled open the driver's door.

"If I was you, man, I'd sit quiet there till the police come down," he said, ushering the driver back into his seat and taking the keys out of the ignition in one easy movement. "You is safe now."

He moved on to where the injured boy lay, the dark pool around his head bigger now and beginning to trickle away towards the gutter, the mini-skirted girl more distraught. He held his umbrella protectively over them for a moment while he looked down at the boy. He shook his head almost imperceptibly before helping the girl to her feet.

"Here's the ambulance now, honey," he said. "You come inside and get dry and then I'll take you down the Infirmary to see how he's doing."

"I'm all right," the girl said, pulling away from the DJ's arm as the ambulance and a police car inched their way through the stragglers and halted beside the victim. "I'm with some friends." But when she scanned the crowd for her friends she could not find them. Suddenly most of the clubbers had melted away.

"Can you tell us who he is," asked one of the paramedics minutes later, crouching beside the injured boy, his feet in the pool of blood and rainwater which now surrounded the victim.

"His name's Jez, Jeremy, Jeremy Adams," the girl said, her voice high with panic. "I'm not sure of his address, but he goes to the grammar school, we're in the sixth form. His dad owns that big warehouse place on Canal Road. And he's going to be absolutely livid that we came clubbing down here."

Back on the steps the DJ took Kevin Mower's arm, let down his umbrella and shook it fastidiously before pulling the policeman back inside.

"Racist little bitch," he said without a smile. "You see her jump when I touched her? My car's out back. We can get through the fire doors."

"Cool," Mower said, turning his back on the incident with a sense of profound relief.

At much the same time that the ambulance pulled away from Chapel Street, siren blaring in anticipation of heroic efforts to save Jeremy Adams' life, a younger boy was crouching under the shelter of the overhead walkways of Holtby House, one of the blocks of crumbling flats which dominated Bradfield's skyline to the west. Stevie Maddison felt sick and he shivered as the chilly rain soaked through his thin jacket and t-shirt. He pulled nervously on his cigarette, shielding the glowing tip with his hand, anxious not to be seen. Unable to sleep, he had called his best friend on his mobile and arranged to meet him, hoping to blag some skunk from the lad he had gone around with at school, in the days when he bothered to go to school. These days he clung to Derek with the frantic clutch of a drowning man, because Derek had been where he was now, stick thin, light-headed and nauseous in turn, desperate for a fix and yet desperate not to have one. Derek had been a heroin user but now Derek was clean. But tonight Derek, who usually answered his urgent phone calls promptly, did not show and his mobile remained on voice-mail, the cool cultured woman's voice seeking messages that Stevie was in no state to give.

He pinched out the end of his roll-up between finger and thumb and was about to turn back towards his home three floors above to resume his elusive search for sleep when he caught a flicker of movement a hundred yards away at the entrance to Priestley House, the most westerly of the three surviving blocks on the Heights. At last, he thought, expecting Derek to emerge from the swing doors but before he could shout a greeting he realised that what he had seen was not someone coming out but three figures in hooded jackets going in, one tall, the others smaller and, he thought, younger. Stevie shrank back into the shadows. He knew most of the drug dealers on the estate only too well, but this group was too far away in the swirling rain for recognition. His heart thumped hard against his skinny ribcage as he watched and waited close to the doors of Holtby, ready to bolt into his burrow like a terrified rabbit at any threat closer to hand. For long minutes he heard only the relentless lashing of the rain against concrete and, far away, the whine of a car being driven until its engine screamed and tyres squealed. Some kids somewhere on the other side of town getting their kicks, he guessed. But then a shout snapped his eyes upwards to the roof of Priestley where, in spite of the rain, he could just make out a figure silhouetted against the reddish glow of the night sky, then another and another, until three or four shapes merged into one and then one became detached, apparently swimming through the downpour, arms and legs flailing, as he fell to earth like a wounded bird.

"Oh God, oh God," Stevie muttered, wondering if this was all hallucination but sure in the sick pit of his churning stomach that it was not. "Oh God, oh God," he said as he waited, back pressed against the wall, until the remaining figures on the roof had disappeared before he pushed open the door to Holtby and slipped inside, to race up the concrete stairs to his mother's flat. "Oh God, oh God," he said as he glanced over the walkway balcony and saw the three figures he had seen enter Priestley House come out again, laughing, hoods thrown back now and at least one dark face clearly recognisable as he clutched a mobile phone to one ear. "Oh God, oh God," he said as he fell onto his sweaty crumpled bed and lay there shuddering, not wanting to know what he knew and terrified of what he didn't. The long scream of whoever had fallen repeated itself like a faint echo in his ears. But what really made him retch with fear and grief was the belief, much more than a suspicion the more he thought about it, that it was Derek who had plunged to earth, that it was his friend who had died.

DCI Michael Thackeray stood in his superintendent's office next morning with a distinct feeling of déjà vu. Arriving in Bradfield from a far-flung corner of the county a few years before, he had learned to live with the glimmer of suspicion which had never seemed to leave Jack Longley's slightly protuberant blue eyes. However much Thackeray thought he had served out his time after almost destroying a promising career some ten years earlier, he had known then that he would have to prove – and keep on proving – to his new boss that he had buried the past and could be trusted. Second chances were hard to come by in the police force and no one had been less convinced than he was himself that he deserved one. But after a couple of years, with those blue eyes watching him every inch of the way, and some successful investigations and even more interesting accommodations achieved, he thought he had seen the suspicion fade for good. Yet this morning it was back and he did not know why. That worried him.

Longley shifted uneasily in his seat and ran a finger round the back of his shirt collar as if it were too tight.

"Grantley Adams, he's been on to the chief constable already," he said. "And that's likely only the start of it."

"Right," Thackeray said cautiously. He knew that Grantley Adams ran one of the largest building supplies firms in Yorkshire, if not in the country, a self-made man employing hundreds, with all the expectations of thanks from a grateful nation that seemed to imply these days. "But this is a road traffic accident we're talking about? Nothing for CID?"

"That's what it looked like. But the doctors are saying the lad was off his head on Ecstasy. That's what's really rattled Adams's cage."

"So it's not the taxi driver he's gunning for?" Thackeray had flicked through the previous night's incident reports as a precaution before answering Longley's pre-emptory summons at a time of the morning when most of CID's officers were contemplating the day's prospects over a cup of tea and a bacon sandwich and a bawdy discussion of the previous night's action – or lack of it.

"No. That's summat to be thankful for. He's been booked for dangerous driving, apparently, but Adams seems to accept that his lad probably wouldn't have noticed an Eddie Stobart juggernaut coming up Chapel Street, the state he was in."

"But he's alive?" Thackeray asked, hoping that the his face gave away nothing of the turmoil inside at the thought of another man losing a son.

"Not so's you'd notice," Longley said. "In intensive care, two broken legs, fractured skull, possible internal injuries. The taxi was moving at quite a lick, apparently."

"So not talking?"

"No chance. But his dad is. Shouting and screaming, more like. He's good at that, is Grantley Adams, when someone's upset him." Thackeray smiled faintly. He could imagine just how good a man like Adams was at throwing his weight about if it suited him.

"So what does he want us to do?" he asked without enthusiasm.

"Find the pusher. Close the club down. Lock up whoever we can find to blame and throw away the key."

"Is that all? Doesn't he know it's likely the lad's best friend who got him the tablets?"

"That's not what our Grantley wants to hear right now."

"Mind you, it'd please the folk at the mosque," Thackeray

said. "I'm told they've been complaining about the Carib to the community relations people for months."

"It'd infuriate the blacks, though," Longley said. "There's no love lost there. If it'd been a black lad got knocked down by an Asian driver I reckon we'd have had a riot on our hands last night. They'd likely had lynched him."

"Presumably the Adams boy wasn't there on his own. Do we know who he was with?"

"Most of his mates melted away, apparently, which no doubt tells you something," Longley said. "His girlfriend hung on, went to hospital with him. Uniform have got the details. They're both sixth formers at Bradfield Grammar. You'd think they'd know better."

Thackeray shrugged non-commitally. Young people and risk went together, in his experience, and he had seen no evidence that affluent middle class kids from the leafy side of town were much different from the rest.

"We're up to our eyes with these burglaries in Southfield. There's been another possibly drug related death up on the Heights. And as far as that goes, I'm still trying to get a handle on Barry Foreman. But I'll put someone onto the girlfriend and see if she knows where the tablets came from. But you know what it's like. This stuff's everywhere. Even if they bought it in the club they probably don't know who the dealer was. They don't wear name badges."

"Aye, well you can leave Barry Foreman and the heroin problem to the drug squad for now. If there's anything in that, they'll cover it in this operation they've got going up on the Heights. So give me something for Grantley Adams and get him off my back, Michael, will you? Check out the girlfriend, check out the club. I reckon Grantley had his lad down for an Oxford degree and next Tory prime minister but one. He'll not want some upstart slap-head from the south to up-stage him for long now our Willy from Rotherham has set a precedent. So he'll want answers if all that's had to be put on the back burner."

"Only son, is he?" Thackeray asked, his eyes opaque.

"A couple of little lasses, I think, but yes, Jeremy's the blue-eyed boy in that family. Nothing's too good."

"Right, I'll get someone to delve into the club scene," Thackeray said reluctantly. "But I don't hold out high hopes."

Longley looked at the younger man with a hint of anger in his eyes.

"Pull your finger out, Michael," he said, not bothering to hide his irritation. "There are times when even you have to bend a bit, you know. It's all politics, of course it is, but these beggars can make life difficult. And this one's got a son in a coma. He's bound to kick up a stink. I'd have thought you'd have understood that if anyone did."

Thackeray's face tightened at that but he did not respond. He did not dare in case his own anger, which burned deep down but with a steady heat, spilled into the torrent of abuse he felt welling up like bile at the back of his throat.

"Do your best," Longley said, aware he had trespassed into areas he normally left well alone.

"Sir," Thackeray said quietly as he closed Longley's office door with exaggerated care behind him. In the deserted corridor outside he took a deep breath to tamp down the fierce emotion Longley had stirred, before composing his face into the impassivity which passed for normality with him and strode back down the stairs to his own office.

Laura Ackroyd parked her VW Golf at the back of Priestley House and took stock. On the minus side, it was getting dark and from the estate's windswept vantage point a scatter of lights, hanging like strings of jewels across the valley, flickered in the wind beneath scudding dark clouds which were still lashing the town with showers. On the plus side, she could not see any of the roaming bands of teenagers who made the estate a threatening place for a lone female after dark. Even so, she got out of the car cautiously and activated the alarm before walking the short distance to the cluster of prefabricated huts which sheltered in the lee of the tall blocks of flats. She pulled up the collar of her coat and wrapped her pashmina more tightly around her shoulders against the biting northerly before setting off across the muddy pathway across the grass.

She had driven from the Bradfield Gazette to the Heights as soon as she had finished work in response to a summons from her grandmother. It was not like Joyce Ackroyd to ask for help and Laura had been alarmed by the unexpected tremor in her voice when she had asked Laura to collect her.

"Is everything all right, Nan?" she had asked and had not been convinced by Joyce's evasive response.

As she approached the Project, which was where Joyce had asked to be picked up from, Laura could see that something was far from all right. The main door to the first of the prefabricated huts was swinging open and appeared to have been decorated by some sort of make-over artist in a more than normal frenzy. Red paint in loops and swirls dripped from the doors and walls and windows, still glistening even in the dim light. As she approached, Laura was not surprised to hear voices raised in anger.

Taking care not to brush against the recent redecoration, Laura stepped inside, pushed her damp and wind-blown red hair out of her eyes and drew a sharp breath. The Project, which she had described to the Gazette's readers when it had opened six months before, was intended to bring the benefits of new technology and modern job training to the dissaffected youth on Bradfield's most unruly estate. Fitted out with computers begged and borrowed from local companies, and staffed mainly by residents of the estate itself, it had appeared to be taming at least some of the intractable young who had been ejected from every school and college and emergency education programme in town.

"Jesus wept," Laura said as she surveyed the devastated reception area in horror. Potted plants had been hurled over the computer on the front desk, smashing the screen and burying the keyboard in dirt, and some of the furniture had been reduced to match-wood before having what was left of the red paint poured all over it. "The little bastards," she said, anger bubbling up inside.

She barely realised that she had spoken aloud, but a silence fell in one of the classrooms leading off the reception area and a door was quickly flung open. To her surprise she recognised the dark-haired man with an unexpected growth of beard who came into the room looking as angry as she felt herself. For a moment they gazed at each other in silence and it was Laura who regained her voice first.

"What on earth are you doing here," she asked sergeant Kevin Mower. "I thought you were off sick."

"You'd better believe it," Mower said quickly, speaking quietly and glancing behind him as if anxious not to be overheard.

"You're not here officially then? Undercover or something? The whiskers are new. Suits you."

"I'm not here at all, as far as Michael Thackeray's concerned," Mower said, too quickly, Laura thought. She raised a sceptical eyebrow.

"He told me you were in rehab."

Mower shrugged.

"I was then. Now I'm not," he said. "Don't look so stricken, Laura. It's not what you think. I'm as dry as the Gobi, clean as the proverbial whistle."

"So what...?"

"Nothing heavy. I was just up here doing a bit of moonlighting, trying to get my head together before I have to decide whether to sign back on or not. And then this. I asked them not to call the police until I made myself scarce. They don't know up here I'm a copper and I don't want the nick to think I've gone soft as well as the other. This being the Wuthering, my mates here'll just think I've unfinished business with the fuzz. I suppose Joyce called you, did she? I asked her not to mention my day-job to the people up here but I hadn't reckoned on her calling you."

"She wouldn't tell me what was wrong. When did this happen?" Laura glanced around at the devastation.

"We close the place at four-thirty, after the afternoon classes finish. Open up again at seven. We were in the back having a coffee and talking things over when we heard some banging and crashing about out here." Mower shrugged. "They can't have been in here more than a couple of minutes," he said. "I don't know why I was so surprised. We should have expected it, I suppose."

"This was some of the kids you hadn't got off the street, then?"

"You can't win 'em all," Mower mumbled. "You'd better come in. Your grandmother hasn't taken it very well, I'm afraid. Donna's plying her with tea and reassurances, but at her age it's hard to cope with, I guess. You met Donna Maitland, didn't you?"

Laura nodded, recalling the local mother who had hauled herself out of the despair and depression which incapacitated so many on the Heights, got herself qualified and had then been appointed as the manager of the Project; a nervous, driven woman whose own nephew had been a casualty of the drug-culture which crippled so many of the estate's young people.

Mower led her through a tidy classroom, untouched by the marauders, and into a small kitchen where Joyce Ackroyd was huddled over a mug of tea at a Formica-topped table beside a blonde woman in a smart blue suit, thin almost to the point of emaciation, who drew hard and frequently on a roll-up cigarette.

"Donna," Laura said quietly. She had been impressed by Donna's energy and her fragility on her first visit. Now the dark circles under her eyes seemed to have deepened in the intervening weeks and her bottle blonde cascade of hair offered a brittle sort of defiance around a carefully made-up, not unattractive face now trembling on the edge of angry tears.

Laura put an arm round her grandmother's thin shoulders and had her hand seized fiercely in return.

"D'you know who would do this?" Laura asked.

"There's no helping some," Donna said wearily. "There's a few skag-heads out there who'd wreck owt just for t'sheer fun of it."

"Will you write something, love?" Joyce asked urgently. "Our budget won't run to putting this lot right. We'll need some extra help."

"I thought the council were backing you," Laura said.

"Only t'running costs," Donna said. She dabbed at her eyes with a tissue and ran her fingers through her hair in lieu of a comb, evidently determined to resume the role of manager in spite of her evident distress. "Capital came from t'Lottery and there'll be no more of that."

"You're not insured?"

"You must be joking," Donna said, angry now. "Have you never heard of red-lining? They drew a red line round the Heights so long ago the ink's pretty well washed out. No banks or insurance companies'll touch us – or any other poor sod up here. Why d'you think the loan sharks make such a killing? They're the only beggars'll help anyone get by. And I don't think they'll be holding a street collection for us."

Laura glanced at Mower.

"Hadn't you better call the police?" she asked. He shook his head.

"Donna'll deal with that shortly. We just thought you might like to take Joyce home before we get into all that hassle. Not that there's much chance of finding the little toe-rags who did it. They'll have had the sense to wash the paint off their hands by now."

"I could give you their names with a ninety-nine per cent chance of being right," Donna said. "But making it stick's another thing. They'll all have been at home wi'their mates – or their mums – if a copper comes asking."

"I'll give Joyce a ride home," Laura said. "If anyone wants to talk to her they know where to find her."

She helped her grandmother into her coat and handed her the stick she needed to walk with now arthritis had made movement difficult.

"It's too late for today but I'll talk to my editor first thing in the morning and come back up to see you," she said to Donna. "I'm really sorry about this. It all looked as though it was going so well."

"It's the first thing we've ever had up here that's got some o't kids off the street and sitting still for an hour or two," Donna said, her voice husky with emotion. "Thrown out of school long ago, most of'em. Given up on reading and writing. But they like computers. Got a bit o'street cred, they have. And because we're on t'spot, not a bus-ride down into t'town, they'll come in, won't they? Come in and stay in, some of'em. We've got a few of them into rehab, and I've real hopes of jobs for a few already. And now this." She lit a fresh cigarette and drew smoke into lungs so damaged that Laura could hear them whistle from the other side of the room.

"Tomorrow," she promised, propelling her grandmother through the door.

Joyce struggled into the passenger seat of the Golf and said nothing as Laura drove her the quarter mile to her tiny bungalow which stood in the shadow of the Heights' three massive blocks of run-down flats. She too was breathing heavily by the time she had opened the front door, turned on the lights and allowed Laura to help her off with her coat and into her favourite armchair by the gas fire. Laura gazed at her grandmother for a moment, absorbing the pallor and the lines of weariness beneath the shock of white hair. But Joyce's green eyes, so like her own, still gleamed with anger.

"I'll get onto the powers that be at the Town Hall tomorrow," she said. "I'll not see Donna defeated."

"Will they listen?" Laura asked carefully. There had been a time when Joyce Ackroyd had been the uncrowned queen of

Bradfield Town Hall, but it was years since she had been forced into retirement by ill-health and she knew that the new faces of municipal Labour regarded the likes of Joyce, an unreconstructed admirer of heroes like Nye Bevan and Tony Benn, with as much incomprehension as she regarded them.

"If we don't make the Project work, they'll privatise it, as like as not, or just close it down regardless," Joyce said. "I want to see it succeed. But we'll need some help. They've got all these schemes for reconstruction, partnerships, I don't know what, but when you want some cash for something simple that actually works you can't get a damn' penny..." For a second she covered her eyes and Laura thought that she had never seen her combative grandmother so depressed.

"You know they found another young lad dead last night, don't you?" Joyce asked suddenly.

"Not the one who was knocked down in town?"

"No, the one who fell off the roof of Priestley House. Overdose, they're saying, out of his head. That's the fifth or sixth this year and no one seems to be doing a damn thing about it. I don't know what that man of yours thinks he's about, but heroin up here is wiping out a whole generation. Aren't the police even interested?"

"I'm sure they are, Nan," Laura said, with more confidence than she felt. She suspected that the kids on the Heights who killed each other quickly with knives or slowly with heroin and crack rated much lower in official priorities than the grammar school boy from a wealthy home who had been run down the night before.

"Well, put a bomb under them for us, will you, love?"

"I'll see what I can do." Laura knew that her grandmother did not altogether approve of her relationship with DCI Michael Thackeray believing, with the same certainty with which she believed in the future of British coal and the need to renationalise the railways, that men and women should have the decency to tie a legal knot before embarking on life together. But she would use the connection ruthlessly if it suited her. Laura had been relieved to discover that Michael took Joyce's reservations in his stride and found it in himself to approve very thoroughly of her.

She made more tea and then slumped into a chair on the other side of the fire and shook her head in mock despair.

"Are you ever going to take it easy?" she asked.

"What do you want me to do?" Joyce snapped back. "Sit in this little box goggling at t'other one till the Grim Reaper pops in to put me in the final box of all? If there's owt I can do to help folk like Donna while I'm still standing I'll do it. And it'll be a pity when they run out of folk like me, an' all."

Laura grinned, shame-faced.

"Will someone at the Town Hall see you, d'you think?"

"Oh, aye, they'll see me all right, if only to shut me up," Joyce said grimly. "Can you give me a lift down in your lunch hour tomorrow, pet?"

Chapter Two

Laura woke early to find herself tucked snugly into the curve of Michael Thackeray's body with one of his hands comfortably beneath her breast. The closeness of him filled her with desire but she could see that it was not yet seven and chose not to rouse him so early. They had both fallen into bed exhausted the previous night and had fallen asleep before either of them could respond to the whispers of their bodies which suggested anything different.

He had come home in a bad mood, although evidently reluctant to tell her why. And he had only seemed to half listen as she had passed on her grandmother's unease about the state of Wuthering, the estate which caused the police as well as the local council the greatest trouble in a troublesome little town which prosperity still resolutely seemed to pass by. But he had not seemed to be very interested. Secrets and lies, she thought ruefully, lies and secrets: they had haunted their relationship since the beginning and even now that they had achieved a sort of truce together she still suspected that their jobs might one day drive them apart in some way which would be hard to forgive.

She did not think too hard about the future at all these days, tiptoeing round it in a way she knew could not be sustained indefinitely. What she wanted and what Michael wanted seemed as far apart as ever. His divorce had drifted into the realms of sometime, perhaps never, and she had avoided talk of children since he had returned to her new flat only slightly shame-faced after their last serious difference of opinion. Apparently relaxed, he was helping her choose rugs and pictures to replace what she had lost when her last home had been trashed. But she knew, and she suspected he knew, that there was too much left unsaid for her to be sure of him any longer. Soon, she thought, they must thrash out where they were going together, if they were going anywhere at all.

Carefully she slipped from his arms and went to take a shower. By the time she emerged, Thackeray was awake, his eyes wary as he watched her come back into the bedroom, throw off her towel and begin to dress.

"It's very early," he said and she was not sure whether there was an invitation there. Once she might have been certain.

"Busy day," she said, pulling on black trousers and a silk shirt of deep green and beginning to brush her tousled copper curls with rather too much vigour. "I promised to take Joyce to the Town Hall at lunch-time so I need an early start. Otherwise Ted Grant will be ranting and raving again. I told you last night."

Thackeray put his hands behind his head and watched her pin her hair up in a severe pleat.

"Tell her we really are working on the heroin problem up there," he said carefully.

"So why don't they think you are?" Laura came back quickly.

"It's out of my hands, Laura. The drug squad do things their own way, you know that. They report to county, not to Jack Longley. I dare say he knows what's going on but he hasn't told me."

"And reassuring the local community isn't part of the game plan?"

"I doubt the drug squad would recognise a community if it jumped up and bit them," Thackeray said.

"Is that what was pissing you off last night?"

"Oh, partly that and partly Jack Longley cuddling up to local businessmen," Thackeray said. "His mates from the Lodge, a lot of them."

"You must be joking?"

"The so-called business community can do no wrong these days. It's official. You know how it is. Longley meets them at his wretched Masonic meetings and every now and again they think they can decide police priorities for him. This time it's Ecstasy at the Carib Club taking priority over heroin up on the Heights."

"The schoolboy who was knocked down?"

"Son of some local worthy, so we pull all the stops out to find the pusher. Chances are the lad got it off a friend who got it off a friend who bought it off someone he'd never seen before weeks ago in a pub he can't remember the name of. But I suppose we'll have to go through the motions to please Grantley Adams."

"Grantley Adams was a mate of my father's," Laura said, suddenly thrown back to a childhood where she had seemed to be constantly at war with her father's ambition to make a million before he was forty. "I remember him coming to the house years ago when I was just a kid. He's quite old to have a son still at school."

"Second family, I think," Thackeray said. "You know how it goes: boredom sets in and he swaps his middle-aged missus for a new trophy wife and another batch of kids."

"And this one's let dad down big time? Still, it must be dreadful for the family."

"Yes," Thackeray said quickly and Laura flinched at the look in his eyes. "But it's police priorities I'm talking here, not family tragedies. Those I never could do much about."

She sat on the edge of the bed and kissed him.

"I'm sorry," she said. "I think work's getting us both down. See if you can get away at a sensible time tonight and we'll go out for a meal. That new Thai place on the Manchester Road is supposed to be very good."

Thackeray relaxed slightly and returned her kiss with interest.

"Things must be looking up if Thai food's arrived in Bradfield," he said. "I thought that was only available in poncy Leeds."

"We could try fusion cooking if you want to go that far…"

"Let me get used to one thing at a time," he said, laughing.

"You know I'm only a roast beef and Yorkshire pud country lad at heart."

"Oh, I think you washed the last traces of muck off your boots a long time ago. And I'm sure that if you really want to get to grips with heroin on the Heights rather than recreational drugs in the pubs and clubs you'll find yourself a way. But watch out for Grantley Adams. I can remember taking a very distinct dislike to him. A bullying man, as I recall. Managed to pat me on the head and tweak my hair at the same time without my dad noticing anything at all. Getting back at me for some cheeky remark I'd made; no doubt some socialist heresy I'd picked up at my grandmother's knee and parroted without really understanding. But very nasty, as I recall."

"I'll bear it in mind," Thackeray said.

The newsroom at the Bradfield Gazette was still quiet soon after eight when Laura got in, with only two reporters on an early shift concentrating on their computer screens. But the early morning peace was soon shattered when the editor, Ted Grant, arrived with the manic gleam in his eyes which Laura knew spelt trouble. Head down, she hoped that it would not involve her brief on the feature pages.

But she was unlucky. By the time Grant had convened the morning meeting and Laura had taken her place at the untidy table in his office alongside her colleagues, she knew that the excitement which had brought a sharp flush to his cheeks and the first signs of sweat to the shirt which strained to encompass his beer belly, would include her. He had placed Bob Baker, the paper's crime reporter, on his left-hand side from where he nursed a contented smirk which boded ill, Laura thought, for the rest of those there.

"We'll make it a Gazette campaign," Grant said. "The war on drugs. The threat to our youth. What can Bradfield do to defeat the evil pushers? You know the sort of thing. Run a hotline for people who want to pass on information if the police are too dozy to do it. The Globe's got it off to a tee, but we can do our own version. We'll collate all the news stories, and Laura, you can run a series of features on families that have been affected. Start with this lad who was nearly killed at this club the other night, Grantley Adams' boy."

Laura opened her mouth to object but, glancing round the table, realised that she was the only one there with any reservations about Grant's plan.

"There's been another death up on the Heights too," she said eventually.

"Aye, well we'll get to that one later," Grant said. "The little toe-rags up there have got nowt else to do, have they? But this lad in intensive care was a high flyer, apparently. Going to Oxford, wanting to be a lawyer. That's a better story for us. See if you can get an interview with his mum and dad – for today if you can, but tomorrow if not."

"Right," Laura said, knowing that facing Grantley Adams again after all these years was unlikely to be a pleasant experience in the best of circumstances, and she would be a long way from those today.

"You don't look too chuffed with that assignment," said Bob Baker a few minutes later, with an unwanted hand on Laura's shoulder and an insinuating whisper in her ear, as they made their way back to their desks. "Surely your boyfriend is going to be chasing this one whatever we run with, isn't he?" Baker, a sleek twenty-five year old with one eye on his career and the other on anyone female who would make eye-contact, was not Laura's favourite colleague. She suspected that he saw in her a chance to pursue both of his objectives at once, not because she encouraged his advances but because he knew that she had a unique line to the police that he might be able to exploit if she did not concentrate hard enough on what she was saying in his vicinity.

"Mr. Adams is an old friend of the family, as it goes," she said sweetly, capitalising for once on her local connections which Baker, a recent arrival, could not match.

"And a crack-down on E? Is that on your boyfriend's agenda?"

"I've really no idea," she said. "We've much better things to do than talk shop after work. Why don't you ask him yourself." She knew that this would annoy Baker whose relationship with Michael Thackeray could best be described in terms of an armed truce.

Baker shrugged and moved away, but not without a parting shot.

"What I don't understand is why Bradfield CID's been cut right out of operations up on the Heights," he said. "Funny, that."

"D'you want to sit in on this one, boss?"

DC Val Ridley hesitated outside the door of an interview room, trim and contained as ever in spite of the dark circles beneath her eyes that Thackeray now regarded as permanent.

"Who've you got?" he asked.

"The girlfriend of the lad who was knocked down in Chapel Street. Jeremy Adams."

Thackeray hesitated and then nodded, curious almost in spite of himself.

"Do we need a responsible adult?" he asked.

"She's seventeen but she's got her mother with her anyway," Val said quickly. "I told them an informal chat. No caution. Nothing heavy. At least she had the decency to hang around after the accident. Most of the little beggars vanished into the night.

"And how's the boy?"

"Still critical." Her voice was flat, without emotion. Thackeray knew that Val was good at that, but very occasionally the mask cracked to reveal a warmer and more erratic human being underneath the chilly exterior. He let her lead the way into the interview room where a young girl with long blonde hair and a sulky expression was sitting at the table alongside a woman almost as slim, certainly as blonde and apart from some faint lines around the eyes not apparently much older.

"Mrs. James, this is DCI Thackeray," Val said. "And this is Louise."

Thackeray took the fourth seat at the table and nodded to Val Ridley to continue. Teenagers fascinated and disturbed him not least because his own son, had he survived, would by now have been hovering on the edge of these turbulent, truculent few years and he had not the faintest idea how he would have learned to cope with that. Badly, he suspected, if Ian had begun to display any of the alarming and often dangerous tendencies to self-destruction he saw amongst the young who crossed his path as a police officer. Would that have given him more insight with a child of his own, or just made him more afraid of what could go wrong? He did not know. But here, at least, he thought, was a child who appeared to have had all the advantages so many of CID's clients had not. Had Louise James slipped over the edge in spite of that? Or was he simply assuming that because she fell into that age range she must be sad, or mad or bad. He smiled uneasily at the girl's mother and tried to concentrate on what Val Ridley was saying.

"So tell me about Wednesday evening, Louise," Val said. "What made you and Jeremy decide to go to the Carib Club?"

"It was my birthday, wasn't it?" Louise said, in a barely audible mumble.

"She doesn't usually go out in the week but because it was her birthday, her seventeenth, we made an exception," Mrs. James broke in quickly. "They get so much homework. They're at Bradfield Grammar, you know…"

"But why the Carib?" Val persisted. "Is it somewhere you've been before?"

Louise glanced at her mother.

"Once," she said. "Once or twice, at a weekend."

"We'd have stopped her if we'd known," Mrs. James broke in again, her voice harsh. "That part of town. That sort of club."

32

"Mrs. James, I'd like to hear what Louise has to say for herself," Thackeray broke in sharply. "If you don't mind."

The girl shot him a glance which appeared almost grateful while her mother turned away, affronted.

"We like the music," Louise said. "And the DJs. Wednesday was Dizzy B. He's cool."

"So you went down there at what time?" Val asked.

"About ten, I suppose."

"Had you been anywhere else first?"

"We had a couple of drinks in the Parrot and Banana."

"No difficulty getting served, I suppose," Val said dryly. "And was it just the two of you went on to the club, or were you part of a larger group?"

"We've tried to bring her up to drink sensibly," the girl's mother said quickly.

Louise ignored her but hesitated, gazing down at her clasped hands on the table in front of her.

"There was a whole gang going on from the pub," she said eventually. "No one I knew very well."

"Names?"

"Just first names. No one from our school. Not close friends."

Thackeray knew the girl was lying and guessed that the two women did too.

"We'll give you a pencil and paper later," he said. "You can have a think about the names of anyone you can remember who was around that evening. Will you do that, Louise?"

The girl nodded, not looking up, and Thackeray knew that the list would be short and the names unidentifiable, but he did not think it worth pressurising the girl at this stage.

"We know from the hospital that Jeremy took at least one Ecstasy tablet during the evening," Val Ridley went on, her voice calm. "Did you know that?"

Louise nodded, a single tear drop splashing down onto the table in front of her. Irritably, she rubbed it away with a finger

"Did you take any illegal substances, Louise?"

Louise nodded again.

"Just one tab," she said, and there was a sharply indrawn breath from her mother. Thackeray shot her a warning glance.

"You think Jeremy took more?" Val persisted.

"I think he had two. He was wild…At the club later he was dancing like a mad-man. I couldn't keep up with him. But we knew what to do. We drank plenty of water…"

"So you know we have to ask, Louise. Where did you get the pills from?"

"They were just passing them round in the pub," the girl said, glancing at her mother. "I'd never had one before but Jez said it would be cool."

"Who was passing them round?"

"Everyone," Louise said, sulky now.

"But someone must have been taking the money for them. These things don't come free."

"I didn't see anyone," she said.

"Did you pay for them, Louise?"

"I never." The girl flushed and more tears came.

"So did Jeremy buy them?"

"No, no, I never saw him pay anyone. I don't know who bought them, where they came from, it was nothing to do with me."

"Right, we'll leave that for the minute, Louise," Val Ridley said, still calm, her voice still low as the girl scrubbed at her eyes with a tissue that her mother handed to her.

"When you got to the Carib, there was someone on the door, right?"

"Two black guys," Louise said.

"And did they check you for drugs?"

"Yeah, yeah, they asked, and looked in my bag. I had a little black bag with me, but we'd taken them by then, so there wasn't anything to find, was there? They were wasting their time."

"Maybe," Val Ridley said. "But inside the club. Did you see anyone offering drugs in there? Pills, cannabis, anything at all?"

Louise shook her head.

"It was dark, and crowded and we were dancing, I didn't see anything much. It was a great night until that happened…" She glanced at her mother.

"It's not fair the way everyone's going on about the drugs," Louise burst out suddenly, her voice choked with anger. "It was that taxi driver's fault. He came round the corner too fast. He could have hit me too, lots of people jumped out of the way. Jez was unlucky that's all. He didn't see it coming. It was nothing to do with drugs. What harm does one tablet do? We had a great time. We were going home. If it hadn't been for that driver no one would have been any the wiser. We'd have been at school the next morning and no one would have known anything about it."

Thackeray stood up abruptly.

"We will want your daughter to sign a written statement," he said to Louise's mother. "And in view of what she's told us about the availability of illegal substances the other night we'll want to be sure that she has nothing else hidden at home – or at Jeremy's home, for that matter."

"What do you mean, hidden?" Mrs. James asked, her voice shrill.

"We'll need to search your house," Thackeray said.

"Oh, Mum," Louise wailed, crumpling across the table and sobbing uncontrollably. "I really, really only took one. I only took one, ever."

"I'll leave you with DC Ridley," Thackeray said and left the room without looking back. A quick search for illegal substances would give Grantley Adams something to think about before he spoke to him, he thought with some satisfaction. For all his sympathy for a father with a child in intensive care, he was not averse to laying down a few ground rules before tackling Jack Longley's Masonic acquaintances. And the first of those was to make clear that no one in Bradfield was above the law.

Chapter Three

Laura held her grandmother's arm firmly as they made their way up the ramp alongside the broad stone steps which led to the massive mahogany doors at Bradfield Town Hall. The Victorians who had built the place had lacked nothing in confidence, Laura thought, any more than her grandmother did. Dressed in her best grey wool suit with a red scarf at her throat, Joyce looked far younger than Laura knew she was. But she could feel the effort that it was taking her to haul herself up the slope in spite of Laura's supporting arm and the rail she was clutching on the other side.

"Where are you meeting him?" she asked as Joyce paused to regain her breath in the doorway.

"In the members' lounge," Joyce said. "It's on the first floor but there's a lift."

Just as well, Laura thought. She could not see Joyce making it to the top of the ceremonial stone staircase, with its ornate fountain on the half-landing.

"Give me my stick now and I'll be fine," Joyce said firmly but when she marched ahead of Laura and pushed the heavy doors they did not budge.

"Let me, Nan," Laura said, ushering her through and pretending not to have noticed Joyce's own attempt. "The lift's round here, isn't it?"

On the floor above Joyce still led the way slowly but confidently, back on territory which had been her own for more than forty years. She tapped her way along the highly polished parquet corridors, the dark wood-panelled walls adorned with portraits of long dead mayors and aldermen in full robes, men who had dreamed their dreams for Bradfield ever since it had burgeoned from a small village of weavers' cottages into a bustling manufacturing town of mills and warehouses and back-to-back workers' terraces during the fifty frantic years of the industrial revolution. Joyce had dreamed dreams here too, trying to alleviate the legacy of slum poverty that revolution had bequeathed the twentieth century, and she had made many of her dreams flesh, only to see them crumble into dust as prosperity ebbed away and grand schemes, like the Heights where she still lived, had decayed and turned sour.

After a walk which Laura guessed she had completed on sheer determination, Joyce opened another heavy wood-panelled door and stepped inside.

"Oh, they've never," she said, standing in the doorway transfixed. The room, set out with armchairs and small tables, appeared to be empty.

"What?" Laura asked.

"They've taken down the chandeliers and put in those horrid little lamps," Joyce said in disgust. "I was never a great one for tradition but I did reckon this town hall was summat to be proud of. They've vandalised it."

"Now then, Mrs. Ackroyd," said a voice from behind them. "I didn't think we'd be seeing you here again." The grey-haired man who had spoken and who ushered the two women into the room with old-fashioned courtesy was not much taller than Joyce herself, but twice as broad. But the breadth was contained within a worsted suit of such evident Yorkshire provenance that Laura almost did what her father had traditionally done with his friends, feeling the cloth of the lapel and rubbing it gently between the thumb and forefinger in appreciation of the quality.

"Len Harvey," Joyce said in surprise. "I thought you'd stood down an'all. Councillor Harvey was leader of the Tory group when I led for Labour," Joyce added for Laura's benefit.

"Aye, well, I did, five year ago. But they've set up this committee on regeneration and my lot reckoned I could represent them. Likely a sign they don't give a tupenny damn, but I must say I'm quite enjoying popping back in here now and then. They've not asked you onto the same thing, have they, Joyce? That'd be a turn-up after all the schoolboys Labour's been putting up recently. Makes me feel a right old fuddy-duddy with my pacemaker and two pairs of specs."

"No, I'm just here for a chat with Dave Spencer," Joyce said abruptly. "I can't get about the way I used to. My hips have given up on me."

The smart tap of footsteps in the corridor outside heralded the arrival of a much younger man, sharp suited, fresh-faced, and with a haircut so close to the scalp that he could have played football for England. He glanced around the room, ignoring ex-councillor Harvey and waving the two women to a table and chairs in an alcove well away from the door. As they settled themselves down, Spencer, with his file and mobile phone lined up in front of him, glanced at the elaborate looking watch on his wrist.

"I'm sorry, Mrs. Ackroyd – can I call you Joyce?" he said. "I've got an urgent sub-committee in fifteen minutes. Something's come up. So perhaps if you just tell me what the problem is I can get back to you later?"

"I think it might take a little longer than that to explain exactly what the problems are at the Project," Joyce said, an obstinate look coming over her face.

"You do know about the Project, Councillor Spencer, don't you?" Laura asked sharply. "The Gazette did a big feature on it about six months ago."

Spencer glanced at her sharply.

"You are?"

Laura told him.

"I didn't make the connection," he said, looking irritated with himself as if his omniscience had been challenged in some way.

"No reason why you should," Joyce said. "Laura's not here as a journalist. She gave me a lift. I'm not as good on my feet as I used to be but there's nowt wrong with my brain."

"And now there's a problem at the Project?" Spencer

asked, altogether more placatory now he realised that the Press was in on the meeting, if only unofficially.

Joyce told him exactly how the Project had been vandalised and, in outline, how their precarious financial position meant that unless they could improve their cashflow the whole enterprise might have to close.

"Training is certainly going to be part of the regeneration project that we're discussing with the government," Spencer said at last. "It's a particular interest of some of our business partners, of course. We've a massive skills shortage building up in Bradfield. Far too many kids still leaving school too soon. Those who do go to university not coming back again to work. We need to address those problems if we're to attract modern high-tech industries to the area. What sort of outcomes are you showing up there? Are they getting jobs?"

"Some are," Joyce said. "Some aren't. If your business friends don't like the colour of their skin it's harder. But you'd be aware of that, of course, on your regeneration committee."

"Of course," Spencer said, glancing quickly at Laura and away again.

"And then there's the problem of drugs," Joyce said firmly.

"At the Project?" Spencer sounded alarmed.

"Not if we can help it, no," Joyce snapped. "But on the estate. Too many kids with nothing to do. Too many pushers. Who do you think wrecked the place for us? It wasn't the ones we were helping, that's for sure. They're good as gold when they come to us. It's the ones who won't be helped. Another lad dead and the Project wrecked, all in two days. What we need is short-term help to keep going and long-term help to get drugs out of the community before any more youngsters die. Can I come and tell your regeneration committee what needs doing up there, before you make any more plans?"

"I'm sure that would be very helpful, Joyce," Spencer said. "But I'll have to put it to them first."

"Can you raise it at this urgency sub-committee you're off

to now, then?" Joyce asked quickly as the councillor glanced at his watch again. He smiled faintly. Her grandmother still did not miss a trick, Laura thought.

"Not appropriate, I'm afraid, Joyce," Spencer said. "It'll have to wait until the next full meeting of the regeneration committee – if they agree. Perhaps in the meantime you can let me have something in writing, including the financial position you find yourselves in now. Our business partners will want to know just what value the project is adding…"

"I've got all that here for you," Joyce said, delving into her bag and bringing out several closely handwritten sheets neatly encased in a plastic document folder. "I didn't think you'd sign a cheque just on my say-so, lad," she said. "I may be old but I'm not daft. You'll find it all here. But I will say one thing. I've worked with folk up on the Heights for the last fifty years, on and off, and this is one of the best projects I've seen for the last thirty. But it's no use the Lottery putting in thousands for the capital costs if we can't insure against theft and vandalism. You can tell your business friends that, especially if some of them are from the banks and insurance companies. They'll know what I'm talking about. And you'd best make sure that they don't sell all your new schemes down the river the same way. Regeneration's all well and good, but when summat goes wrong you've got to be able to pick up the pieces."

She struggled to her feet, ignoring Laura's arm.

"I'll be hearing from you shortly, then, shall I, Councillor Spencer?"

Spencer got up and took a step towards the door, clutching Joyce's folder as if it was giving off a faintly unsavoury smell.

"I'm sure," he said. "I'm sure." And he was gone, the door slamming behind him.

Joyce looked around the room with some satisfaction. On the far side, Len Harvey peered around his *Daily Telegraph* with a wicked grin.

"Not lost your tongue then, Joyce?" he said.

"Think they know it all, these sharp young men," Joyce said.

"Same with us," Harvey said more soberly. "Trouble is, I think some of them know nowt. Doesn't matter what party they belong to, they're all t'same. They're ambitious, I'll give you that. Full of big ideas but all mouth and no trousers, I reckon, a lot of them."

"Well, we'll see," Joyce said, following Laura slowly to the door. "If they can't solve a simple problem like we've got just now on the Heights, then I reckon you're right. Business partners! Since when did business do owt for the poor? Unless there's a fat rate of interest in it for them."

DCI Michael Thackeray closed down his computer, stubbed out his half-smoked cigarette and sat for a moment in the half-light of the winter evening, with the rain beating against the window as it had done for weeks, reviewing an unsatisfactory afternoon. Superintendent Longley had marched into his office halfway through it as Thackeray expected he would. His face was flushed and his expression as angry as the DCI had ever seen it.

"I've just had Mrs. Adams on the phone," Longley had said, without preamble.

"Sir?" Thackeray said, his face impassive.

"Did you have to search the bloody house?" Longley asked. "I told you to handle this with kid gloves and you choose to use a bloody great sledge-hammer. Did you go down there yourself?"

"Val Ridley was in charge," Thackeray said. "I told her to handle it sensitively. She's no fool. She knew the implications."

"That's not the impression I got from Mrs. Adams complaining about coppers in hob-nailed boots tramping around her home when the lad's life is on a knife-edge. And I can't say I blame her, either."

"You wanted the drug aspect investigated, sir," Thackeray had said as mildly as he could manage. "Unless we eliminate the two kids we know took Ecstasy that night we don't know

41

where to begin looking for the dealer. And unless we'd moved quickly we'd have had the parents doing a search before us and destroying any evidence there might have been. I told Mrs. James we'd need to search. I sent the teams out immediately so she couldn't warn the Adamses."

"And did you find any evidence?" Longley had asked, more quietly now, but still flushed.

"A small amount of cannabis in Jeremy Adams's bedroom."

"Bloody hell." Longley had sunk into a chair, breathing heavily, while he took in the implications of this news.

"Did you inform the parents?" he asked eventually.

"You'll have to check with Val, but I don't think so, no. Mrs. Adams took off for the hospital before the search was competed, apparently, leaving the cleaner to lock up the house. They probably don't know yet."

"A small amount, you say?"

Thackeray had reached into his desk drawer and handed Longley a plastic evidence bag containing some screwed up paper which Longley opened and sniffed suspiciously.

"Not much doubt about that then? Though you'd have difficulty making a charge of dealing stick," he said.

"Maybe." Thackeray did not try to hide the challenge in his eyes and eventually Longley looked away.

"I'll keep this," the superintendent said, putting the bag into an inside pocket. "If the lad snuffs it, it won't have any evidential value any road, will it? If not, we can think about what to do about it when he's in a fit state to be interviewed. Right, Michael?"

"Sir," Thackeray had said, wondering what sort of a slippery slope Longley was threatening to slide down and determined he was not going to slide down it with him.

"A close friend, is he? Grantley Adams?" he ventured.

"He's not a bloody friend of mine," Longley said angrily. "Just a bloody acquaintance at the Lodge. But they've invited me to sit on this committee looking at the regeneration of the

Heights, so I don't want to queer our pitch there. It seems like a worthwhile thing for the Force to be doing, wouldn't you say? Opportunities to build in security, consult on policing, community-minded, all that?"

"I'm sure it's all of those things," Thackeray conceded. "Though there've been more schemes to regenerate that estate than there've been modernisations of the Force. Pulling the whole lot down, like they said they would, might be a better bet."

"Aye, well, that might be on the agenda, as I understand it. But never mind that. What about the bloody Carib Club? It might have been better to concentrate your efforts there, rather than going for a couple of respectable families who seem to be the victims rather than the villains in this mess, wouldn't you say?"

"Perhaps," Thackeray said. "Val Ridley and DC Sharif are down there now, as it goes."

Only slightly deflated, Longley had departed, leaving Thackeray in a foul mood which was not improved by the mountain of paperwork which he tackled for the rest of the afternoon. According to the new management jargon, he was now Bradfield's "crime manager" and it was not a job he thought particularly suited him. By five o'clock, with dusk settling over the square outside, he was sitting in his car deciding to make one last call before going home and it would be as unannounced as he had determined his officers' raids had been earlier in the day.

Unannounced and unofficial.

The boss was in his office at Foreman Security Services when Thackeray arrived. With barely a nod of greeting, Barry Foreman crossed the room to the cocktail cabinet and waved a bottle of Scotch expansively in his visitor's direction with a hand heavy with gold rings.

"You're off duty by now, I take it?"

Thackeray shook his head, certain that the offer was intended to rile. Foreman was as tall as he was himself, though perhaps without the rugby-player's breadth, but he dressed with a style and at a cost which Thackeray could only marvel at. If proof was needed that Foreman had interests which went far beyond the modest security company which was his only ostensible source of income, his vanity provided it. Those rings, the Italian suit, the hand-made leather loafers on which he padded across his thickly carpeted office, the silk tie that Thackeray knew he should recognise as the signature of some designer or other, all spoke of money and plenty of it. There was a new breed of criminal abroad – and the DCI had no doubt Foreman was a criminal although he had failed so far to prove it – computer literate and intelligent enough to keep well clear of the dirt that supported their lifestyle. While Thackeray assumed that it was the drug trade which funded Foreman's extravagances, he admitted that it could just as easily be people trafficking, or some financial scam which bridged the gap between legitimate and illegitimate business worlds. He had trawled the man's record with inexhaustible patience, wasting his own time as well as the police force's, but Foreman had no criminal record and he could find no evidence apart from the vaguely circumstantial, to implicate him in any illegal activity.

Foreman was waiting for his answer, a faint smile on the thin lips, the eyes offering a chilly challenge, the bottle still poised.

"Not for me," Thackeray said. Foreman shrugged and poured himself a large one.

"That little gypsy scrote with the shot-gun got sent down, I see," he said as he dropped a couple of ice cubes into the drink and tasted it. "Didn't even call me as a bloody witness in the end." The faint note of complaint suggested that he would have enjoyed taking the stand.

"He pleaded guilty, but they don't look kindly on fire-arms offences," Thackeray said. "How are Karen and the babies?" The two men had not met face-to-face since the day Foreman's girlfriend and her twin girls had been besieged briefly by the boy with a shot-gun though the security boss had seldom been far from Thackeray's thoughts. Foreman shrugged again and Thackeray wondered if he had imagined the flash of anger in his pale eyes.

"She buggered off, didn't she? Took the kids with her. I can't say I was sorry. How am I ever going to know who's kids they are?"

"You didn't have the tests done then?" The paternity of Foreman's children had been thrown into doubt by the doctor who had helped the couple conceive them.

"She wouldn't have it, would she? Scared of the results, I dare say," Foreman dropped heavily into his swivel chair behind an extensive desk unsullied by paperwork and waved Thackeray into an armchair. "Stupid cow."

Thackeray watched as Foreman sipped his drink. The heavy, bland face gave nothing away and as Foreman told it there was nothing to give. But Thackeray had never glimpsed a spark of humanity behind those normally cold blank eyes.

"So what can I do for you, Chief Inspector?" Foreman asked eventually.

"The Carib Club," Thackeray said. "Do you look after the doors for them?"

"Nope," Foreman said. "Nowt to do with me that place. They make their own arrangements, as far as I know. Keep themselves to themselves, those black lads, don't they? I heard they had a bit of trouble the other night. Just shows, they might be better off using FSS, mightn't they?"

"You must hear a lot of things in your line of work," Thackeray said mildly. "What about the supply of Ecstasy? Your lads hear anything about that lately?"

"At the Carib? Or generally?"

"Whatever?"

"There's a lot of it about, I'm told. Kids can't have a night out without it. I'd tan their backsides for them if they were mine. As to where they get it, I can't help you there, Mr. Thackeray. As I think I've said to you before, I know nowt

45

about the supply of drugs, and if any of my lads give me as much as a whiff that they're dealing they're out. Ecstasy, hash, crack, Charlie, I'll not tolerate it. More than the company's reputation's worth."

Thackeray smiled with as much sympathy as he could muster for a man who, in his book, had a reputation so fragile that it might shatter if a breath of wind disturbed it. But it had to be the right breath of wind and so far he had not managed to generate even an echo of the hurricane he believed Foreman and all his works deserved.

"You'll keep me informed if you hear anything," he said. "Anything at all."

"Of course, Mr. Thackeray," Foreman said, knocking his drink back and getting to his feet. "Anything I can do to help."

Chapter Four

"You don't have to pretend you're in love with me and all that crap, you know," Donna Maitland said as Kevin Mower rolled out of her bed and slipped into his jeans.

"Sorry," Mower said, pulling up his zip viciously. Donna slid from under the duvet, naked, blonde hair straggling down her back and her face, stripped of make-up, revealing fine lines that were usually carefully concealed. She was not quite the woman Mower had first seen belting out 'I Will Survive' at a karaoke night at one of the local pubs, but he had learned that in many ways she was much more than that woman throwing musical defiance at the world had appeared to be. Dozens of women from the Heights performed nightly on the pub and club circuit, casting off their bras and squeezing into too revealing dresses to exchange their pain and disappointment for a moment of glamour and whoops of drunken enthusiasm from the audience. He knew now that Donna was different. She saw life on the Heights as a challenge and had learned slowly and painfully that occasionally she could win and he admired her for it. But admiration and sex in the afternoon did not equate to anything more. They both knew that and most of the time accepted it. It was only occasionally Mower caught that look of longing in Donna's eyes before they turned away from each other, he in sudden anger, she in embarrassment.

She pulled a blue silk nightdress over her head to conceal breasts that were beginning to droop and a stomach still flat from fevered dieting but not free of stretch marks, and reached out until Mower sat back down on the bed beside her and put an arm around her waist companionably.

"What is it about you?" she asked. "I've been watching you, you know. This weren't just summat that came up on me today. I've watched you wi't'kids and seen you come alive wi'them. And then when you come back to t'bloody adults you switch off, dead as summat that fell off back of a bin lorry. What's that all about?"

"It's a long story," Mower said uneasily, getting up again to pull a sweatshirt over his head and moving out onto the balcony of the fourth floor flat where an icy blast from the Pennines made him recoil. Donna followed him, pulling a robe around herself and standing beside him shivering as they both gazed down at the littered car-park below. Donna's lips tightened and she looked away so that the sergeant could not see eyes filled with tears which were only partly caused by the wind.

"And a story you're not going to tell some slag you just picked up on a night out slumming on t'Heights?"

Mower reached out and pulled her closer.

"Don't do that to yourself, Donna," Mower said. "You don't deserve it."

"So why won't you tell me about her? I know there's someone else. I can see it in your eyes when you get into bed. It's not me you really want. Dumped you, did she?"

Mower shuddered slightly as the wind threw a flurry of needle sharp sleet in their faces.

"It wasn't like that," he said, turning and urging Donna back inside.

"So you dumped her and now you're regretting it?"

"She…" Mower hesitated. "You don't need to worry about her. She died."

"Oh, Jesus, I'm sorry," Donna said quickly, her eyes filling with tears again. She dashed them away and began to get dressed, pulling clothes on quickly to cover flesh she did not want Mower to inspect too closely. Mower stood with his back against the balcony door looking at her, wishing he could give her what she so desperately wanted and knowing that he never could. He followed her into the living room where she began a furious tidying away of the previous night's mugs and glasses which covered the coffee table.

"You don't need to be sorry for me. It's over now," he said.

"Aye, but it's never over, is it?" Donna said. "My sister lost her lad. He were t'first to OD on smack. Too pure, they said, as if that made it any easier. She'll not get over it. Not ever. Why d'you think I'm so gutted that the Project's getting trashed by t'minutes. It's to stop kids like our Terry getting hooked. And my Emma, for that matter, though she's little yet."

Mower glanced at his watch. Emma was Donna's eight year old daughter and as far as he knew she did not know of his existence. It was a situation he preferred to maintain.

"She'll be home soon, won't she? I'd better go."

Donna glanced out of the window again to where a straggle of school-children could be seen making their way round the corner of the neighbouring block of flats.

"Just let me get my coat on, it's coming down like stair-rods out there," she said. "I'll walk down with you. I don't like her coming up them stairs on her own. You never know who's about." Donna went back into the bedroom and within minutes had slipped into a jacket and carefully repaired her make-up and hair.

"Will I do?" she asked with an attempt at coquettishness as she came back into the living room.

"You'll do fine," Mower said, kissing her gently on the lips and opening the front door of the flat for her. They made their way along the rain-swept walkway to the concrete stairs which led to ground level.

"You wait there," Mower said. "I'll watch her safely up."

"I'll be back over t'road at seven," Donna said, her face determined again. "I've got a babysitter sorted. And Kevin…"

Mower glanced back.

"I didn't mean owt," Donna said. "Just good friends, right?"

"Right," Mower said, with what he hoped was the right degree of enthusiasm. He set off down the stairs without looking back and by the time he had reached the ground floor a small fair child in school uniform had made her way into the hallway where the single lift boasted an out-of-order sign.

"Your mum's at the top, Emma," he said quietly, but the child gave him a frightened look and hurried up the stairs, her school bag banging against her bare legs painfully as she ran. Mower stood at the bottom for a moment looking up until he heard Donna greet her daughter loudly enough for him to hear. It was not until the echo of their footsteps along the walkway above had died away that he groaned and thumped his fist hard against the concrete wall in a vain attempt to assuage the pain which still consumed him. A drink, he thought, would be good. Two would be better. Six better still. The sleet which was now battering against the doors would not deter him but he guessed that the kids who were waiting for him at the Project just might.

Laura Ackroyd stood on the top step of the Carib Club trying to keep out of the rain and watched the group of Asian boys on the other side of the road with some anxiety. They were a perfect example of what the police used to call loitering with intent, she thought, as one of the teenagers kicked a soft drink can across the road in her direction and fell back against the opposite wall laughing hysterically. She knocked for the third time on the club door and was just about to turn away when she heard the sound of movement inside. Eventually with much shooting of bolts and turning of keys in locks, the door inched open a crack and a voice demanded to know who she was and what she wanted.

"I had an appointment to see Darryl Redmond," Laura said, pushing her Press card into the gap in the door and straggles of damp red hair out of her eyes.

"Safe," the voice said and eased the door back sufficiently for her to enter before slamming it shut again.

The interior of the club was gloomy, lit only by the emergency lights over the exits and a faint glow which filtered out from an open door on the opposite side of the cavernous room.

Laura had never visited the place before. The Carib was an addition to the Bradfield scene since her own student days at the university when she had gone clubbing with the best. These days an exhausted evening with Michael Thackeray slumped in front of the television and an occasional meal out made up the sum total of her social life. Middle age, she thought, must be creeping up, and she did not much like the prospect.

The young black man holding a broom in one hand who had let her in led her across the dance floor, past the enormous sound system and into the lit room on the other side.

"The reporter woman," he said to the two black men who were sitting in a cramped office, one light-skinned and short, with a tight, neat haircut, and a small goatee, the other taller, broader and darker and with a shock of dreadlocks down to his shoulders. The bigger man raised a fist in greeting while the other waved her into a chair.

"I'm Darryl Redmond. This is my DJ from last night, Dizzy B. You're Laura, right? You want to write about the club?"

Laura nodded.

"You gonna give us a bad press?" Redmond asked, his eyes unfriendly. "This thing with the boy and the taxi was nowt to do wi'us, you know? We're getting all this hassle and it was nowt to do wi'us."

"That's why I wanted to talk to you," Laura said. "I wanted to get your side of the story." Persuading Ted Grant that the club might even have a side of the story had been a gargantuan struggle that morning, but she had prevailed eventually by suggesting, with a sweet smile, that even a night-club might sue if the Gazette suggested it was a source of illegal drugs without allowing it any right of reply.

"Oh, yeah," Dizzy B said sceptically. "And how do we know you'll tell it like it really is?"

"You have to trust me," Laura said. "Believe me, the Gazette could have sent someone a lot nastier than me." She tried her most trustworthy smile but it did not seem to impress her listeners.

"There's nothing to tell, any road," Darryl said. "We tell our door people not to let drugs in. You can't ever be sure it works. An' there's nowt you can do with kids who've popped pills before they even got here. That boy didn't get his Es in my club. I can tell you that for a fact. Maybe some ganja slipped in on Saturday but that ain't no big deal. But no Es. And nothing harder either."

"I had a good view of the dancers," Dizzy B said flatly, dark eyes amused rather than anxious. "I don' see no dealers in here that night though some of the kids maybe were high. A few brothers smokin'. Nothin' more. An' I had a frien' wit' me who's a copper so I was keepin' a good eye open. A very good eye. I didn' want no trouble that night."

"Police?" Laura's surprise was obvious.

"You think we can't have friends in the force?" Dizzy B asked, grinning broadly and abandoning his West Indian accent. "You should get out more, lady. I was in the Met myself for a little while. But the music called stronger."

"There was a policeman inside the club all night?"

"Right," Dizzy B said.

"And two good men on the doors," Darryl insisted. "Though I reckon I'm going to have to get different security if I'm going to keep my licence here. Barry Foreman's been on at me for months to give him the doors. Maybe that's the price I'll have to pay."

"He's reliable, is he?" Laura asked, recalling her brief acquaintance with the security boss and thinking that reliability was not the first word that sprang to mind.

"He has friends in high places," Darryl said. "That's enough, isn't it?"

Laura was about to explore that interesting avenue when there was a crash from the far side of the club and an outraged shout from the man who had let her in earlier, who was now sweeping up around the DJ's dais.

Darryl and Dizzy jumped to their feet, ran to the main doors and flung them open to find themselves faced with flames from some sort of fire which had been lit outside. While Darryl turned back for a fire extinguisher, Dizzy stamped on the burning rubbish and succeeded in kicking most of it away from the wooden doors and down the steps before it could do any serious damage. Outside the narrow street was deserted.

"There was a gang of Asian lads out there when I arrived," Laura said, gazing at the smouldering mess on the pavement in horror.

"Surprise me," Dizzy B said, standing aside to let Darryl douse the last of the fire in foam. "Darryl was just telling me that the Asians have been trying to get him closed down for months."

"Why should they want to do that?" Laura asked.

Darryl shrugged.

"There's no love lost between the two communities, you should know that if you live in Bradfield," he said. "And we're the wrong side of town here. The premises are cheap but we're very close to the mosque. A bad influence, the old men in white pyjamas think. Might give their little girls the wrong idea entirely."

"Just because we all have dark skin you think we all the same..." Dizzy B mocked Laura. "But if this place is anything like London, you've probably got the Asian gangs just as deep into drugs as anyone else – buying and selling."

"So who's your friend in the police then?" she asked waspishly. "Kevin Mower, I bet. He was in the Met."

"Yo, you're well informed," the DJ said.

"He's a friend of mine."

"Close friend or just friend?"

"Just friend," Laura said.

"Ah," Dizzy B said. "And was the amazing Rita a friend of yours too?"

"I never met her," Laura said. "But it was a big thing when she was shot, front page story in the nationals, the lot. She was very beautiful. Kevin was devastated."

"So I'm told, so I'm told," Dizzy B said, glancing away.

As the club's cleaner appeared with his broom and began to sweep away the debris of the fire into the running water of the gutter, a car cruised slowly down the street and stopped beside them. Laura was surprised to recognise DC Val Ridley with DC Mohammed Sharif – universally known to colleagues as Omar, an alternative he seemed to approve of – beside her.

"Did you call the police?" she asked Darryl.

"No point," the club proprietor said, surprised.

"Well, you've got them anyway," Laura said as the two officers got out of their car and crossed the road.

Val nodded at Laura without much warmth.

"Just leaving, are you?" she asked.

"Looks as though I'll have to," Laura said, realising she would get no further now. "Some kids just lit a fire here. Dangerous that."

Ridley and her companion looked at the still smoking rubbish.

"Did you see who it was," Sharif asked.

"There was a gang of lads outside when I arrived," Laura said. "Asian lads."

"Most of them are round here," Sharif said without acrimony. "Could you identify any of them again?"

"I doubt it," Laura said. "I wasn't taking much notice. They just seemed to be larking about at that stage."

"It's not the first time it's happened," Darryl Redmond broke in. "We don't seem to get much protection."

"I'll get one of my crime protection colleagues to call," Val Ridley, the sarcasm heavy. "In the meantime, can we get on?"

"The guest list seems to be wide open this morning," the club proprietor said, following the two officers and Dizzy B inside and leaving Laura facing the doors again, frustrated in her morning's work.

But when she got back to the office it did not seem to matter. Ted Grant waved her into his office with an unusually benign look on his face.

"Owt or nowt in that?" he asked, barely giving her time to reply before pointing at his flickering computer screen where Laura could half see a front-page layout. "Bob Baker came up with the goods any road," Grant said and she knew that the editor had used his increasingly frequent tactic of setting one reporter up against another to see how far he could push them into sensation. He spun the computer monitor round in Laura's direction with a wolfish grin so that she could read the headline: "Imam lashes 'Satanic' clubs."

"Got an interview with the top man at the mosque and some good quotes from the local councillors. The Asians are launching a petition to get the place closed down. You can add a couple of pars at the end if you got owt of interest from the club people. You'll just catch the edition if you're quick."

"They say they do their best to keep drugs out," Laura said, but she recognised a deaf ear turned her way as clearly as if Ted Grant had worn a Position Closed notice on the offending orifice and she shrugged again.

"I'll do a short add on," she said. Ted Grant beamed as kindly as his habitually belligerent countenance would allow.

"You can get back to your features then," he said. Laura gritted her teeth although she knew that she was being told with crystal clarity that the girls should keep out of the big boys' games. Bob Baker, she thought, would have to be seen to, and the sooner the better.

Chapter Five

DCI Michael Thackeray waited with ill-concealed impatience in the well-appointed ante-room of the headmaster's secretary at Bradfield Grammar School. It was the first time he had ever been inside the school which stood in mock-classical splendour in leafy grounds on the outskirts of the town. From the moment he had entered by the heavy mahogany doors, obligingly held open for him by a tall Sikh boy in turban of regulation school navy blue, and found his shoes squeaking on the highly polished parquet floor of the corridors, he had recognised the smell of what money could buy. Somewhere in the distance he could hear a choir singing, the young boys' voices pure and clear, a sound from his own past which sent a shiver of recognition down his spine.

He knew the school accepted girls these days, a sure sign of the competitive times, but the building still reeked of male exclusivity. From his own modern and slightly tatty country comprehensive school you could imagine students moving on to work in offices and factories, garages and farms. Here the atmosphere spoke of similarly panelled lawyers' and accountants' offices, the great wool exchange which had once been the hub of this part of Yorkshire, even the gentlemen's clubs of London and Parliament itself. The school had narrowly missed producing a prime minister but the gold inscribed honours boards listing scholarships to Oxford and Cambridge would have easily taken that in their stride. This was solid, expensive, traditional education and if the students found it rather dull even they probably reckoned that was a fair price to pay for well-nigh guaranteed security later.

Thackeray had come alone, knowing that brow-beating the headmaster of this particular school was more than most of his detectives would be able to do. And brow-beating was certainly his intention if it came to it. The latest hospital report on the condition of Jeremy Adams was not encouraging and, in spite of his reservations about superintendent Longley's motives, he owed it to the boy to make some gesture towards tracing the source of the drug which looked as though it might have killed him. And the best place to start, he was sure, was amongst the sixth-formers at his school.

He glanced at his watch and then at the attractive middle-aged woman who was busy at a word-processor on the other side of the room. She smiled at him sympathetically and, he thought wryly, possibly slightly hopefully. The name on the door had indicated that she was Miss Raven – there were no concessions to politically correct language here in spite of the recent influx of girls, he noticed – and Miss Raven wore no wedding ring.

"He shouldn't be too long," she said. "He has the chairman of governors on the phone. This business with Jeremy is not what any school wants to hear these days. It frightens the horses – or in this case the parents."

"It was not only Jeremy who was involved," Thackeray said without letting too much sympathy creep into his voice. A desperately sick student merited rather more than a revamp of the school's marketing strategy in his book. Miss Raven pursed her lips, picking up his disapproval.

"His parents must be distraught," she said. "I hear he's on life support."

Thackeray nodded, unwilling to get involved in a discussion of the medical details. He did not need reminding of the horrors of watching the professionals lose a battle for the life of a much-loved son. It was an experience he had relived every night for years until he had met Laura, who seemed to have the capacity most of the time to lighten the darkness.

At that moment the communicating door between Miss Raven's office and the head's study was flung open and a tall, broad-shouldered man with a head of gleaming silver hair and a ruddy, out-of-doors complexion hurried in, hand outstretched in Thackeray's direction.

"Chief Inspector, I'm so sorry to have kept you waiting," he said. "David Stewart, headmaster for my sins. And I think you're here to discuss some of the less creditable activities of some of our sixth-formers? Do come in. Tea, Felicity, I think? Will that suit you, Chief Inspector?"

Thackeray stood up and found, unusually, that he was in the company of a man as tall as he was himself and almost as broad, and about his own age. There was something about him which was familiar and brought a half-smile to his lips. This was, he knew, a rugby school, just as his own less exalted establishment had been, and he had a faint suspicion that he had once upon a time brought David Stewart down heavily and kneed him fairly unmercifully into the mud.

Settled in the Head's study in a comfortable chair close to the coffee table where Felicity Raven soon deposited a tray and poured them cups of tea from a silver teapot, Thackeray took a moment to look around the elegantly furnished room with its view over the extensive playing fields.

"Were you a pupil here yourself?" he asked, accepting a cup and saucer.

"I was, as it happens," Stewart admitted. "Played rugger out there with far more enthusiasm than I had for my A Levels. But I scraped into university and teaching seemed like a good bet for someone with my sporting interests. And you? Are you an old Bradfielder too? I don't remember…"

"Arnedale," Thackeray said shortly. "But I played rugby here once or twice."

"Ah yes. We did play Arnedale, even after…" Stewart hesitated. "I don't think they compete in our league any more."

"Not many comprehensives do, I imagine," Thackeray said dryly. "The rugby team was a hang-over from the grammar school days when I was there. A lot of lads preferred soccer even then."

"Pity," Stewart said. "But I suppose I'm biased." He gazed fondly at the playing fields. "Great days," he said.

"Jeremy Adams," Thackeray said, breaking into Stewart's

nostalgic moment fairly brutally. "Did you have any idea he was indulging in illegal substances?"

"I did not," Stewart said. "And I understand Louise James was with him. I have to say I'm astonished, though perhaps that's naïve these days."

"Have you spoken to Louise?"

"Not yet. I'm seeing her with her parents on Monday. I'm afraid I'll have to ask her to leave."

"That seems harsh for something which happened out of school," Thackeray said. Stewart glanced out of the widow for a moment without speaking.

"That's easy to say, Chief Inspector, and I know the police don't do much about young people using drugs these days, but our parents expect the highest standards. After the publicity there's been, my chairman has already indicated that we can't afford to take her back. Or Jeremy, for that matter, should he recover. Our reputation depends on us taking a strong line. We're in a cut-throat market."

"Have you said anything to your other sixth-formers yet?" he asked.

"Not yet. Everyone is waiting to see what progress Jeremy makes."

"You make it very difficult for them to contact the police with information if they think they'll be expelled if you find out," Thackeray said. "I'm pretty sure there were others out celebrating with Jeremy and Louise but no one has come forward yet. I want to ask you to urge them to contact us. We need to find the source of the Ecstasy tablets. It's the least we can do for Jeremy's parents. You can tell the youngsters they can talk to us in the strictest confidence."

Stewart nodded enthusiastically.

"Of course, of course, we can do that," he said, although Thackeray had no confidence at all that exhortations from the headmaster would have much effect on his clubbing sixth-formers who must know very well what was going to befall Louise James.

"And you won't threaten them with any sort of consequences here as a result? You can't assume that just because they were at the club they took drugs as well."

Stewart looked more doubtful at that, as well he might, Thackeray thought. You could probably count the number of young people who went clubbing without the use of illegal stimulants on the fingers of one hand.

"Parents will talk," Stewart said. "You know what the grapevine's like, Chief Inspector. If it's drawn to my attention that someone else is involved I don't see how I can avoid taking some sort of action."

"It's not helpful at the moment," Thackeray said.

"Well, I'm sorry," Stewart insisted. "I'll turn as deaf an ear as I can – but I can't afford to harbour known drug users. It does the school no good at all."

And with that Thackeray had to be content. He drove away from the school in a dissatisfied mood and instead of turning back into town and on towards Laura's flat he joined the stream of rush hour traffic heading for the suburbs and beyond. His objective was a street of run-down semi-detached houses on the very edge of the town with a view from generally untended gardens over the moorland countryside between Bradfield and the commuter village of Broadley. Turning off the main road, he drove gingerly over the rutted surface and parked outside one of the last houses in the row and sat for a moment contemplating the muddy garden, the broken fences and the light spilling from the uncurtained front window. The last time he had been here an angry youth with a shot-gun had been threatening the family inside the house. Since then the son who had been threatened had been gaoled, as had the attacker he had provoked, and he fervently hoped that the authorities had shown enough sense to send them to different institutions. Where the rest of the family had gone he needed to discover, although as Superintendent Longley kept reminding him, the basis for his inquiries was flimsy, little more than a hunch which in a junior officer he would himself have dismissed with contempt.

He locked his car carefully and knocked on the door, which offered neither knocker nor bell-push, several times before it was eventually opened by a middle-aged woman, with a cigarette clutched in one hand and the collar of a fierce-looking Staffordshire terrier in the other.

"Oh, it's you Mr. Thackeray," Jean Bailey muttered pulling the growling dog back into the house. "Just let me shut this beggar up and you can come in." He waited while doors opened and shut at the back of the house and eventually the woman beckoned him inside. She evidently bore him no grudge for arresting her son because she waved him into the front room with a smile and sank back into the armchair from which she had been watching TV, turning the volume down very slightly with a remote control,

"Bloody dog were Nicky's idea," she said. "Security for me, he said. But the beggar's more trouble than he's worth. Let him run out on t'green and he's off for hours at a time. I can't catch him, can I? And if you keep him on a lead he pulls your bloody arm off. He'll have to go."

"I was keen to have a word with Karen," Thackeray said. "But Barry Foreman says she's left him. I thought maybe she'd come back home."

Jean shook her head.

"I've done my bit wi'babies," she said, lighting a fresh cigarette and flinging the match into an over-flowing ash-tray on the cluttered coffee table. "Nappies, bottles, screaming in t'middle o't'night. I can't be doing with all that again. I told her. She'd made her bed, she'd have to bloody lie on it."

"So do you know where she is?" Thackeray asked, slightly shaken by this lack of grandmotherly solidarity. But Jean only shrugged.

"Barry said she were talking about going to London," she said. "I reckon she's got some new man in her life. You'll be seeing her in t'Globe next wi'some footballer with a tattoo on his bum."

"London? With two young babies?"

"Aye, well, I didn't know t'twins were going with her, did I? I thought he were keen to keep them, Barry. He can afford a nanny or summat, can't he? Any road, she'll want to be somewhere where he can't find her, won't she? He's got a vicious temper on him, has Barry Foreman."

"Has he now?" Thackeray said carefully. "He always seems as smooth as silk when I talk to him."

The woman glanced away and shrugged slightly.

"You ask our Nicky," she said. "He were a damn' sight more scared of Barry after that business wi't'gippos than he was of you lot."

Even if that were true, Thackeray thought, and he had no reason to doubt Jean Bailey's assessment of her son's state of mind, there was little chance of the already jailed Nicky expanding on any threats Foreman might have issued to his girlfriend's brother. He changed tack.

"Has Karen got money of her own? I don't imagine Barry sent her on her way with a generous redundancy cheque, do you?"

"Karen never had owt, as far as I know. Spent it as fast as she earned it when she were living here. If she had one pair of shoes she had fifty, all t'colours o't' bloody rainbow. If she's gone she'll have found some beggar to pay her fare, you can bet on that."

"But you haven't heard from her?"

"Not a friggin' word," Jean said, drawing hard on her cigarette. "Not for months now. She never were one to keep in touch, weren't Karen. Only when she wanted summat. You know how it is?"

Thackeray suddenly felt very cold although the room was stuffy. No one seemed to be worried about Karen Bailey and her twin girls, barely six months old: not their father, not their grandmother and certainly not their uncle banged up in

Armley for violence which still sickened Thackeray to think about. So why was he so certain that they ought to be? Perhaps he was going soft, he thought, but he didn't really believe it. If only for his own peace of mind, he knew he needed to track Karen and her children down.

Laura got home that night tired and irritable. She had spent the best part of the afternoon at the Infirmary waiting for the interview which had been promised by Grantley Adams, only to have the man brush her off without a word of apology at five o'clock as he strode angrily out of the hospital, stony-faced and unbending. His wife, a fragile-looking woman much younger than her grey-haired husband, who had been following almost at a run, hesitated when she saw Laura with her tape-recorder at the ready.

"We can't stop now," she said. "Grantley has a meeting in half an hour he can't miss."

"How's Jeremy?" Laura had asked, but the boy's mother had shrugged wearily, pushing wisps of what Laura guessed would usually be elegantly coiffed hair out of her eyes.

"There's no change," she said, and scuttled after her husband who had glanced back impatiently from the swing doors. She had tried calling the Adams family home a couple of times later but had only got an recorded message telling her that Grantley and Althea Adams and family were not available. Eventually she drove out to Broadley and parked outside the Adams's substantial stone house, set well back from the road, and pressed the answerphone on the heavy iron gates. Somewhat to her surprise, Mrs. Adams responded and opened first the gates and then the front door. But it turned out to be an unsatisfactory encounter. Althea Adams had taken her into the kitchen and poured herself a gin and tonic which she drank quickly with shaking hands while she made Laura a coffee. Somewhere else in the house the sound of pop music indicated the presence of the Adams daughters but they did not appear and Jeremy's mother seemed almost incoherent with anxiety.

"I only came home because of the girls," she had said. "I ought to be at the hospital. I shouldn't really have let you in. Grantley would be furious…"

"Your husband couldn't have cancelled his meeting, with Jeremy so ill?" Laura asked curiously, but Mrs Adams simply shrugged.

"It was very important," she said.

"You don't work yourself," Laura asked.

"I used to before we were married. I was an accountant. I worked for Grantley for a couple of years, that's how we met. But there's no need now and with three children there's a lot to do here." She smiled faintly. "Grantley's first wife had her own career but I don't think that worked out very well. He's a very demanding man. I should know. I worked for him before his divorce."

"And neither of you had any idea Jeremy was into drugs?"

"No of course not," Mrs. Adams said sharply. But when Laura suggested that a profile of the family might help others in a similar situation, she panicked.

"Grantley would hate that," she said. "In fact he'd hate you being here. Perhaps you'd better go now."

And with that Laura had to be content, although she knew it would in no way satisfy Ted Grant's desire for an in-depth interview for the next morning's first edition. But before she could get too broody about the fragile state of her career, her mobile rang and she heard her grandmother's voice again, full of emotion.

"Have you got time to come up to the Project after work, pet?" Joyce asked. "I won't keep you long but there's someone I'd like you to meet." Laura had smiled to herself as she agreed. Even at almost eighty her grandmother, with the bit between her teeth, was a formidable force. So for the second evening running she had ground her way up the steep hill to the Heights and picked her way across the puddled pathways to the Project where she found Joyce and Donna Maitland drinking tea with a small dark man with deep pouches under fierce black eyes.

"This is Dr. Khan," Donna said. "He wants to tell you about the drug problems up here."

"Donna tells me you're going to write something in the Gazette," Khan said. "It's time someone took some notice of what is happening on the Heights. The problem is getting out of control."

"I know there's been a spate of deaths from overdoses...."

"Twelve years old one of them was," Khan said, evidently outraged. "But there have been other deaths. The boy who went over the top of the flats the other day, another who was killed by a car. I think they are all connected. It is an epidemic. And apart from this place, and Donna here, no one is taking it seriously or doing anything to help. I can't get kids into rehab when they need it. I can't persuade the police that some of these deaths are tantamount to murder."

"The younger children carry knives, some of the older ones have got guns," Joyce broke in.

"My nephew was fourteen," Donna said quietly. "Started sniffing glue, moved on to heroin. I'm frightened to let our Emma out of my sight..."

"Murder?" Laura concentrated on the doctor with exhaustion written all over him. "What makes you say that?"

"I've no evidence," Khan said. "Just rumours, sideways looks. I wasn't called to all the deaths, but I've treated some of the bereaved families. Everyone assumes that all the kids who have died brought it on themselves. That they were rubbish because they were junkies. But that is not my impression. The mother of one of the boys who died of an overdose says he was not on drugs, that he hated them, that he worked hard at school and had ambitions. The boy who fell off the roof was not a user, apparently. They haven't held the inquest yet so I don't know what they found at the post-mortem. But his mother is adamant he was not a junkie now, even if he had been once."

65

"You think there's some sort of war going on between dealers?" Laura asked doubtfully. "No one's suggested that publicly. There's not been any shooting."

"Yet," Donna said bitterly. "All t'kids are saying there's guns on the estate."

"I don't know what's going on, and I don't see any signs of anyone trying to find out either," Khan said. "What we really need to do is get a campaign going to tackle the problem up here. Some of the families are keen to help…"

"If you can do it without using their names," Donna broke in. "Don't underestimate just how bloody scared people are."

"But we need some backing," the doctor went on. "Not a lot but some funds to get started, and we need some publicity. That's where we thought you could help. You could write about it in the Gazette."

Laura had listened to Dr. Khan's complaints with a growing sense of unease. She thought of the effort the police seemed to be putting into investigating the incident at the Carib Club, and about Thackeray's scarcely veiled lack of faith in the drug squad's efforts on the Heights, and wondered if she could persuade Ted Grant to let her write about Donna's fears and Dr. Khan's campaign. To catch his interest she had to have a good story and that, she thought, would involve some serious research.

"Where's Kevin Mower today?" she had asked, a germ of an idea forming in the back of her head.

"He doesn't tell me what he's doing," Donna said, and Laura could see the pain behind her carefully composed façade. "I've a genius for hooking bastards who don't tell you what they're doing, didn't you know? He's not due in here today, any road."

Laura had taken that unasked for piece of information on board with no more than a sympathetic glance. It was not the time, she thought, to fill Donna in with details of Mower's chequered history. So she had driven home, increasingly determined that she would pursue Dr. Khan's problems and find a story she could realistically sell to her unsympathetic editor, and wondering how far her own man was willing to share his plans with her and how safe it would be to share hers with him on this particular occasion.

In the end the decision was made for her. She had cooked a meal without much enthusiasm but Thackeray was late and she ate alone, too hungry by nine o'clock to wait any longer. It's a bit soon to be behaving like an old married couple, putting the dinner in the oven and waiting with a rolling pin behind the door, she thought wryly as she sat in the silent flat listening for the sound of a car outside. When he finally arrived, she had switched on the TV and curled up on the sofa to watch a documentary about the melting ice-cap in Antarctica. And as if that were not sufficiently gloomy, she could see from a quick glance at Thackeray's face as he hung up his coat that he was in a dark mood too.

He flung himself onto the sofa beside her, lit a cigarette and zapped the TV off.

"Where would you run to if you had two young babies and no obvious means of support?" he asked.

Laura shrugged.

"Some sort of women's refuge?"

"I'm not sure she was running away from violence, though her mother thinks it's possible" Thackeray said. "Anyway, I've checked the local women's centres out. She's not there."

"Perhaps she's got money. What makes you think she hasn't?"

"Because this is Barry Foreman's girlfriend we're talking about and I don't reckon he's the sort of man who'd let her have more than peanuts for spending money. And according to her mother she's never ever had two pennies of her own to rub together, even when she lived with her."

"New boyfriend?"

"With two tiny babies?"

"Some men like babies," Laura said, and could

immediately have bitten off her tongue. She turned to Thackeray and reached out a hand which he avoided.

"Sorry," she said. "That was stupid of me."

Thackeray looked at her for a long moment, although what he saw was not Laura's stricken face but a peacefully sleeping infant in another mother's arms. He shook himself sharply.

"I'm the one who should be sorry," he said. Impulsively she leaned over and kissed him and the kiss turned into a longer embrace.

"I'm all right," she said, when they came up for air. "*It's* all right. We'll get by."

"I'd hoped we'd do a bit better than that," he said.

"We will, we will," she said and kissed him again, and this time they did not break off.

Chapter Six

Alderman Sir Jebediah Hustler, whose portrait gazed down from above the ornate stone fireplace in Committee Room B at Bradfield town hall, would have felt at home amongst the grey suits and iridescent ties which assembled there the next morning for a meeting of the Heights Regeneration Zone Action Committee – HR-Zac for convenience. Jebediah had been a man who combined a harsh regime in his mills and the rows of back-to-back hovels which he rented to his workers with a shrewd self-interest when it came to local government. If there was owt in democracy for the masters, then Jebediah wanted his share, whether it came in the shape of prestige and a knighthood or harder currency. The cold blue eyes set in a face of florid self-satisfaction almost entirely surrounded by well-combed iron-grey hair and whiskers, could have been overseeing the proceedings of HR-Zac, and would certainly have presided over its deliberations with approval.

Councillor Dave Spencer who was actually in the chair was a less imposing figure, but he dressed with as much vanity as his Victorian predecessor and watched with equally sharp and self-interested eyes as his hand-picked committee took its seats around the highly polished boardroom table – not least to make sure that the regulation complement of women and ethnic minorities was present. It was so much more convenient when they could be combined in the figure of one Zufira Ahmed, a director of her father's import-export business and a governor of Sutton Park school, he thought, as Miss Ahmed took her place and slipped her long white head-scarf back from her dark hair, letting it trail elegantly across her dark-suited and much admired breasts.

Spencer had made sure that Zufira's father's support for the regeneration project was assured before he had secured the daughter's nomination. Dave Spencer prided himself on his business savvy. If only he had not committed himself to a career in politics when he was sixteen and still filled with anti-Thatcherite zeal, he thought, he might have been on one of those rich lists himself, at least for the county of Yorkshire. Still, he consoled himself, there was time. He did not have to go on chivvying dozy officials and timid councillors into the twenty-first century forever. As his girlfriend, who was in management herself kept telling him, it was where the chivvying might lead which was important at his stage of career, after all.

Spencer tapped his pen against the carafe of water in front of him to bring the meeting to order.

"Glad you could all make it," he said. "And I'm delighted to welcome a new member to our ranks. Superintendent Jack Longley from Bradfield police HQ, who I'm sure will give a very welcome perspective to our discussions. Welcome, Jack. We're glad to have you on board. Let me introduce you to the rest of the action group: Grantley Adams you may know – and all our sympathy goes out to you and Althea at the moment of course – no change there, Grantley?"

Adams shook his head sourly, glancing round the table and reserving a particularly vicious glare for Jack Longley.

"And next to Grantley is Geoff Wright from Wright and Purser up at Long Moor, another of our generous industrial sponsors, Zufira Ahmed, from Ahmed Trading in Aysgarth Lane, Steve Brady from the town planning department here at the town hall, Jim Baistow from Baistow Construction, Jude Laythwaite from education and leisure services, and Barry Foreman who runs his own security company. I've had apologies unfortunately today from the housing department and from Ray Hayter of the Afro-Caribbean community liaison committee. And from our Tory representative, Mr. Harvey. No surprise there, I suppose, as there's not much in this for them – politically speaking, of course. You'll soon get to know everyone, Jack, and although we don't expect you to be carrying a police cheque book you can rest assured we'll value your contribution as much as anyone's."

Jack Longley had nodded dourly at each of the committee members as they were introduced but he glanced down at his council blotter before meeting Barry Foreman's bland smile of welcome. He was sure that Thackeray's suspicions of the man were unlikely ever to be proved, even if justified: and Foreman was embedding himself into Bradfield's establishment too securely to be vulnerable to anything but a case of the most cast-iron variety. But Longley was not above hedging his bets. Thackeray was not given to wild flights of imagination and experienced enough to pick up a faint odour of corruption which others might miss. Longley gazed resolutely into the sharp blue eyes of Jebediah Hustler on the wall facing him and did not look away until the rest of the introductions were completed.

Spencer zipped through the printed agenda quickly and it was obvious to Longley that his own presence at the meeting was purely cosmetic. Many of the crucial decisions around rebuilding the Heights and upgrading the infrastructure in that part of town had already been taken in principle and most of the business people round the table had evidently committed funds to the programme and been allotted roles in its implementation, subject to Whitehall approval. That some of them might add financial gain in the long term to the undoubted kudos their involvement brought in the short did not seem to cause anyone any unease. Longley increasingly wondered what he was doing there. He was not used to playing a violet of the shrinking or the hothouse variety. But as Councillor Spencer announced item ten on the agenda his antennae quivered and he decided that as he was there, at Spencer's invitation and with the Chief Constable's approval, he might as well make his presence felt

"Right, we'll turn to youth policies now," Spencer said briskly with a glance in Longley's direction. "As most of you know this has been one of the most difficult areas to tackle as it involves so many agencies: education, youth service, the courts, the police, probation, community groups, social services – you name it they're all in there – all failing together." Longley kept a straight face although the little sally was greeted with chuckles of approval from the businessmen present. Zufira Ahmed merely looked pained. Those who knew Longley better might have been concerned at the way his almost bald crown flushed slightly under the electric lights but Spencer did not know him well enough to be perturbed.

"Not to put too fine a point on it, kids on the Heights are running wild and no one so far has come up with a means of cutting crime and getting them into employment," the councillor went on. "So we're open to suggestions, the more innovative the better. What we need to build into this scheme is something to get the kids off the streets and into jobs so that whatever we invest doesn't get vandalised the moment the construction workers move out."

"Performance in the schools is improving..." Jude Laythwaite, the representative of the education department said tentatively.

"But how long will that take to work through, Jude?" Spencer came back sharply. "We need results now not in ten years' time." In ten years' time, Longley thought unsympathetically, Spencer's political career might have been destroyed by the impact of the lawless young. He was aware that the councillor's sharp gaze was now focused in his direction.

"What chance more intensive policing, superintendent? Residents up there complain they never see a bobby until there's a crisis."

"We have a community officer up there most of the time," Longley said mildly. "Like everything else, it's a question of resources. I'd have thought your best bet was that project they've already started up there, give the kids some skills to get decent jobs..."

"That's just an amateur effort, isn't it?" Barry Foreman put in unexpectedly. "Not enough capital, not enough security, as I hear it. What you need is summat much more hard-edged and professional."

"As it happens the Project is seeking some extra funding from the council right now," Spencer said, without enthusiasm. "They've had some trouble with vandalism..."

"Just what I'm saying," Foreman said. "You can't have tin-pot prefabricated classrooms where any little toe-rag can barge in off the street and chuck computers around. Stands to reason. You need it done properly."

"With respect, Chair, I think Mr. Foreman's right. This is something the college could do much more effectively," Jude Laythwaite said. "At the moment it's just a few untrained people who live locally. There's one old girl who's eighty if she's a day. If we get approval for the private finance initiative and rebuild, I'm sure accommodation could be provided for these sort of activities and for proper staffing instead of amateurs who've just strolled in with their own agendas."

"And how long will that take?" Longley asked. "I thought you were looking for quick results?" He glanced at Spencer who was watching the exchange with a faintly satisfied look in his eyes.

"Well, we are," Jude Laythwaite came back quickly. "But I rather think that's where the police could be helping. Half the problem is these gangs of marauding youngsters drugged up on God knows what up there." The education officer was evidently not prepared to give an inch of her professional territory.

"If you locked a few more of them up there wouldn't be half the problem, would there?" another voice broke in. "If we're seriously going to put some private sector housing up there we've got to make the place safe. Folk won't pay good money to live in a jungle." The speaker was Jim Baistow, head of the largest of the local construction firms and Longley guessed that he had a sharp eye on the chance of his company building some of the new housing on the Heights. The views alone would be worth an extra ten thousand on a decent house on the hill, he thought. All you needed to do to make a killing was to subdue some of the current residents – or better still, perhaps, get rid of them altogether.

"I'll take back what you say to headquarters," Longley said, face flushed, unable to conceal his anger any longer. "But if the success of this project depends on more police officers on the Heights, then I think you're on a hiding to nothing. We don't have the resources. In the meantime it might do some good if the council paid some attention to security in those tower blocks, to the inadequate street lighting, and to keeping kids in school during the day instead of letting them play truant and wreak havoc around the neighbourhood. You can't rely on one or two police officers to solve all the problems that exist on the Heights. All we can realistically do is pick up the pieces when things get out of hand. You need a coordinated effort up there. And I wouldn't have thought rubbishing this computer project the locals have got going was a very bright idea. Surely what you need is exactly that sort of community involvement. If you've got it, flaunt it. Isn't that what they say? Don't uproot the bloody thing just because it doesn't fit your bureaucratic model. Christ, I thought it was the police force which was supposed to be behind the times."

The rest of the committee gazed at Longley in amazement for half a minute before a babble of members tried to take him up at once.

"Order, order," Dave Spencer said, tapping the water carafe with his pen again and again before the meeting calmed down.

"Well," he said, when silence was restored. "Thank you for that very interesting contribution, Superintendent. I'm sure that's given us all some very useful talking points to take back to our constituencies with us. Perhaps we can defer this discussion until our next meeting when perhaps we will all have had the chance to come up with some constructive suggestions for youth work on the Heights. Does that seem reasonable?" Longley glowered at the chair but the rest of the members nodded or mumbled their assent and Spencer moved quickly on to the next business, with an encouraging smile.

The meeting dragged on for another half hour with Longley increasingly convinced that he had nothing useful to offer. When it broke up he found himself waylaid by Jim Baistow as he gathered his papers together.

"Interesting point you made there about policing," Baistow said. "I'd like to bend your ear some time about the possibilities of private security up there, something Barry Foreman over there has raised a couple of times."

"Really?" Longley said noncommittally. Foreman was obviously another one with his eye on the main chance.

"Are you interested in the horses at all?" Baistow changed track so suddenly that Longley could only look at him with some bemusement.

"Racing," Baistow explained. "I've got a box at York in a couple of week's time if you'd like to join me. Some of the other committee members are coming. Should be a grand day out."

"Thanks, but no thanks," Longley said ungraciously. "I'm not a betting man." He turned away only to find himself following Barry Foreman into the lift. Longley hesitated for a moment before he stepped inside, afraid that Foreman would refer back to his outburst in the meeting but to the superintendent's surprise he too took an entirely different tack.

"All right, is he, that DCI of yours?" Foreman asked pleasantly enough as he pressed the button for the ground floor. "Thackeray?"

"As far as I know. Why shouldn't he be?" Longley said carefully, a tiny niggle of unease at the back of his mind.

"It's just that he popped in to see me for no apparent reason the other day," Foreman said. "I thought he looked stressed out, to be honest. Involved in this big operation on the Heights, is he? I thought it was a bit rich you pleading poverty just now when you've got all that going on up there."

"I know nowt about any operations on the Heights, Mr. Foreman," Longley said. "And if I did, I wouldn't be at liberty to discuss them with you."

"Oh, I see. All a bit hush-hush, is it," Foreman said, tapping the side of his nose and smiling. "Say no more."

"I've no idea who's been putting that about…"

"Oh, well, you pick things up in my trade, you know. Quite a few of my lads have been in the Force at some time."

And most of them have been thrown out of it, Longley thought grimly but said nothing as the lift doors opened and he followed Foreman out into the entrance hall. He wondered if the drug squad knew that their operation had been compromised. One way and another he needed a long session at county HQ and he did not think that his superiors would be too pleased with what he had to tell them.

"There's enough there to make two spliffs at the most," Dizzy B said angrily as DC "Omar" Sharif turned up his not very carefully hidden stash of cannabis at the back of the drawer beside the bed in his hotel room. "You'd have difficulty weighing it."

"It's an illegal substance," Sharif said without sympathy. "You're nicked."

"Look, I've been in the job myself. I know you don't have to do this. It's not even an arrestable offence any more."

"That may be how they carry on where you come from. Here it's different. In any case, I know damn well you've got form. You were done for possession with intent to supply. I've every right to arrest you on suspicion of dealing."

"Checked that out, did you? That was bollocks, anyway," Dizzy B said. "I was going on tour. Needed a decent stash. Some over-enthusiastic copper got carried away. I only got a fine, man. The magistrates had more sense than you lot'll ever have"

"Then you can take your chances with another lot of magistrates, can't you?" Sharif said. "Perhaps you'll be lucky again.

But I wouldn't bank on it. Soft isn't the name o't' game in Yorkshire."

"What are you doing turning me over anyway?" the DJ asked as he flung his leather jacket round his shoulders and prepared to follow the DC downstairs. "I've only been in Bradfield five minutes, and I won't be here again in a hurry, I can tell you."

"We're checking up on everyone connected with the Carib Club," Sharif said. "You just come under the general heading of associates. There's folk in this town want that dump closed down. And if you're the excuse that's just fine by me."

"In other words you're just fishing, man," Dizzy said with disgust.

"Oh, no, it's you idle bastards go fishing. We go tiger hunting. And if you know who the tiger is in this particular jungle you could do yourself a lot of good by filling us in. Guarantee your ticket back to Manchester or London or whichever swamp you surfaced from, I'd say, instead of a spell at Her Majesty's. Know what I mean?"

"Up yours," Dizzy B muttered as he took the back seat offered in DC Sharif's unmarked car. DC Val Ridley glanced round at him from the driving seat.

"To what do we owe this pleasure?" she asked Sharif as she started the engine.

"What do you think? Do they ever go anywhere without their stash?"

"That could be construed as a racist remark," Dizzy B said.

"Could it?" Sharif asked with a smile that could have been construed as a sneer in the DJ's direction. "I thought I was talking about musicians. Colour don't come into it, bro!"

At the police station the DJ found himself being processed behind two men he recognised.

"They're not leaving anyone out then?" he said to one of the two doormen from the Carib.

"Got us out of bed, man."

"And they've brought Darryl in, an'all," his companion said.

"Let's have less chat and more attention to what's going on here," the custody sergeant said, waving the two doormen towards the cells. "Name?"

"David Sanderson," Dizzy B said abruptly as he listened contemptuously to Mohammed Sharif's summary of his arrest and emptied his pockets with all the familiarity of one who had not only stood in front of a custody desk but behind it as well. "Can we get this over with? I've got things to do, places to go."

"CID want to talk to him about other matters, sarge," Sharif said quickly as the sergeant glanced quizzically at the tiny amount of cannabis the DC handed him in a plastic evidence bag. "When Val Ridley's ready."

"My guest, Mr. Sanderson," the sergeant said, gesturing towards the cells where the Carib's doormen had already been incarcerated. As Sharif personally slammed the heavy door behind his prisoner, the two men's eyes met in mutual dislike through the peep-hole before Sharif closed that too.

"Paki bastard," Dizzy B Sanderson shouted loudly enough for Sharif to hear before flinging himself angrily onto the bunk on the other side of the cell. "Let's see the race relations industry sort that out, shall we?"

Four hours later Dizzy B was sipping a vodka and cranberry juice in Bar Med, the stylish new café bar which had just opened in premises near the university that had once been a bank. Kevin Mower leaned back on his tubular steel chair and grinned sympathetically.

"You and Omar didn't hit it off then?"

"Bastard thinks we're all just down from the trees," Sanderson grumbled. "Less than an eighth I had. There was no way they could make out I was dealing. I accepted a caution, but they kept me there two hours trying to get me to grass up my supplier. Did I buy it in Bradfield? Did I buy it at the club? He's in London, for God's sake. What's it to them?"

"They seem to be going over the top about the Carib," Mower said, pulling a face over his orange juice cocktail. "There's no sense in it when it's the kids up at Wuthering who are really running out of control. It's awash with the hard stuff up there."

"Look at this," the DJ said, flinging a copy of the Bradfield Gazette across the table in Mower's direction. "Who gave them all that? Someone's got a hotline to the local rag." The front-page carried a photograph of him under the headline "DJ in drugs bust" and a short item on his recent compulsory trip to the police station.

"I told you. There's people want the Carib closed down, not least the local mosque," Mower said.

"So your mate Omar likely leaked it? He'll be well in at the mosque, I guess."

"I wouldn't jump to conclusions," Mower said quickly. "Bob Baker their crime reporter's always snooping around the nick. He could have picked it up from anyone. There's a few clubbers around who could have recognised you on your way in."

"Too many, by the look of it," Sanderson said bitterly. "What is it with this town?"

"I'll see if I can find out what's going on," Mower said. "In the meantime, you can do me a favour."

"Oh, sure, like I'm right into helping the police with their inquiries just now."

"Come on, this has got nothing to do with the police. I'm putting in some hours at a computer club for disaffected kids, a lot of them black. If you came up to visit you'd give my street cred a boost and they'd be right chuffed, as they say up here. What do you say?"

Dizzy B groaned but finished his drink.

"Community bloody service, is it now? What did I ever do to you, man?"

"Better than digging old ladies' gardens," Mower said without much sympathy.

Chapter Seven

Laura stood on the muddy grass at the centre of the Heights and gazed up at the three dilapidated blocks of flats in something close to despair. The driving rain which had beaten down on Bradfield all morning had only just eased off and the concrete sides of the building were streaked with dark, damp patches. She could see a woman in a red fleece pushing a baby in a buggy along one of the walkways three floors up in Priestley, immediately above the rain-tattered bunches of flowers which lay on the concrete where the boy called Derek Whitby had fallen from the roof to his death. In the other direction she spotted a couple of youths, hoods drawn around their faces so tightly that only their eyes were visible, sauntering out of the doors of Holtby, leaving them swinging open behind them instead of securely locked as the council intended. She watched them watching her as they made their way under the relative shelter of the balconies towards the bus-stop on the main road which skirted the estate. She knew they were young enough to be in school and was equally sure that was not where they were going.

It was the third day in a row that Laura had driven up the steep hill to the Heights during her lunch-hour and today, as she had waited at the traffic lights to turn onto the estate, she had admitted to herself that she was seriously worried about her grandmother. Joyce was looking as old and frail as Laura had ever seen her. Even the sparkle was beginning to disappear from her eyes. Laura knew she was depressed about the vandalism at the Project but guessed that she was finding her inability to pull strings at the Town Hall to push-start the rescue attempt she had set her heart on was even more to blame for her depression.

She followed what had once been a footpath, but which

now resembled a quagmire, towards the Project. It had been the wettest winter on record and she knew that the ceaseless rain was getting to people in unpredictable ways. As January slid gloomily into February the tempers of even the most equable souls were beginning to fray, and equable was not an epithet she would ever apply to herself or to Michael Thackeray. She knew that the tension in their relationship was growing rather than receding as they had both hoped it would, and the knowledge was as dark and heavy as the rainclouds which rolled incessantly down from the high moors to the west.

Donna met her at the door of the Project. She had tied her hair up in a scarf, like a war-time factory worker, and was wearing a sleeveless t-shirt under paint-stained dungarees.

"Watch yourself, pet," she said by way of greeting as she stood aside to let Laura into the reception area which reeked of white spirit. Her smile was warm, though she looked tired.

"We've got most of the red paint off, but if you light a match the place'll go up like a bomb," she said.

"Don't give the tearaways ideas," Laura said. "Is my grandmother here?"

"In t' back with Kevin," Donna said. "He's brought some mate of his from London with him. A DJ? To talk to t' kids?" Donna rolled her eyes to heaven in mock despair at the preoccupations of teenagers and waved Laura on into the building.

Laura made her way into the small kitchen where she found Joyce in animated conversation with Mower and Dizzy B, one white head and two dark ones, and, unexpectedly, three pairs of laughing eyes.

"Did you know your amazing grandmother saw Louis Armstrong in the 1950s?" Mower said, glancing up as Laura came in. "Satchmo himself and I didn't even know she was into jazz. The boss would be impressed."

"There's lots of things I don't know about what Joyce got up to in her misspent youth," Laura admitted with a grin.

"She's not old enough to have been a suffragette but you can bet your life she'd have been chaining herself to railings if she'd had the chance."

"Tried that at Greenham Common," Joyce said tartly.

"She told me she was on the first Aldermaston march too, and every one after that, and the riot in Grosvenor Square," Laura said. "Though I'm sure that's not for police consumption. I bet MI5 have still got her on their files."

Mower put a finger to his lips and glanced at the door to where Donna could be heard belting out 'Look for the Hero Inside Yourself' as she worked.

"We don't know any coppers here, remember?" he said. "And certainly not any spooks."

"They came to interview me once, MI5," Joyce said unexpectedly, a wicked gleam in her eyes. "When George Blake escaped. You remember? The Russian spy? Thought I might know summat about it."

"And did you?" Mower asked.

"Well if I did, I don't think I'd tell you, even after all these years," Joyce said primly. "What you youngsters forget, though, is that we won most of those battles in the end. Only the miners lost and I'll never forgive some folk who should have known better for that."

Mower grinned, and glanced at Dizzy B.

"This is Laura," he said. "A chip off the old block." Mower looked happier behind his piratical black beard than she had seen him for months, Laura thought, and her own heart lifted slightly in response.

"I've met the reporter lady," the DJ said, a wary look in his eyes. "Was it you who put me on the front page of your rag this morning?"

Laura shook her head.

"That was our enterprising crime reporter, Bob Baker," she said. "Nothing to do with me." Dizzy B glanced at Mower uncertainly.

"You can believe it," Mower said. "Baker's got someone at

the nick in his back pocket and the brass would dearly love to know who. It's been going on for a while."

"I thought that sort of thing only happened in American crime novels," Dizzy B said.

"Well, if you imagine the Gazette's paying anyone to leak stuff I should think again," Laura said. "Getting your bus fare to the town hall paid by my boss is like getting blood out of a stone. I don't think even Bob Baker could persuade him to bribe coppers, not because of any moral scruples, you understand, but because he's too damn tight with the petty cash."

Joyce stood up suddenly, as if irritated by the younger generation's chatter.

"Have you heard anything from the town hall about funding for this place, pet?" she asked. And when Laura shook her head her face tightened and aged perceptibly.

"I can't get any sense out of that lad Spencer," she said. "One minute it's all in hand, and the next he's making excuses. I don't think he gives a tuppeny damn about the kids up here when it comes to the point. Calls himself a councillor but all he's really after is a safe seat at the next general election. And he'll more likely get that by buttering up businessmen than by looking after the folk who elected him, more's the pity. They've lost sight of what they're there for, a lot of them. It's a disgrace."

"I'll talk to the guy who covers the town hall when I go back to the office," Laura said. "He must have some idea of what's going on."

"I reckon they've got some scheme for rebuilding up here which ignores what the locals want," Joyce said bitterly. "You'd think they'd have leant from the mistakes we made when we built these flats. Thought we knew best. Never asked folk if they actually wanted to live in prefabricated concrete rabbit warrens. You'd think they'd know better than to make the same mistake again."

"I'll check it out, Nan," Laura said feeling helpless. "Do you want me to run you home now?"

Joyce shook her head vigorously.

"There's a couple of young lasses coming in with their babies at three," she said. "We're going to do some reading. They're worried out of their heads because they're being told to help their kiddies with books and all that and they can barely read themselves."

"What are you like?" Laura said, giving Joyce an enthusiastic hug.

"There's always summat to do," Joyce said, her eyes shining again. "It'd be nice to think things have got better for folk up here, but there's not much sign of it."

"Give it time," Laura said, although she knew that Joyce had already given it a lifetime.

"Do you have some time?" Mower broke in. "You know what you were talking about with Dr. Khan? Dizzy met some kids this morning he'd like us to talk to. One of them's a mate of the lad who went off the roof of Holtby House. You said you wanted to write about what's going on up here. They might make you some good copy."

Laura glanced at her watch and nodded.

"Half an hour," she said.

"You'll have to go without me then," Mower said. "I've got some kids coming in to work on the computers in five minutes." Laura glanced at Kevin Mower with affection.

"Michael won't know where you're coming from when you get back to work," she said.

"If," Mower said so softly that Laura was not sure she heard him.

"Anyway, I'm sure Dizzy and I can cope for now," she said.

Laura followed the DJ out into the relentless rain. As they hurried in silence across the muddy grass towards Holtby House there was a dull explosion of splintering glass behind them. Laura glanced back and saw that there was a smashed bottle on the concrete where a smashed bottle had not been before. She glanced up at the walkways of Priestley House above them but could see no one. Dizzy B shrugged.

"Someone round here doesn't like strangers," he said.

"It's getting worse," Laura said. "It's more threatening than it's ever been."

"It can't be bad if they're pulling these stinking places down, can it?" Sanderson said as they pushed open the swinging doors of Holtby and set off up the steep concrete stairway where the justice of his epithet became immediately apparent. They hurried to the top and stepped slightly breathlessly out onto the walkway where the slanting rain struck them again with icy force but at least the air smelt clean.

"Of course it's not bad," Laura said. "It's what they replace them with that's the issue. And what's going to happen to the people who live here now. That's what's bothering my grandmother."

"You mean they might dump them on some other sink estate?"

"They're talking about building private housing up here. In that case there may well be a problem re-housing the tenants. They're not the sort of people who can afford to buy."

"Yeah, yeah, we've seen all that in London. Put some gates on the council estates, turn the hallway into an atrium, paint the railings round the balconies bright colours, call the flats apartments and flog them off to yuppies. Not only do you upgrade the property but you get lots of middle-class voters in as well. Before you know it you've guaranteed your majority on the local council and put a Tory MP into Parliament as well."

"Only here it's the other lot that's trying to gentrify the place," Laura said. "That's what's driving my grandmother bananas."

They stopped outside the last door on the landing, a flimsy stained affair reinforced with strips of metal around the lock. Dizzy knocked hard but there was no response.

"If his mother's not around he may not come to the door," Dizzy said. He pushed the letter-box experimentally but it would not budge. It had been sealed shut on the inside. Dizzy cupped his hands against the door and shouted.

"Stevie! Stevie. It's me, Dizzy B. Are you in there, man?"

The silence inside the flat continued and Laura was about to give up when they heard footfalls on the walkway behind them and turned to see a tall fair-haired woman bundled up in a black puffa jacket hurrying towards them, looking anxious.

"Oh, it's you," she said when she recognised Sanderson. She glanced more suspiciously at Laura and seemed less than impressed when she introduced herself.

"I don't think we've owt to say to reporters."

Dizzy glanced at the pharmacist's bag which the woman carried.

"You'll get no peace up here until you talk to someone, Mrs. Maddison," he said. "The police and the newspapers are the only ones who can help you, and if you won't talk to the police then why not give the Gazette a try. Laura won't identify you if you don't want her to, will you Laura?"

"Dizzy thought that a feature about your son would get some official attention directed up here. It's about time, isn't it?" Laura added with her most persuasive smile.

"Official attention? That's a bloody joke, isn't it? The only attention we get is when they come to arrest t'kids who take stuff and leave t'dealers running around to get t'little 'uns hooked an'all."

"So you have to stop it," Dizzy said. "Come on, Lorraine. It is Lorraine isn't it? You've got to draw a line somewhere."

"Did Stevie say he'd do this?" Lorraine Maddison asked, her face still clouded with suspicion. "I just went to get his methadone from t'chemist. It takes half the day to get down to town on t'bus but I told him not to answer t'door to no one."

"I told him I'd come back again," Dizzy said. "Ask him if he'll see us. Please?"

Still looking doubtful, the woman unlocked the door with two keys and led them into a darkened living room where they could dimly see a figure curled up under a blanket on the sofa.

"Stevie, love," she said. "Here's Dizzy B back with a lady who wants to talk to you. D'you want to do that, son?"

Slowly the figure stirred and they could make out Stevie Maddison's face, grey and strained, the cheeks sunken and the eyes so bloodshot that he seemed to have difficulty focusing on his visitors. He glanced at Laura's tape-recorder and shrugged, his whole body shrinking as though he could not even find the energy to acquiesce or dispute their presence.

"Dizzy B, man," the boy said faintly, trying to feign an enthusiasm he clearly did not feel. "You again. I never found that demo tape I promised you. My mate Derek's rap. When I feel a bit better…"

"Later, Stevie," Dizzy said. "It'll be fine later."

"Take your medicine, lad," Stevie's mother said, handing him a small glass with some liquid in it. The boy drank and sighed heavily.

"It's no bloody good, this stuff," he said to Dizzy. "They tell you it's as good as t'real thing, but no way. I'm turning into a right wreck." With difficulty he hauled himself upright, revealing emaciated arms, scarred and reddened by continuous infection, and a hollow chest within an over-large t-shirt. He shivered convulsively, although the room was warm and airless. This wrecking of a life, Laura thought, must have begun long ago.

"You want to stop more kids getting into this mess?" Dizzy asked, his voice harsh.

"That'd be summat," the boy said. "But there's no way you can stop it. It's the way it is. You try to stop it and you end up dead, one way or another."

"Is that what happened to the boy who fell off the roof?" Laura asked gently.

Stevie shuddered and wrapped his arms round himself, shivering more violently.

"He were a friend of our Steven's," Lorraine Maddison said. "They were in t'same class at school. When they went to school"

"He went to rehab," Stevie said. "They don't like that."

"Who doesn't like it?" Laura asked angrily.

"The dealers, of course," the boy said contemptuously. "They don't like losing customers, do they? They don't like rehab, do they? They don't like projects, they don't like employment schemes, they don't like people getting their lives together... Bad for business, know what I mean?" For a moment or two he looked animated but the light in his eyes soon began to fade.

"Is it the dealers who are trashing the Project?"

"'spect so," Stevie said, his interest waning. Laura turned to his mother.

"Why isn't Stevie in rehab?" she asked.

"Stevie won't go for treatment. He's too scared of what they might do to him, so we're trying to do it on our own," his mother said. "Any road there's a waiting list for places, isn't there. He might be dead before one comes up. Donna at the Project persuaded him to give it a try but even she couldn't find him a place in a clinic. Months he had to wait, getting worse all t'time."

"She's all right, is Donna," Stevie muttered unexpectedly. "She's cool."

"Tell us about the boy who fell off the roof, Stevie?" Dizzie asked. "What was his name again?"

"Derek, Derek Whitby. He were my best mate. And he didn't fall, man."

"I thought he was high..." Laura began.

"So he was high. Maybe he was, more likely not. I don't think he was using again, man. Last time I saw him he were clean. Any road, he didn't fall," Stevie said. "I was there. I saw him."

"You mean he jumped? Killed himself."

"I don't mean that, neither. I mean he were pushed. I were down below. I'd been waiting for him. I saw him on t'roof wi' some other lads. But there were nothing I could do. I were too far away. I saw him up there and I saw him pushed over t'edge. I heard him scream all t'way down."

"Who? Who pushed him?" Laura asked but the boy just looked at her contemptuously again. It was obvious that there were some things he was never going to tell them, even if he knew.

"So what did you do, Stevie?" Sanderson asked quietly.

"I ran, didn't I? I went back home, didn't I? I thought them bastards'd be coming for me next."

"Have you told the police this?" Laura asked. The boy looked at her again and held a shaking hand up in front of his face.

"This stuff maybe goin' to kill me," he said. "And maybe not. But if I talk to t' police I'm dead. Any fool knows that on t'Heights. See nowt, say nowt, that's the way it is."

"I think it's time you went," Stevie's mother said quietly from the other side of the room where she had been listening to her son as intently as her visitors had. "This lad's going to stay alive. I'll make sure of that."

"But if Derek was murdered...That's what he's saying?" Laura began.

"He's saying nowt," Lorraine Maddison said, glaring at her visitors defiantly. "He knows nowt. That's the way you stay alive round here. If the police want to find summat out they're on their own. And if you tell them owt about what Steven's said, we'll just deny it. There's no help for it. That's the way it is on Wuthering."

Reluctantly Dizzy B led the way back down the damp and stinking staircase.

"He knows who it was," he said. "I'm bloody sure he knows, but unless the police are prepared to get him and his mother off the estate he'll never talk."

"I thought that's what the police did with witnesses," Laura said.

"Sometimes," Dizzy said. "But at the moment the local nick doesn't even believe this Derek boy was murdered so they won't be taking any interest at all, will they?" Just inside the doors to the block he hesitated.

"You up for talking to Derek's mother?" he asked. Laura glanced at her watch. Her lunch-hour was rapidly running out but her instinct was to follow where the story led and risk Ted Grant's wrath.

"You know where she lives?"

Dizzy nodded.

"Your amazing granny told me," he said with a grin.

"Is there anything she doesn't know?" Laura asked with genuine wonderment.

"I doubt it," Dizzy said. "He actually lived in the block where he fell off the roof. His parents are still there, poor sods."

"So let's do it," Laura said, the laughter fading from her eyes. Picking their way across the soggy grass they made their way to the identical entrance of Priestley House, the most westerly of the three blocks of flats on the Heights and the most exposed to the wind and rain. Most of the cellophane wrappings had been blown off the flowers which had been left in tribute to Derek Whitby, and the pale carnations and roses were gradually disintegrating into the mud, a frail memorial to real flesh and blood, Laura thought.

"It's like bloody Siberia up here," Dizzy complained, pulling the collar of his fleece up to his nose.

"They're not joking when they call it Wuthering," Laura said. "And the buildings soak up water like a sponge. They should have pulled them down years ago but they've never been able to find the money – or the commitment. There's some who believe that the people who live up here don't deserve anything better."

Inside the bleak entrance hall where the lifts displayed the familiar out-of-order signs and a couple of hypodermic syringes rolled into a corner in the draught from the open door, she glanced up the staircase quizzically.

"How far this time?" she asked. "I'm not fit enough for this. I've been skipping my exercise lately, putting on the pounds."

Dizzy B glanced at her appreciatively.

"You look fine to me, woman," he said. "Number ten, first floor. Think you can manage that?" He led the way up again and onto another puddled landing where the wind howled like a banshee between the panels of the walkway. Leaning against the gale, eyes half closed against the driving rain, they staggered to the door of number ten and knocked. This time the door was opened quickly, though held on a restraining chain, and two dark eyes peered through the gap.

"Mrs. Whitby?" Laura said. "I'm from the Gazette. I'm writing about the drug problem on the estate and I wondered if you could spare me five minutes?" The eyes widened slightly and for a moment Laura thought that the door was going to be slammed in their faces but eventually the chain was eased off and the door pulled wide to reveal a middle-aged black woman in a formal dark dress who glanced anxiously along the landing before beckoning her two visitors inside.

"You wan' to be careful, girl," she said. "It ain't safe for folk like you to be roun' here asking questions like that." She glanced at Dizzy B her eyes full of accusing anxiety. "You should know better than to bring her here, man," she said.

"We're OK," Dizzy said. "We'll be fine. But we just saw Stevie Maddison and that boy's not fine. Is that the way your Derek was before he died?" Laura thought that Dizzy B's casual brutality would dissolve Mrs. Whitby in front of their eyes but after turning away from them for a moment, her shoulders slumped and her plump features almost collapsing in misery, she turned back with a spark of anger in her eyes.

"He was like that," she said at last. "For a long time he was like that. And then he decided he want to change. And believe me we did everything we could to help that boy. An' Donna from the Project. She a brave lady, that one. She helped me an' Derek. I tol' the police. Derek was not a junkie no more. But out there there's people who do the opposite. They don' want no one to change. They like things just the way they are with these kids. Lots of profit in it for them if things stay the same, I dare say. They come knocking at my door with cheap offers for Derek, special deals… Can you believe that? Like travellin' salesmen? I tell them he not a junkie, that's he's clean and I intend he goin' to stay clean, and then suddenly he's dead, high on something, they say, and falling off a roof. Is that convenient for someone? After all the trouble he went to get himself clean, booking into rehab, everything? Can you believe that is what really happened?"

"What do you think happened, Mrs. Whitby?" Laura asked quietly, switching on her recorder again.

"I think he was killed, that's what I think. That's what Stevie says and I believe him."

"And have you told the police that?"

"I told the police that. And they don' believe me, do they? They don' want to believe me, maybe. Maybe the dealers pay them not to believe me. That's what I think. So now we goin' home. We'd decided that before Derek died. Since 1965 my family been in this country, my mother and father came on the boat all that time ago, and it's been nothin' but trouble all the way. Derek was my youngest boy, my last child, and I've lost him, and there's no justice for black people in this country so we going back to Jamaica. It's all over here, finished. My man is giving up his job at the end of the month. I stopped already when I was helpin' Derek get clean. I worked at the Infirmary but I'll not go back, I haven't the heart now." She crossed the room and took an envelope from behind the clock on the mantelpiece.

"We've bought our tickets," she said. "We've one too many now."

"I'm sorry," Laura said. "When do you fly?"

"At the end of next month. The coroner say we can fix the boy's funeral for next week. There'll be an inquest, but it was an accident, they sayin'. I don't believe that, but what can we do?"

"So if we can persuade the police to look at Derek's death more seriously you could help them?"

"Why they listen to you when they won' listen to the boy's own parents?" Mrs. Whitby asked bitterly.

"I think there are people who know things who haven't talked to the police yet," Dizzy B said, his face grim. "D'you know who might have been threatening Derek?"

"I know what they look like, but I don' know no names. You have to ask the kids. In the end it's the kids who have to stop this trade. The good Lord knows, it took me long enough to persuade Derek to give it up but in the end I succeeded. I prayed for him and prayed with him, and in the end I thought I'd won. And then…" She shrugged and turned away again to hide the raw emotion which overcame her.

"Come here," she said suddenly drawing her visitors to the window which overlooked the bleak spaces between the flats. She turned out the light so that they could not be seen from outside and pointed to where a small group of hooded men and youths huddled in the gloomy shadows under the inadequate shelter of the balconies of Holtby House.

"They dealing there in broad daylight. We never see a policeman trying to stop them. They fearless, those men. They brazen with it. They wait for the kids coming home from school – and soon them they trap don' bother going to school no more. They ain't afraid of no one. That black boy there, see, the tall one. I know he is called Ounce."

"Ounce," Dizzy said. "That's a seriously odd name."

"That's what they call him. He come and he go in a big car and I reckon when he come the drugs come with him. That's how it was with Derek. He was twelve when they got hold of him. A little boy."

"Do you have a photograph of Derek I could use?" Laura asked. "I'd like to make his story the centre of my feature about the estate."

Mrs. Whitby flicked the lights back on and took a school photograph of her son, smiling tentatively at the camera, from the mantelpiece.

"I pray to God it do some good," she said, pressing the picture into Laura's hand. "It won't bring my son back but maybe it will help some others."

Chapter Eight

Laura lay in bed the next morning, rigid with an anger that had not been dissipated by a restless night's sleep. She listened to Michael Thackeray moving around in the bathroom next door and wondered whether reopening their differences again in the grey half-light of morning was worth the risk of deepening the rift between them in the unpropitious cause of changing a mind that had seemed set in stone the previous evening.

She had got home from work already seething. When she had returned to the office she had braved Ted Grant in his glass-walled watch-tower at the end of the newsroom and outlined the results of her researches on the Heights. He had not seemed impressed, and after she had played her tape-recordings of the two distraught mothers to him he had merely opened his office door and summoned Bob Baker, the crime reporter, from his computer with his customary bull-like bellow.

"It's as likely nowt as owt," Grant had said as the younger man glanced inquiringly at the editor. "Laura reckons folk up on the Heights are putting that lad Whitby's death down as murder. What do the police think?"

"What I hear is that Mrs. Whitby's gone off her rocker since the lad died," Baker had said dismissively. "He's a bit of a militant, the father. The Anti-Racist League, works for the council and took them to court over discrimination, all that stuff. Complaints about police harassment a couple of years ago. Nothing substantiated, of course. They see discrimination round every bend, some of these people."

"That's not fair," Laura said. "I've got a witness on that tape who says he saw the other boy pushed over the edge of the roof."

"Black, is he?" Baker asked.

"No, he's not, as it goes," Laura snapped.

"On drugs then?"

"Getting off them, actually. Or trying. He saw what happened and he's scared out of his wits."

"And has he told the police that?" Baker asked. "Because my information is that there's not a scrap of evidence that it was anything but an accident. Derek Whitby was high as a kite, fooling about on the roof, went too near the edge and bingo! He's mince-meat."

"And the other lads who were on the roof with him have come forward to confirm that, have they?" Laura asked sweetly, but Baker just shrugged.

"You know what it's like up there. They won't confirm their own names if they can avoid it," he said.

"Well my information is that the dealers up there are using all sorts of violence to keep the kids in line, and that this was just the most vicious instance," Laura said.

Ted Grant had glanced at his two warring journalists with something like a smirk of satisfaction. Suddenly he pushed Laura's cassette tape in Baker's direction.

"You have a listen to this, Bob," he said. "Then have a word with your contacts up there, and in the Force. Laura's too busy with other stuff to get stuck into a crime story right now – *if* there's a story there, which I very much doubt."

Laura opened her mouth to protest and then closed it again. She knew from the glint in both men's eyes that it would do no good and would only provoke further humiliation. As she spun on her heel to go, hair flying, face set, she heard Baker's low laugh and Grant pull open a drawer in his desk.

"I had my invitation this morning to join this committee to redevelop the Heights," she heard him say. "That was a good move to put my name forward. It'll give us the inside track on a lot of good stories up there."

"I thought you'd be pleased," Baker said. "It was Barry Foreman's idea. Thought you'd be an asset."

"Close the door, lad," Grant had said suddenly, realising that Laura was still within earshot.

White-faced with suppressed anger she had made her way back to her desk, pounded out the last few hundred words of the feature she was working on and had stormed out of the office a good hour before she should have done to drive back up to the Heights as fast as she could weave her Golf through the heavy late afternoon traffic. If remaining on the Gazette meant being passed over in favour of flash young men ten years younger than herself, she wondered how much longer she could hang on. All her half-buried ambition to get out of Bradfield came flooding back. Joyce, she had long ago decided, she could take with her if she decided to move and apart from her grandmother there was only one other person to keep her in her home town any longer. Unfortunately, in spite of their differences, Michael Thackeray remained the most important person in her life. She had pounded the steering wheel in frustration as she waited at the traffic lights to turn onto the Heights again.

Not many cars ventured into the narrow streets beneath the flats and there were few people about on foot in the wet winter dusk as she parked. More aware than usual of the brooding bulk of the estate and the menacing shadows beneath the walkways, she hurried to the Project where she found Donna drinking tea with Kevin Mower in the brightly lit back room.

"Your gran's gone home, love," Donna said, stubbing out her cigarette into her saucer and lighting another. "She looked right tired this afternoon so I told her to go and have a rest. I reckon she's trying to do too much, you know."

"Try telling her that," Laura said. "The day Joyce stops fighting will be the day we need the undertaker."

"How did you get on with Dizzy," Mower had asked and Laura told them everything they had learned from their visits to Stevie Maddison and Derek Whitby's bereaved mother.

"D'you think Derek could have been pushed?" she asked

when she had finished. "He can't have been able to see that clearly in the rain and the dark."

"Anything's possible with some of the scumbags we have to live with up here," Donna said bitterly.

"Do you know this man they call Ounce? Mrs. Whitby's sure he's behind the dealing."

"I've not come across him, though I've heard the kids mention the name. We…" She hesitated and glanced guiltily at Mower. "I'll ask around. See what's being said. But I guess if the police didn't investigate Derek's death straight away they'll not be right interested now. The lad's funeral's next week."

Laura glanced at Mower who almost imperceptibly shook his head. So he still had not told Donna that he was a policeman, Laura thought, even though that unexpected pronoun had hinted again at a much closer relationship than was apparent to the naked eye. She smiled slightly.

"I'll chase Bob Baker so we get a story out of it somehow," she said. "That's a promise."

But when she had got home and turned to the person she had hoped would be her closest ally in an attempt to expose what was happening on the Heights, she met a lack of enthusiasm that at first surprised and then infuriated her.

"You're taking a real risk knocking on doors up there," Thackeray had said, propped up on the pillows beside her in too unyielding a position for Laura to feel able to get as close to him as she usually did. He took up their debate where they had left it earlier in the evening. "Especially if you're with someone who may well be a dealer himself. David Sanderson has form for drug use, and he's up to his eyes in the Carib Club which seems to be awash with the stuff."

"It's not a bit of dope we're talking about up there, is it?" Laura said. "These kids are dying from heroin overdoses, crack cocaine, cocktails of the real hard stuff. Dizzy B's just as horrified by what's going on as any of us. He's a nice guy. And he's not too impressed by the attitude of some of your people, as it goes. Says he was nicked by a racist DC, an Asian. Who would that be then?"

"Sharif," Thackeray said shortly. "Just arrived from Leeds, but he's a Bradfield boy. And if Sanderson's got a complaint he should make it through the official channels, not go broadcasting his grievances to the Press and God knows who else."

"I'll tell him," Laura had said, her temper on a very short fuse. "So stick to the main issue, Michael. What's being done about the heroin crisis on the Heights? Why do people think a murder's being covered up? Why does everyone up there – including Joyce, incidentally – think no one gives a damn about their kids? Is everyone just waiting for the flats to be pulled down and hoping that the problem will disappear with them? It's not very likely, is it? It'll just move somewhere else."

"Laura, Laura, you're jumping to conclusions again. I never said nothing was being done. But I can't tell you about everything we're doing, you know that. It's not all my responsibility. As far as I'm concerned I'm still trying to discover who got the Adams boy so far out of his head on Ecstasy that he walked in front of a taxi."

"Is he still unconscious?" Laura asked.

"As far as I know, yes. But slightly improved, apparently."

"But if this other boy, Derek Whitby, was pushed off the roof that would be murder and surely that would be your responsibility, even if the drug squad is up on the Heights," she had persisted.

"I never said anything about the drug squad," Thackeray came back irritably. "And I've absolutely no evidence that the Whitby boy was murdered. Bring me the witnesses, and then we can talk about it. In the meantime, please don't take risks up there. You're right on one count at least – the place is run by the dealers and some of them are very unpleasant indeed. They'd think nothing of throwing a reporter off a roof if she got in their way."

"I can look after myself," Laura had said, with more

confidence than she really felt. "And I think I can get you the witnesses."

Thackeray groaned.

"You are the most pig-headed person I have ever met," he said.

"And you love me for it," Laura had come back quickly, reaching a tentative hand for his. But he had pulled away.

"Just now I'd like to go to sleep," he said. "You're not the only one who's had a bad day." And with that she had to be content. In the cold light of morning, finding herself alone in the bed, Laura had quickly realised that she had not forgiven him for his lack of understanding and she guessed – as he had not roused her with his usual kiss – that he felt much the same.

"Damn and blast," she muttered into the pillows, before burying her head under the bedclothes and remaining there without moving until she heard the front door close behind him. "Oh, Michael," she said to herself as she shrugged herself into her bathrobe and wandered into the kitchen for orange juice. "Are we ever going to make this work?"

Thackeray carried his ill-humour to the office with him. His track record with women, he thought as he drove into town, didn't bear thinking about. His marriage to the sweetheart he had met at sixteen had collapsed early into acrimony on Aileen's part and heavy drinking on his. By the time their son Ian had been born it had been too late to rescue much from the wreckage and he had been too drunk most of the time to notice that his wife was sliding into the suicidal depression which soon claimed her sanity and the life of their baby. Since then he had drifted from one brief unsatisfactory relationship to another until he met Laura Ackroyd and rediscovered the sort of intense happiness which he thought had slipped beyond his grasp for good. And now he found himself wondering how long it could last – and how long he could last if she left him. He knew she was frustrated by her job, by

Bradfield and increasingly, he felt, by his own limitations. They paddled endlessly around the jagged reefs of his fears: of commitment, of permanence, of having another child. He adored her for her resilience, her determination and her humour, but these were the very things he was afraid he was wearing down. She deserved more, and he was very afraid that he would never be able to give it to her.

He parked his car in his space at the central police station and made his way gloomily to his office where he flicked idly through overnight reports. The name Adams caught his eye and he saw that Jeremy, who had been in the Infirmary for almost a week now, had regained consciousness. Squaring his shoulders to face the day's work, he picked up the phone and asked DC Val Ridley to come in to see him.

"Can we interview the Adams boy today?" he asked when she had presented herself, all brisk efficiency in a dark suit and a powder blue shirt which matched her wary eyes.

"Possibly," she said. "But doting dad says he wants his solicitor to be there."

"Taking no chances then?"

"He wouldn't would he, boss?"

"Let me know when you get a slot to see him," Thackeray said. "I might come with you. If they feel the need to put up their big guns perhaps we should do the same."

Val Ridley smiled faintly as if she approved of that but she did not comment.

"Did you hear about the trouble at the Carib Club last night?" she asked.

And when Thackeray shook his head, she expanded.

"Running battles between the black kids coming out and some Asian youths who were evidently waiting for them outside."

"Serious, was it?"

"Serious enough. Half a dozen charges of affray, a couple of ABH, three in hospital with minor stab wounds. And a whole chorus of the great and the good on the local radio this morning calling for the place to be shut down. Including the local mosque, of course." Laura usually listened to the local radio news as they snatched breakfast together, he thought, but this morning he had made sure he was not there when she woke.

"You're not suggesting it was a put-up job, are you?" Thackeray asked with half a smile. "I mean, if you want to get a place a reputation for rowdiness there's no easier way than providing a bit, is there? What was your impression when you interviewed the owners?"

"It didn't seem to be any worse than half a dozen other clubs on the patch," Val said.

"And young Sharif? Would he agree with that assessment?"

"Omar's a bit uptight about these things," Val said carefully. "The Carib's very close to Aysgarth Lane. There's been a long history of trouble between the black and Asian youngsters there. Omar's not just aware of that, I guess he was probably part of it when he was at school. The older generation seemed to be doing their best to damp it down but I'm not so sure now."

"I heard Omar didn't endear himself to the DJ when you arrested him yesterday," Thackeray said, to Val Ridley's evident surprise. "Over the top, was he?"

"I don't think so, sir," she said, not daring to ask how he had come by his information. "Not much love lost, but nothing you'd need the race relations thought-police for."

"The last thing I want with this Carib row going on are allegations that the police are taking sides, or being racist in any way," Thackeray said. "Keep an eye on Sharif, will you? And on anyone else who might raise the tension – by accident or design."

"Sir," Val Ridley said, her face expressionless, and Thackeray knew that she did not like the order, although whether that was because she thought he was over-reacting or because she did not want to mother a younger colleague, he could not tell. She probably suspected that he would not have asked any of her male colleagues to do the same, and she was probably right, he thought wryly.

Ridley hesitated by the door.

"Have you heard anything from Kevin?" she asked at last. "When he's coming back."

"He's got another couple of weeks before he needs to make a decision," Thackeray said. Another boss might have teased her about her interest but that was not the way he worked. "Last I heard he was doing fine."

"He's a good copper," Val said defensively.

"I know that, Val," Thackeray said. "Don't worry. I'm not looking for an excuse to get rid of him."

She nodded and closed the door quietly behind her, leaving Thackeray to contemplate his economy with the truth. Val Ridley, he guessed, still carried a torch for Kevin Mower, in spite of the sergeant's near contemptuous lack of interest, but he saw no reason to cause her unnecessary anxiety about his future. But while he would be happy to have Mower back on his team he knew there were those above him in the hierarchy who might not be so keen. When it came to the crunch, he knew that he might have to fight for Mower's future career. And he owed him that, at least.

For the rest of the morning he ploughed through the paperwork and it was not until lunch-time that Val Ridley knocked on his door again and dropped a copy of the first edition of the day's Bradfield Gazette on his desk.

"I thought you'd like to see that, boss." The headline jumped out at him

"Drug club facing closure".

He read Bob Baker's front page story with growing anger before taking the stairs two at a time to superintendent Jack Longley's office. Longley raised an eyebrow as the DCI was admitted to his sanctum.

"Summat up, Michael?" he asked mildly.

"I just wondered who the police spokesman was who's

allegedly said we're considering taking action on the Carib," Thackeray said, spreading the paper in front of Longley just as Val Ridley had spread it in front of him. Longley cast an eye over it.

"Gone to town a bit, has he?" he murmured. "He was trying to get hold of me last night, but I got the wife to tell him to go through the Press office. I'd nowt to say to Baker. I'd like to know who has been blabbing in that direction, mind."

"So *are* we considering closing the place down? On the say-so of Grantley Adams? The black kids will play merry hell. It's the only place they really call their own."

"If we do close it, it'll be when I say so and on my say-so, not Adams's, or the imams from the mosque. But yes, after the little fracas last night, following on from the accident, uniform's not happy. They thought they might try out these new powers to close rowdy pubs and clubs. D'you have a problem with that?"

"Not if the trouble stems from the club itself and not from people trying to get it closed down by making sure there's trouble there," Thackeray said.

"Yes, well, it has to be said that Barry Foreman says his door-policy will keep the trouble-makers out."

Thackeray found it hard to conceal his astonishment at that.

"I met him at this regeneration committee they've asked me on," Longley said quickly. "He rang me yesterday and we had a chat about the Carib. He reckons he can keep the drugs out."

"Does he?" Thackeray said, not bothering to hide his scepticism. "That's not what I hear happens at the other clubs where he does the doors. Word is that selected dealers get in with no questions asked. His own men, no doubt. We just don't have the evidence to prove it."

"Aye, well, I've told you before, he's well in now, is Foreman. If you reckon he's anything other than a respectable businessman you'll have to find some cast-iron evidence to prove it."

"And the Carib?" Thackeray said, his unease growing.

"My feeling is that we give the Carib one last chance to see if Foreman's as good as his word. But if we get trouble on the streets again we'll be under a lot of pressure."

"My guess is you'll get trouble on the streets either way," Thackeray said. "It's a no win situation. In the meantime, it looks as if we'll be able to interview the Adams boy shortly. He's regained consciousness, apparently."

"Has he?" Longley said. "That's good. You'll go and see him yourself, will you?" It was not phrased as an instruction but Thackeray had no doubt what was intended.

"I'll see if I can find the time," he said, grudging what he had already decided to do anyway. "Don't worry, we'll get the kid gloves out, but if he's been dealing he'll get no favours from me."

"Of course not, Michael," Longley said, unembarrassed.

By mid-afternoon Thackeray found himself waiting with Val Ridley outside a side-room off a ward at the Infirmary. Through the frosted glass windows it was possible to see the shapes of several people moving about the small room and when eventually the door was opened by Grantley Adams himself, they found Victor Mendelson, one of the town's leading solicitors, sitting on one side of Jeremy Adams's bed, and his mother on the other, with an anxious-looking young nurse hovering at the end of the bed.

Thackeray nodded to Mendelson, who was the father of one of his few close friends in Bradfield, the friend who had introduced him to Laura Ackroyd at a dinner party, every minute of which he still remembered well. He introduced himself and Val Ridley to the boy on the bed, who was watching the proceedings from beneath a swathe of bandages with surprisingly wide-awake eyes considering he was supposed to have been unconscious for days. Thackeray nodded to the boy's parents and then held the door open wide.

"If you'll excuse us, we'd like to talk to Jeremy alone please. Victor will represent his interests very ably, I'm sure."

Grantley Adams, face flushed, opened his mouth as if to object but his wife got to her feet quickly, took his arm and urged him into the corridor as Victor Mendelson held up a placatory hand. The nurse followed the parents out of the room.

"How are you feeling, Jeremy?" Thackeray asked after introducing himself and taking a seat on the other side of the bed from the lawyer. "You're quite sure you feel fit enough to answer some questions about the night of your accident?"

The boy nodded.

"I'm not sure I remember much," he said.

"It's not the accident I'm so interested in as what happened before," Thackeray said. "There were plenty of witnesses to what happened outside the club. What I'd like to know is where you came by the drug which was found in your blood stream when the hospital came to do tests. In other words, where did you get the Ecstasy from?"

"I'm not sure my client should answer that," Victor Mendelson said.

"It's all right," the boy came back quickly. "Honestly, I can't remember. That whole evening is a blur."

"You can't remember whether you took it before you went to the club or while you were in there?"

"What does Louise say?" the boy prevaricated.

"I can't tell you that," Thackeray said. "I want you to try to remember without any prompting."

Jeremy shook his head and then winced and passed a hand which was shaking slightly across his eyes.

"I can't recall, you know. I'm sorry."

"Can you recall whether it was the first time you'd taken Ecstasy?" Thackeray asked.

"Oh, yes, it must have been. It's not a habit or anything like that. It was Louise's birthday, a celebration. We must have decided to give it a try."

"You mean she supplied it?"

"No, I don't mean that at all," the boy said with a startled look at the lawyer. "But it's difficult to remember."

"And what about the cannabis? Is that a habit?"

Victor Mendelson made to intervene but Thackeray shook his head sharply.

"We found some in his room," he explained.

Jeremy Adams shut his eyes and sighed heavily.

"Just now and again we'd have a spliff," he said. "Honestly, it was nothing. We never took it to school or anything. Just in the house, usually."

"And did your parents know this was going on?"

"No, of course not."

"And who supplied you with the cannabis?" Thackeray persisted, although he knew he would not get an answer.

"Oh, friends of friends, you know. It's not difficult to get hold of. No regular dealer or anything. It's harmless enough. You know that."

Thackeray ignored that.

"So you can't tell me the name of anyone you've bought illegal drugs off – ever?" he snapped. "These things just came into your possession almost inadvertently?"

The boy glanced at his lawyer and shook his head helplessly.

"That's the way it is, you know?" he said. And Thackeray almost believed him.

Outside in the corridor he found Grantley Adams waiting, his broad face still suffused with colour. His wife fluttered to one side of him like a nervous bird. Adams opened his mouth as if to launch a new tirade but Thackeray was determined to get in first.

"We won't bother Jeremy again until he's recovered," he said. "But we may well want to talk to him again at some point, Mr. Adams. He doesn't deny he's been taking illegal drugs."

"Did he tell you where he got the stuff? The Ecstasy?" Adams asked.

"No, he didn't," Thackeray said. "Nor where he got the cannabis we found in his bedroom. Did you know he had cannabis in the house, Mr. Adams?"

"Of course I bloody didn't," Adams said. "I'd have tanned his backside for him if I had, never mind how big he's grown. What I want to know is where he's been getting it from. I'd put odds on it being that bloody club."

"That's what we'd like to know too," Thackeray said. "But hasn't it crossed your mind that Jeremy may not just have been buying drugs, but selling them too. That he may have been a dealer..." Mrs. Adams gave a faint moan at that.

"You what?" Adams said, his face becoming even more flushed. "What the hell are you suggesting now, man?"

"I'm not suggesting anything, Mr. Adams," Thackeray said, aware that Victor Mendelson had followed him out of the ward and was watching him with what appeared to be a thin smile. "You have every right to know what line our inquiries might take when Jeremy's a bit more able to recall what he's been involved in recently. As I think you've said yourself, drugs are a menace and those who deal in them need to be identified."

Adams appeared to deflate suddenly and turned a sickly shade of pale. He glanced at his lawyer for help but Mendelson was studying the no-smoking notice on the other side of the corridor with unusual interest.

"Thank you for your help," Thackeray said to no one in particular and led Val Ridley away down the long hospital corridor at a brisk pace leaving Adams to berate his lawyer in a fierce whisper.

"That was a bit over the top, wasn't it, boss?" Val said as soon as they were out of earshot. "You don't really think the boy's been dealing, do you?"

"I haven't the faintest idea," Thackeray said. "The whole thing is a complete charade. He'll never tell us where he got the Ecstasy and his cannabis stash isn't even worth cautioning him for. But Adams himself was the one screaming for retribution. It doesn't hurt to let him know just where that might lead."

Val glanced at her boss with some curiosity. She recognised

a bombastic bully in Adams when she saw one but she had not often seen the DCI react so overtly to such a challenge. Canteen gossip, in this case originating she guessed with Kevin Mower, suggested that Laura Ackroyd has been known to indulge in a spliff now and again – although how Kevin had come by that piece of compromising information she could not begin to guess. Perhaps Kevin had shared one with her. She would not put it past him. Or perhaps the reporter had been passing round a relaxing joint at home these winter nights, Val thought with a secret smile.

"We waste too much time chasing kids with dope," she said cautiously. Thackeray glanced at her as they waited for the lift.

"Maybe," he said. "Though in this case you're certainly right. If Grantley Adams didn't regard himself as the great moral arbiter for the whole of Bradfield…"

"Or its grand master, more like," Val said sharply. "We wouldn't be here, right?"

"I couldn't possibly comment," Thackeray said.

Thackeray let the detective constable go back to police HQ without him and made his way through the long hospital corridors and down a back staircase to where the mortuary and pathology departments lived discreetly separate lives in the basement. Amos Atherton was not in his office, and after glancing through a small window into the main operating room, Thackeray saw the pathologist untangling his bulky frame from green blood-stained overalls. He nodded at the DCI through the glass as he struggled out of his boots.

"Give me two minutes, lad," Atherton mouthed, holding up his fingers in a Churchillian salute.

Thackeray waited in the corridor wondering whether he could get away with a cigarette immediately beneath the large red no-smoking notice on the tiled wall. It was not a place he had ever felt comfortable. Too many memories stalked the infirmary corridors for his peace of mind, and they were not just of people he had met professionally, lying naked and ultimately exposed in the room behind him, victims of a second assault under Atherton's dispassionate scalpels and saws, although those ghosts were bad enough. Once he had roamed these tiled depths for hours, without authority and crazed with grief and alcohol, while a pathologist – and he had never dared ask Atherton if it had been him – had ascertained the cause of death of his tiny son. Upstairs his wife had lain comatose hooked up to life-support machines, and while every fibre of his being had wished Ian back to life, he had just as fervently wanted Aileen dead. In the end the cries of pain he was hardly aware he had uttered had brought officialdom in his direction and sympathetic but firm hands had led him away. He had never set foot in the hospital again without a shudder of fear and shame.

Atherton's two minutes were up and the pathologist shambled out of the morgue straightening his jacket across broad shoulders and making a vain attempt to button it across his ample stomach.

"Now then?"

Thackeray hesitated for no more than a second.

"The lad on the Heights who fell off the roof," he said at length. "Open and shut, was it? Nothing to suggest it might not have been an accident?"

"Ah, now I'm glad you asked me that. I've been meaning to complete the report and get it back to you," Atherton said, looking slightly flustered. "I'd been expecting to find him full of heroin. The tolerance these kids build up never ceases to amaze me. But even though he had plenty of old scars and track marks on his arms, the blood tests came back clean."

"His mother's insisting he was murdered," Thackeray said shortly.

"Well, I can't say that's what I concluded. There were no injuries I could find that weren't consistent with him simply hitting the ground from a great height. He could have been pushed, I suppose, but I'm not sure that's what the coroner will decide, on the evidence we've got. He could have just been fooling about up there, the way lads do. All I can tell you is that he wasn't high on drugs, for what that's worth."

Thackeray shrugged.

"It's probably nothing. Though in the natural course of events, there's too many people dying up there. Take each case on its own and it looks like an overdose or some other sort of accident. Take them together and you begin to wonder."

"If you want to kill an addict there's one foolproof way to do it," Atherton said. "And that's to give them an overdose, or a dose full of rubbish like sink cleaner. Who's going to ask questions any road? Most folk just write it off as no more than they deserve. And kids on the Heights all get tarred with the same brush. Are the police any different?"

"Probably not," Thackeray admitted.

"Now if it's Grantley Adams's son, then a few stops get pulled out…" Atherton offered with a tight smile.

Thackeray groaned. "Not you as well," he said.

"Bit close to the mark, is it?"

"I'd not have wasted half a day on it myself, to be honest," Thackeray said. "Essentially it was a traffic accident."

"It's all politics, lad, you should have learned that by now. Why do you think this department's still stuck down here in the bowels of the earth with equipment that bloody Burke and Hare would have found familiar. It's because I won't play their games and butter up the chief executive of the hospital trust on the golf course like some folk I could name. Golf clubs, Masonic Lodges – if your only outside interests are a bit of course fishing and a ramble on t'Pennine Way on a Sunday afternoon you're out of the loop. QED."

The thought of Atherton rambling across Town Hall Square, let alone the wild moorland paths of the Yorkshire hills brought a faint smile to Thackeray's normally impassive features.

"Pull the other one," he said.

"Aye, well, I was young once. So why else have you come?"

Atherton asked, steering his guest towards the stairs and the faint clatter of the hospital tea-room above. "I reckon it's not to buy me a cuppa and a Penguin biscuit."

"A favour," Thackeray said quietly.

"Oh aye?" Atherton said non-commitally, though his eyes said "You too?" He stopped short of the top of the stairs and put out a broad arm to bar Thackeray's way.

"You remember the dodgy doctor at the May Anderson clinic I crossed swords with earlier this year?" Thackeray asked, his voice low.

"No one in the business will forget that bastard in a hurry," Atherton said. "Bloody General Medical Council hasn't got round to striking him off yet, you know."

"I know," Thackeray said. "But it's one of his patients I'm interested in. Medical opinion seems to reckon that he couldn't possibly have been experimenting with clones, is that right?"

Atherton nodded wary agreement.

"So we're left with the case of Karen Bailey. She had twins at the clinic and the whole thing left her wondering who the hell the father was – assuming there was one."

Atherton said nothing but his eyes narrowed and he kept his arm firmly in place, blocking the stairs. Thackeray hesitated.

"Her boyfriend says they never had tests done to establish paternity," he said at last.

"He must be the only man on earth who doesn't want to know," Atherton said.

"It's hardly credible. And with twins…" He shrugged.

"I don't believe him," Thackeray said. "Would she come here for tests?"

"The May Anderson has some arrangement with our labs, I think," Atherton said. "Unless she had it done privately somewhere else. I suppose you want me to root around in the records for you, do you?"

"I'd be grateful."

"Aye, so you should be," Atherton said. "Of course, you realise that if all they did was a simple blood test it won't tell you who the father actually is, if it turns out it can't be who it ought to be? You'd need DNA samples for that and I doubt they'd go to the expense of getting that done. Chances are they'd not have a sample to match against anyway if the actual father was keeping his head down."

"Money might be no object, but if the father's not who it should have been that's all I need to know," Thackeray said. His mind clouded for a second and he felt an emptiness in his gut that took his breath away.

"You all right?" Atherton asked.

"I'm fine," Thackeray said, trying to drive away the image of a baby's face gazing at him wide-eyed from beneath the surface of his bathwater.

"I'll not promise," Atherton said. "But I'll see what I can do. You look as if you need a holiday, lad."

"It's booked," Thackeray lied.

Chapter Nine

Laura Ackroyd set up her tape-recorder on the polished table which dominated councillor Dave Spencer's spacious office and smiled sweetly at the councillor himself and his even younger press officer who sat opposite her, as she recalled the first rule of journalism according to Jeremy Paxman which was to ask why these bastards were lying to her. She had no particular reason to distrust Spencer, who had granted her request for an interview about the new development on the Heights readily enough. He had all the attributes she admired in a politician. He was young, and evidently energetic and open-minded, ready to find solutions to problems without relying on dogma to give him the answers. And however much the lack of ideology might upset her grandmother, Laura could see no reason to object to any strategy which brought results for Bradfield's less prosperous citizens, as Spencer and his colleagues claimed their policies did. And yet as she pulled out her notebook and her list of topics she wanted to discuss with him, she felt uneasy. All the Italian-suited charm, and crop – haired openness across the table did not impress her as much close up as it had at a distance. Might there after all, she thought, be something to hide? But if there were, she was not sure that she was skilful enough to discover what it was.

"So what can we tell you, Laura?" Spencer asked. "Ted Grant says he wants to give this the centre spread so we've brought you up some of the outline plans which you can reproduce. They're on display downstairs, of course, but not many people make the effort to come and look." He glanced at the young woman at his side. "Jay here is going to do a flyer which will go out to all the residents of the Heights so that they know exactly where we are coming from with this."

"Fine," Laura said, switching on the recorder, bristling at his tone.

"Let me talk you through," Spencer offered kindly. "I don't suppose you're used to reading this sort of stuff. These outlines here are where the existing blocks of flats stood. They'll all come down, of course, when we get the go-ahead, and not before time. They'll be replaced by low rise housing, here, and here and here." He ran a finger along the lines which indicated new streets. "And here we have a new primary school to replace the Victorian slum down the hill."

"The one where the ceilings are always falling down because the roof leaks?"

"St. Michael's. That's it. This will be much more convenient for the families, and a good modern building. That's pure planning gain, of course. And here, a health and community centre, to replace those awful huts, and there an outpost for the further education college to provide courses at that end of the town."

"And this is all going to be low rent housing, councillor?" Laura asked. "So the tenants of the flats can stay?" The right to buy council properties had proved a dismal failure for tenants in the tower blocks of Wuthering as no financial institution could be persuaded to grant mortgages on the damp and rotting dwellings which had been due for demolition for ten years or more, even if anyone had been prepared to buy them.

"Do call me Dave, by the way," Spencer came back. "But, no, this is a public-private partnership and in any case the new thinking is that we should mix the types of accommodation so that we don't recreate these sink estates…"

"And the old people's bungalows? They're not in such poor condition." Laura thought of her grandmother's fury if her small but comfortable home were to be demolished.

"They come down too. That's a prime site they're sitting on, worth a lot of money to the council, and the existing density's too low for the new developers."

"So how many of the original tenants will be re-housed on the Heights?" Laura asked.

"Well, that sort of detail will be thrashed out in the

consultation. No definite decisions have been taken. And the developers will want a say, of course."

"Approximately, Dave?" Laura persisted.

"Well, I should think when the plans are finalised some-where between two-thirds and a half of the tenants will be re-housed elsewhere. It's inevitable when you take these high rise blocks down that some people will have to move on."

"That's an awful lot of people," Laura said quietly. "Have they any idea they'll be moved out to make way for more affluent residents?"

"As Councillor Spencer said we're working on the full con-sultation procedures as we speak," Jay said enthusiastically. "We'll be leafletting up there, having a public meeting, all long before the planning committee commits to definite deci-sions."

"This is all the council's land?" Laura asked.

"Oh, yes," Spencer said.

"So why isn't it possible simply to pull down the old blocks and replace them with enough new houses to accommodate the whole of the existing community?"

"Well, as I said, it doesn't work quite like that these days. There's a presumption in favour of mixed developments. And then the government likes the thing to be done in part-nership with the private sector and inevitably the private sec-tor wants houses to sell. Bradfield will do very well out of this. It's a fantastic way of involving local business and get-ting investment without massive borrowing. We will get the public buildings a modern community up there needs while our private partners will get land for their housing in a prime site. The views from that hill will be a major selling point…"

"I'm sure they will," Laura said. "So let me get this clear. Your private partners put money in?"

"They buy the land – cleared of course – which gives the council a nice little windfall…"

"How much is the land worth then?"

"Oh, I'm not sure, but I've heard twenty million mentioned,"

Spencer said. "Can't be bad for Bradfield, that. Then on top of that the developers build the new housing and other facilities."

"And then some of the housing is sold? So how much will the private houses go for then?" Laura asked.

"Well, they are thinking at the moment of executive town houses, with small gardens and reserved parking, so we're talking top of the range."

"So not many of the current residents will be buying those?"

Spencer looked irritated for a second and then smiled faintly.

"The indefatigable Joyce has been briefing you, has she? No, as I said, this is intended to be a mixed development." He ran his finger across the map again. "Private housing here at the east side, overlooking the town. Quite a valuable proposition, that. And public housing further back to the west."

"And the rest belongs to the council: houses, school, health centre and so on?"

"No, not exactly. We lease what we want back from the developers and they maintain the facilities for us. For thirty years in the first instance. It's a way of getting private investment into public facilities. Brilliantly simple really. It's definitely the way ahead."

"But your business partners will do very well out of it, won't they? They get to do the building for you, sell the private housing, lease back the social housing and community stuff to the council – they can't lose, can they? But do you actually save public money in the long run? Is it cheaper?"

"In the short term, yes, much cheaper," Spencer said.

"But not long term?" Laura persisted.

Spencer did not answer. If I can find a tame accountant, Laura thought, I'll work out just what this does cost in the end.

"Who are these partners exactly?" Laura asked.

"That's not for public consumption yet," Spencer said. "It'll be a consortium. There's a couple of groups interested. City

Ventures is one. Blackstock Holdings another. But there may be more by the time it goes out to tender."

"Local businesses?"

"Oh, yes, some of them. It all boosts the local economy, one way or another."

"So there'll be an open competition for the contract?"

"Probably," Spencer said. "We may have a favoured bidder, but that's all in the future."

"And what about the project that the women are running up there for the school drop-outs, the one my grandmother was so anxious about? That will be housed in the new college facilities, will it? Or in the community centre?"

Spencer glanced at Jay, who looked disconcerted.

"I'm not sure any provision has been made for that sort of facility, although Mr. Foreman did say that he would be interested in helping with facilities for young people in difficulties," she said. "Of course, with the new executive housing on the Heights we're hoping that a lot of the problems they have currently up there will be ..." She hesitated.

"Dispersed," Spencer said cheerfully. "That's the word Jay's looking for. One of the difficulties we have currently up at Wuthering, as you must know, is the sheer concentration of problem families and difficult kids. They'll undoubtedly be dispersed by this new development. And a very good thing too. It'll be much easier for the schools and other agencies to deal with these kids if they are not concentrated in one place, and in one or two schools."

"But much harder for the parents to organise self-help schemes like the Project," Laura said. "And where exactly will they be dispersed to? They'll get nice new houses somewhere else, will they? Or not?"

"Well, we have no other major redevelopment schemes in the pipeline so I expect most will move onto older properties elsewhere. That's inevitable, really," Spencer said. "We've no shortage of vacant properties which are in better condition than the flats up at Wuthering. So everyone gains."

"I thought most of your vacant properties were vandalised and impossible to sell," Laura said, feeling almost as outraged by Spencer's plans as she knew Joyce would be when she heard the details.

"Not at all," Spencer said. "In any case, any property people move to will be made fit before they move in. We'll have the funds for that too, when the land on the Heights is sold to the developers."

"Not really much in this for those who have to move though, is there? The community broken up, lots of people moved out to areas they may not want to go to? Won't this be a difficult scheme to sell to the people on the Heights, Councillor Spencer?"

"Oh, I think we'll manage, Laura," Spencer said easily. "I don't really anticipate any difficulties. The crucial decisions will be taken by the planning committee once the regeneration committee has drawn up its final plans and has costed the whole project."

So I guess that's all sewn up already, Laura thought.

"Well, it's certainly an interesting scheme," she said.

"Well, I know your editor thinks so. You know we've asked him to sit on the regeneration committee, don't you. We're sure his input will be extremely valuable."

Laura nodded weakly, not willing to admit to knowledge that she was not supposed to have.

"Terrific," she said.

"Call me if you have any more questions when you come to write your feature," Jay said, passing a wad of glossy brochures across the table to Laura. "This is what we've prepared so far."

Laura glanced at the sketches of town houses set amidst trees and neatly parked BMWs which appeared on the front of the publicity material and thought of the fate of cars currently left parked for more than half an hour on the Heights. She smiled sweetly, green eyes opaque as she caught Spencer's gaze.

"Fine," she said. "And when does your consultation begin?"

"After the next meeting of the committee," Spencer said. "Ted indicated that he would use your feature the day after that."

"And there was I thinking we were an independent newspaper," Laura said stabbing off her tape-recorder with an angry jab. Dave Spencer's expression hardened for a second and then he smiled, without warmth.

"I'm sure no one is going to compromise your independence, Laura," he said. "You're a chip off the old block."

"I'll get my grandmother to contact you again about funding for the Project, then, shall I? I don't think she's had an answer on that yet."

"Of course," Spencer said. "We'll see what we can do about that. Perhaps Barry Foreman would come to the rescue with a bit of persuasion. You never know."

"I'm not sure that's quite what she had in mind," Laura said.

"No, I'm sure it isn't," Spencer said, distinctly waspish this time. "But even the dinosaur tendency is going to have to shift its arse in the end, you know. Perhaps you could tell her that before she comes badgering me again?"

"D'you fancy lunch?" Laura asked when she was back at her desk and finally got through to Michael Thackeray. There was a long enough silence at the other end of the line to cause her heart to sink.

"Michael," she said softly.

"The Warp and Weft in half-an-hour," he said at last, naming a pub where they were unlikely to meet any of his colleagues or hers. He was already sitting at a corner table when she arrived, surrounded by an array of old wool mill relics, now collectors items rather than anything with much bearing on Bradfield's economy. He had a glass of tonic and ice in front of him and a similar glass which Laura hoped contained vodka as well as tonic on the opposite side of the table. Laura slipped off her coat and dumped it on an empty chair and leaned across the table to kiss his cheek.

"I've been confining my inquiries to the town hall this morning," she said. "Am I forgiven?"

"Of course you are," he said, wondering whether there were any circumstances in which he would not forgive this woman who still sent his heart lurching, and other men's heads turning, when she walked into a room, copper hair flying and eyes sparkling. "But you mustn't expect me not to worry if you take risks."

"I know," she said, her expression sober. "Anyway, I'm into the murky waters of local politics this morning. Physically safer but not that much cleaner, I suspect. Did you know that they're going to pull down the flats up at Wuthering and turf most of the residents out. They'll have to make do with surplus accommodation no one else wants while yuppies move in up the hill. They're even planning to pull the old folks' bungalows down. Joyce will go bananas when she hears."

"She'll be out with her protest banners again, then?" Thackeray asked, though with affection.

"'Fraid so," Laura said. "She's already in the whiz-kid Spencer's bad books for trying to get him to fund the IT project up on the Heights that keeps getting trashed. You know, Spencer said something very odd about that. Wasn't Barry Foreman the guy with the twins who nearly got shot out at Benwell Lane last year? The security company boss?"

"What about him?" Thackeray asked, hoping that Laura's antennae would not pick up the spark of excitement she had fanned into life.

"Spencer said he wanted to work with "the youth". Has he taken up philanthropy or something? I mentioned it to Ted Grant and he seemed to think Foreman was God's gift to the poor and needy too. Not the impression I got when I met him, I must say."

"Jack Longley told me Foreman had got himself involved

in the regeneration committee up there," Thackeray said carefully. "But I thought it was a donation they were after rather than anything more hands-on."

"Ted Grant's got himself appointed onto that too," Laura said. "Are they recruiting the great and the good, or just those who like to imagine they are?"

"The rich and the influential, more like," Thackeray suggested. "And Grant will be a useful ally to have if there's going to be a lot of protest up there."

"I'd like to be able to say that my respected editor couldn't be bought but I reckon that's wishful thinking. He's never been out looking for the radical campaigning journalism awards, hasn't Ted. And he's done his damndest to make sure none of the rest of us are in the running either."

"With limited success in your case," Thackeray said, not quite able to keep a note of disapproval out of his voice. "So is this your next campaign then? Hands off the Heights? Save our local eyesore?"

Laura drained her drink and gave Thackeray one of her most beatific smiles.

"You're pushing your luck, Chief Inspector," she said. "No one's going to mind if they blow those flats up tomorrow. It's what happens next that matters."

He got up and planted a kiss on the top of her copper curls.

"Let me get you a sandwich," he said. "And then you can tell me how Joyce is going to lead her troops into battle against the town hall. All we poor coppers'll get is the blame when the protests turn nasty and a few rioters get their heads clouted." Laura watched him shoulder his way through the lunch-time crowds with a rugby player's ease, and felt a sudden surge of emotion. She knew how determinedly Thackeray wanted to protect her but she wondered if he knew how she too felt that protective urge, not to shield him from physical harm, which he if anyone, she guessed, could cope with, but from the sort of damage which his marriage had inflicted. There came a point in any relationship, she thought, when it became almost impossible to envisage life without the other half of it, and she guessed she had reached that point with Thackeray. Although whether that resolved anything in the long term she was less sure. You might cleave to a rock, but that didn't mean that in the end your grip might not slip and the tide dash you to pieces on its jagged edges.

Michael Thackeray did not go straight back to his office after lunch. Instead he picked up his car, made a call on his mobile and headed out of town to a pub set back from the traffic on the Manchester Road. The man he had arranged to meet was sitting alone at a table at the back of the lounge bar and glanced around anxiously when the policeman came in. He was a small tired-looking individual in a grey suit which had seen better days, his collar dusted with dandruff, his fingers yellowed by nicotine. His pale blue eyes flickered nervously from Thackeray to the other customers in the bar and back again.

"I'm not too keen on meeting like this," Stanley Wilson said as Thackeray pulled out a stool and sat down opposite him. "I know you did me a favour…"

"And one deserves another, Stanley," Thackeray said, without a flicker of sympathy.

"You could get me into a lot of trouble."

"And you could get into a lot of trouble if you're caught again with an under-age lad. You only got away with it last time because anyone would have taken Malcolm for twenty if he was a day. And he was obviously willing enough."

"You'd not have got a conviction," Wilson said bitterly. "Malky wouldn't 'ave hung around for a court case."

"You were willing to take a chance, were you?"

Wilson shook his head imperceptibly.

"Exactly," Thackeray said. "So in return for that caution, which was more than you deserved, I need some information. You're still working for Barry Foreman, are you?"

Wilson nodded gloomily.

"I'm only t'bloody dogsbody in that office," he muttered. "I don't get to hear owt important."

"It's not Barry's books I'm interested in at the moment," Thackeray said, although that was not strictly true. "I wondered if there was any word in the office about his girlfriend? Karen? And the kids?"

Wilson shook his head in some bemusement. "She buggered off, didn't she? That's what I heard."

"With the babies?"

Wilson's eyes flickered round the room again.

"You can't imagine him keeping two kids on his tod, can you?" he asked. "Word is they weren't his, any road."

"So Barry hasn't talked about the twins since Karen left?" Thackeray persisted.

"He never talked about them much before she left," Wilson said. "I reckon Rottweilers'd be more chuffed to be dads. Funny thing was, he seemed to be quite looking forward to it before it happened. He must have thought they were his then, mustn't he? But after, he were wild about summat. He never said nowt. He never does, does 'e. But you could tell he had one o'them moods on 'im. That's the time to keep your head down wi'Barrry. He's an evil bastard when he's crossed."

"Did you ever see him with Karen? Or the twins?"

"Nah," Wilson said, lighting a fresh cigarette from the butt of the previous one. "He's not the sort who'd bring kids to the office, is he? Not your new man." Wilson sniggered, choking on his cigarette smoke. "Karen used to come in now and then," he added, wiping tears from his eyes. "She came in once in a right mood. You could hear them at it all over the office. Summat about her credit card being withdrawn."

"When was that?" Thackeray asked, his eyes sharpening. "Before the twins were born or after?"

Wilson screwed up his face as if in pain and allowed Thackeray to refill his pint glass at the bar before he came up with a reply. He took a long pull at his drink.

"After they arrived, I reckon. I remember her being

pregnant. Like a barrel, she were. But not this time. She had one of them slinky trouser suits on, tight fit, belly button on show, all that. Back to normal, you might say. Looked as if she'd been shopping. It must have been after t'kids were born. It's not that long ago."

"And that's the last time you saw her?"

Wilson nodded.

"I want you to ask around and see if anyone else has seen Karen – or the babies – since then," Thackeray said. Wilson turned his glass on the wet ring it had made on the table and looked dubious.

"Ask around who, Mr. Thackeray?" he asked. "They'll think I'm soft in t'head. Why would I be asking around after Barry's tart? Me, of all people?"

"Keep it casual," Thackeray said. "The women in the office always know what's going on with the boss's love life. Keep your ears open and see what you can pick up. The girls'll trust you, won't they? I want to know if Karen was seen in Bradfield later than that row over the credit card. OK?"

"Summat in it for me, then, is there?" Wilson avoided Thackeray's eyes and his voice took on a whining note.

"You've had all you'll get out of me," Thackeray said, getting to his feet. "Call me on my mobile if you hear anything of interest." He scribbled the number on a beer mat and thrust it towards Wilson. "I've not forgotten Malcolm, Stanley, even if you have."

Wilson watched Thackeray as he walked swiftly towards the door.

"Fuck you," he said softly under his breath, but he put the mat in his pocket just the same.

Glancing into the main CID office on his way back to his desk, Thackeray's attention was caught by a flushed looking DC Mohammed Sharif standing by Val Ridley's desk. Ridley caught his eye.

"You decided to close it then," she said.

"Close what?"

"The Carib Club. It's all over the Gazette. Didn't you know, boss?" Sharif said triumphantly.

Thackeray glanced at the paper Val pushed in his direction and soon picked up the same triumphant note in Bob Baker's story, in which Grantley Adams and the imam at the local mosque vied for the credit of closing down the den of iniquity on Chapel Street. His face tightened but he said nothing as he finished with the paper and folded it neatly.

"Can I borrow this?" he asked.

"Sure," Val said. "I hear uniform isn't very pleased. Reckon it'll cause more trouble than it prevents."

"They should be pleased there's one less source of drugs in town," Sharif said. "D'you want us to follow up on the DJ, Sanderson, boss? He has to be dealing. I can smell it."

"It could just be that your sense of smell's a bit off," Thackeray said. "And that could worry me a lot, Omar."

Thackeray went upstairs to Superintendent Jack Longley's office and barely waited for the secretary to clear his visit before pushing open the door.

"I see we went ahead with closing down the Carib," he said, dropping the newspaper with its banner headline in front of Longley. "The drug squad's charged someone, have they?"

"Not to my knowledge," Longley said. "It's a voluntary move. And temporary. Let's just say that they were persuaded, shall we? Seven days peace and quiet while things calm down."

"Whose idea was that, then?"

"Mine, as it goes," Longley said tetchily. "We've interviews to complete. And I want the place searched thoroughly. Sniffer dogs in, the lot."

"And you want Adams off your back."

"Amongst others," Longley admitted. "But he's not the only one. As far as I can see the only person who wants the place kept open is Barry Foreman, and that's only because he's persuaded them to let him take over the security there."

"A bit like asking the fox to mind the hen-house," Thackeray said.

Longley looked at the DCI and wondered how far he was beginning to let his prejudices cloud his judgement.

"Aye, well, I've told you what I think about that," he said, mildly enough. "It's evidence you need."

Thackeray looked at his boss's bland expression for a moment, wondering whether to share his worries about Karen Bailey and her children but at a loss to summon up a single concrete piece of evidence for his fears so he decided against it.

"He'll trip up eventually," he said.

"Maybe."

"I'll guarantee it," Thackeray said.

Chapter Ten

Kevin Mower leaned across the boy at the computer screen, a burly youth in dark tracksuit and baseball cap, and flicked a key.

"Use the spell-check," he said. "Look, it brings up the underlined word and suggests the correct spelling."

"Oh, yeah," the boy muttered, evidently astonished by the power of the technology. "If we 'ad this at school I mighta' got me GCSEs. It were the writing and spelling that did for me every time."

"Everyone uses word-processors now," Mower said. "If you can get to grips with this you'll find it much easier. Then you can do a course at the college if you want to later on."

"They won't tek me at t'college," the boy said, successfully replacing Hites with Heights.

"Of course they will if you put in a bit of practice here," Mower said cheerfully. The boy shrugged uncertainly.

"Mebbe," he said, but he returned to the slow jabbing at the keys which Mower had interrupted with a dogged determination which few of the Project's clients had showed when they tentatively sidled in through the doors. Mower glanced across the room at Donna who was helping a tall black girl at another keyboard. Their eyes met and Mower smiled faintly. It was a long time since he had experienced the satisfaction that he gained from helping these kids on the Heights, and he had begun to wonder whether this was not a road he might be persuaded to follow. It seemed to him it might be more productive than helping to dump them in the crime schools which passed by the name of young offenders institutions.

At that moment the door opened and the dreadlocked head of Dizzy B Sanderson appeared in the gap. A ripple of excitement ran round the young people at the computers but Mower quickly ushered the visitor out into the reception area.

"He'll be here to talk to you when you break for lunch," he said to the class. "I won't let him go away."

Dizzy flung himself into one of the dilapidated armchairs from which the smears of red paint had been more or less removed and sighed dramatically.

"This town does my head in, man," he said. "You heard about the club being closed down?"

Mower nodded.

"I read about it in the Gazette," he said. "It seems a bit drastic."

"Some copper came over all heavy, persuaded Darryl to volunteer to close for a week."

"D'you know who the copper was?" Mower asked cautiously.

"Some guy in uniform. Not one of your lot. But Darryl says he'd got the whole thing sussed – new people on the doors, some local firm that does most of the clubs round here."

"Barry Foreman's mob?"

"That's the one."

"I've come across Foreman before. A nasty bit of work, if you ask me. I reckon if he's helping your mate Darryl out there must be something in it for him," Mower said.

"Protection, you mean? Is he into that?"

"I don't think we're sure what he's into, though my boss is convinced there's a drug connection. But we've no evidence. As far as we know he does doors, does some secure deliveries, that sort of thing. I've no doubt we'll have his lads patrolling the streets up here before long if all this new stuff goes through. Then we'll see whose side he's on."

"Yeah, well Darryl seemed happy enough with him. Anyway, it's all safe and sorted, and then the Old Bill comes on all heavy anyway. As Darryl hears it, those kids got their Es in some pub, nowhere near the Carib at all. I saw no one dealing that night and I get a good view of what's going on round the dance floor. There was some dope. You could smell that. But I didn't see anyone selling anything stronger. They've got no grounds to close the place. But the local rag's running this campaign, stirring things up, and they don't want to know when Darryl wants to say his piece. Don't want a few facts to get in the way of a good story."

"Who's doing it? Bob Baker?"

"Yeah, that's the guy. All this stuff about the father of the kid who got knocked down. If you ask me that's just an excuse to get at Darryl and the black kids. I reckon it's the blasted Asians at the back of it. If you want to find a racist in this country that's where you should look. That Asian guy of yours who arrested me was no better than he should have been."

"Young Sharif?" Mower said. "He's new. I don't know him well. He arrived just as I…" He hesitated seeking the right word for his departure from CID.

"That's the one," Dizzy said. "DC Sharif."

"Have you made a complaint?"

"What's the point?" Dizzy asked. "You know how long it takes and I don't think I'll be coming back to Bradfield again after this little lot, so you can sort DC Sharif out yourselves. I'm planning to go back to Manchester tomorrow and then to London so I thought I'd just look in on your kids one more time. I brought them some vinyl."

"They'll like that," Mower said, glancing at the case of records that Dizzy had dumped beside his chair. "We've got a hi-fi system locked away somewhere. It's too risky to leave it out when there's no one here."

"Tell me about it," Dizzy said. "So, are you jacking in the job, then?"

"I don't know," Mower said. "I've got another couple to weeks to make up my mind."

"Do it, man," Dizzy said. "I never regretted it. Stay in and you'll end up dead or damaged – if you're not already."

"Damaged, anyway." Mower smiled wryly.

"So get a life," Dizzy said emphatically. "If the head-banging hurts, give it up, for God's sake."

"It's not as easy as all that," Mower said. "I owe people."

"You owe yourself more," Dizzy said flatly. "If you don't look after yourself no one else will."

"Maybe," Mower said. He glanced at his watch. "We break for lunch in five minutes. Have a chat to the kids and then we'll go for a pint."

Dizzy leaned back in his chair with his hands behind his head and stretched his long legs.

"Sounds OK to me," he said. But even as he closed his eyes, there was a commotion at the door and Mower sprang to his feet in alarm as a couple of young boys in school uniform burst in.

"Is Emma Maitland's mum here?"

"She's been right sick down by Priestley."

"She needs her mum, quick!"

Mower's heart lurched as he took in the urgency of the children's voices.

"I'll get her," he said and hurried back into the classroom where Donna looked up in alarm.

"Can you come? It's Emma," Mower said. The colour drained from her face, turning it putty coloured beneath her careful make-up. She grabbed her coat and bag from the teacher's desk and hurried to the door. In the reception area, Mower took hold of Dizzy B's arm and thrust a set of keys into his hand.

"Mind the shop for us, can you? We've got an emergency," he said. "Don't leave the place unlocked, for Christ's sake. See the kids off the premises and if you've gone when I get back I'll catch up with you later on your mobile."

Donna was already running awkwardly across the muddy grass between the Project and Priestley House on too high heels and Mower had to sprint to catch up with her. A small crowd of children were huddled around a small figure on the ground close to the main doors and as the adults arrived they drew away uncertainly, leaving just one girl supporting Emma's head. Mower shouldered in front of Donna and leaned over the child, who seemed to be unconscious.

"She were right sick," her friend said.

"What's she taken?" Mower asked harshly as he lifted Emma's eyelids gently.

The other girl glanced away, her expression guilty. Before Mower could intervene, Donna had seized her by the shoulders and shaken her hard.

"Come on, Kiley, what's she had? Is it drugs? What is it? You must know."

Kiley pulled away, her pale face sulky and her eyes full of tears.

"It weren't drugs," she said. "We'd not do drugs. It were just a drink. I thought it were fizzy pop. A man gave it us when we went for some chips. I didn't like it, though, and Emma drank most of it. An' then she went all funny and I thought I'd teck her home, like, and find you. But she couldn't stand up, could she? And then she were right sick."

Mower thrust his mobile phone into Donna's hand.

"Get an ambulance," he said. While Donna punched in 999, he put his coat round Emma and pulled her upright.

"Come on, sweetheart," he murmured. "Come on, wake up." The child's eyes flickered slightly but did not open. He glanced at Donna who was sitting on her heels in the mud, her face rigid with fear.

"Ambulance is coming," she whispered. "What d'you reckon?"

"She'll be fine," Mower said with more confidence than he felt. "Some sort of alcopop, I should think. Though what stupid beggar's been handing them out to kids I can't imagine. But I'll bloody well find out, I promise you."

In the distance they could hear the siren of the approaching ambulance. Mower put his arm round Donna.

"Come on," he said quietly. "She'll be OK."

"And if she's not?" Donna said, her voice reduced to a dry croak. "She's everything I've got."

132

* * *

By the end of the afternoon Mower had driven Donna home, leaving a pale but conscious Emma settling down to sleep in the children's ward at Bradfield Infirmary. Donna led the way wearily up the long concrete staircase to her flat and flung herself into a chair, tears streaming down her cheeks.

Mower perched awkwardly on the arm of the chair and put an arm round her.

"Come on, lover," he said. "It's all over now. She's come to no harm. They've only kept her in overnight as a precaution."

Donna shuddered.

"So they say," she said. "They'll have social services round as soon as my back's turned. They'll take her away from me, Kevin. You don't know the half of it."

"Perhaps you'd better tell me then," Mower said quietly.

"It were when she were little. Her dad and I were in a terrible state, rowing and breaking up and getting back together and rowing again. He was unemployed and drinking and there was no money in t'kitty. There were no end to it. One night Emma were fast asleep in her cot and her dad buggered off at the end of a blazing row and I ran off after him. I weren't out long. I swear I weren't. Not more than half an hour. But when I got back the stupid old bat who lived next door had sent for t'police because Emma were crying, and then social services turned up, and they took her away, had her examined and everything. They gave her back next day, because there was nowt wrong with that baby. Even her dad worshipped her, and there wasn't much he worshipped apart from a bottle of booze, believe me. But they put her on some register and it were years before she were taken off. You have to believe me, Kevin, I've done everything by the book for that child. Every jab at the doctors, every toy and book she should have, every bit of reading practice and homework from school. I've done everything I could to live that night down and then some. And now…"

"It's all right," Mower said. "You only have to look at Emma to see she's a well cared for child. This is just a stupid thing she's done herself. She should never have taken the drink from this man. But no one's going to blame you. You weren't there. Kids do these things."

"I don't know what she were doing out of school. She's supposed to have her dinner at school not go gallivanting round t'neighbourhood for chips."

"Yes, well, I think maybe her mate Kiley has some explaining to do," Mower said. "Where does she live? Is it far?"

"Just down below. Number 18."

"D'you feel like coming down?" Donna shook her head angrily, scrubbing what was left of her mascara off.

"I'll say summat I shouldn't if I get involved with the bloody Hatherleys," she said. "I don't like my Emma being so friendly with Kiley and her sister, but what can you do when they live so close?"

"Make a cup of tea for yourself and put a slug of whiskey in it," Mower said, getting to his feet. "I'll see if I can find out just exactly what went on at lunchtime."

Closing the flat door behind him he stood for a moment, taking deep breaths of the cold air and gazing unseeingly out at the glittering early evening lights of the town below. From the moment he had arrived with Donna at the Infirmary and been addressed by the harassed nurse as Mr. Maitland while Emma was wheeled into the resuscitation room for urgent treatment, what Donna left unsaid had hammered at his consciousness with much greater clarity than what she actually put into words. *Emma needs a father* was the message he was getting loud and clear. And with that he could not argue, although he was equally certain that soon he would have to tell Donna very bluntly that he could not be the father she wished Emma had. He was not looking forward to that.

In any case, he doubted the underlying logic behind Donna's panic: she seemed to believe that none of this would have happened if Emma had a father. Fat chance, he thought.

On the Heights, this sort of accident could happen to any child at any time. It was not a safe place to be, and the presence or absence of fathers did not necessarily make much difference to a child's safety.

He pulled the collar of his fleece up closer round his neck and shivered himself back to the immediate problem, where, he thought wryly, he could at least perform one paternal duty for young Emma and try to find out how she had managed to drink herself unconscious in her school dinner-hour. He ran quickly down the first flight of stairs and made his way to number 18, from where a loud and indeterminate noise seemed to shake the door in its flimsy frame. He knocked a couple of times without response and then banged hard on the kitchen window where he could see the silhouette of someone outlined against the drawn curtains. The noise inside the flat did not diminish but eventually the door was edged open a crack and a woman's face peered out.

"Mrs. Hatherley? Is young Kiley in?" Mower asked. "Emma Maitland's mum asked me to come down and talk to her about what happened at lunchtime. She's very grateful Kiley had the sense to get help. Saved Emma's life, I reckon."

"Who are you, any road?" the woman asked, without a flicker of friendliness in her eyes.

"I'm Emma's uncle," Mower replied, knowing the codes of the estate. "I just brought Donna back from the Infirmary. They're keeping Emma in tonight, but she's OK. No harm done."

From behind the woman the noise of television or hi-fi, or possibly both, diminished a decibel or so and a male voice could be heard calling angrily for the door to be closed. When the woman did not respond, a volley of curses was followed by the appearance of a large, shaven-headed man in jeans and a sleeveless t-shirt who pushed the woman out of the way and scowled angrily at Mower.

"Yer what?" he asked.

Mower repeated his request to talk to Kiley but met with

even less co-operation than he had from the woman he presumed was her mother.

"If I could just ask Kiley a couple of questions. Whether the bloke was black or white, for one. There's a lad called Ounce…"

"Don't I know you?" the man broke in aggressively. "You're the fucking fuzz."

"No way, mate," Mower said quickly. "Not long out of nick, me."

"He says he's Donna's bloke," his wife put in tentatively.

"Fuck off, any road," the man said and slammed the door in Mower's face. As he turned away he was aware of a child's pale face watching him with frightened eyes from the kitchen window.

Exasperated by the limitations of being without a warrant card in his pocket, and by the implications of what Kiley's father had said, Mower leaned over the balcony again, fingering the beard which had not protected him as well as he had hoped. He considering his options which had suddenly become very much more limited than they had been even half an hour before. If he had been half-recognised once, he had no doubt that he might be again and the news that Donna Maitland was seeing a copper would travel round the estate within hours. It would inevitably reach her ears sooner rather than later, only adding to the emotional turmoil she was already in. The news itself would not necessarily upset her, he thought, but the fact that he had deceived her undoubtedly would. The kids at the Project would not greet the revelation with unalloyed joy either, he thought bitterly, as they jumped to the conclusion that he had been spying on them. He pulled out his mobile and called up Dizzy B.

"Where are you, mate?" Mower asked.

"Waitin' for you in the pub like you said. It's been a bloody long wait, man."

"Do one thing for me will you?" Mower asked. "Those kids you were talking to with Laura Ackroyd. See if they

136

know who got Emma Maitland pissed out of her head this lunchtime. Someone must have seen something, and if I know anything about the Heights, no one will tell me. My cover may be blown – such as it is – and I've got some things to sort out with Donna."

"Sounds like bad news," Dizzy said. "Give me an hour, right?"

"Right. And Dizzy. Ask them if it was an accident, will you? Or if someone's got it in for Donna. That's the really scary thought, OK?"

As Mower walked slowly back up the stairs to Donna's flat he was surprised to hear voices he recognised on the landing above. Taking the last few steps two at a time he found Laura Ackroyd helping her grandmother slowly along the walkway. They turned in alarm at the sound of his footsteps and laughed in relief when they recognised him.

"You made us jump," Joyce said cheerfully. "You won't find me up here after dark as a rule. But I wanted to see Donna and find out how Emma's doing."

"She's fine, thank God," Mower said. "The doctors said it was a good job she was sick or it could have been much worse."

"How did she get hold of the booze. Was it her mother's?" Laura asked cautiously.

"No, it bloody wasn't." Mower's response was angry enough to startle the two women. "Some idiot gave it to them apparently, but the other girl didn't like it so Emma drank the lion's share."

"How old is she?" Laura asked.

"Eight," Mower said, his anger suddenly out of control. "Booze at eight! What do they get for their ninth birthday on this god-forsaken estate? A shot of heroin? When do they start pulling the bloody place down, because it can't be soon enough for me."

"Well, that's a sore point, too," Joyce said. "You could get rid of the drink and the drugs without pulling the whole community apart and punishing us all. And I do mean you, Kevin. We might as well be on the moon, I sometimes think, for all the attention we get from the police."

"Come on, Nan, I don't think this is the time or the place…" Laura began but Mower took hold of her arm urgently.

"I'd be grateful if you didn't link me to the police when you talk to Donna. She's going to have to know very soon, but I'd rather tell her myself."

Laura looked at the sergeant curiously.

"Unravelling, is it, your cover?"

"No comment," he said sharply. "Tell Donna I'll be back in a couple of hours. I've some things to do. OK?"

"Fine," Laura said, taking her grandmother's arm again. "We'll keep her company till you get back."

Later Laura drove her grandmother the short distance from Priestley House to the small bungalow, one of the row perched on the brow of the hill overlooking the town. Laura had never thought of the tiny properties as in any way "desirable" in estate agents' terms, but on a clear night, with the view across the town in the valley below sparkling like a scatter of jewelled necklaces thrown carelessly down on black velvet, she suddenly saw the potential of the site through Councillor Dave Spencer's – and his developer friends' - eyes and knew with a depressing certainty that Joyce and her elderly neighbours would not win their battle to stay put.

Joyce opened her front door.

"Come in a minute?" she asked. Laura glanced at her watch and shrugged. They had waited more than an hour for Kevin Mower to return to Donna Maitland's flat and it was late now even by Michael Thackeray's standards for supper at home.

"I must call Michael," she said, pulling out her mobile. But his phone was switched off and she could only leave a message to say that she would be even later home.

"Can't the beggar cook?" Joyce said, struggling out of her coat with inelastic difficulty. "Even my Jack could cook in an emergency, all those years ago before the war – egg and chips, any road."

"He does sometimes," Laura said irritably. "Don't worry. I can pick up a take-away on the way back."

Joyce sank into her favourite chair and Laura switched on the gas fire. She could see that her grandmother had exhausted herself but she knew better than to suggest that Joyce was doing too much to help her friends at the Project. One acerbic exchange was enough for one evening, she decided, although she knew very well that her own father was as much use in a kitchen as the proverbial bull in a china shop. What Joyce had evidently accepted as a welcome bonus from her husband during their brief marriage, she had not bothered to pass on to her fatherless son.

"Have you had your tea?" Laura asked. Joyce nodded.

"I eat early. It's an old habit from when I used to be out at a meeting almost every night. No time for leisurely dinners then, so I never got into the habit."

"They're not listening to you at the town hall, are they?" Laura said. Joyce shook her head and glanced away.

"They don't seem right interested in the Project," she admitted. "They'd rather draw up their own grand schemes without asking anyone up here what they really want. Do you know how much Len Harvey reckons the land up here is worth on the open market? Twenty million. Just the land. You can't believe it, can you? Even Len's shocked and he's a blasted Tory. I don't think we spent more than a million tearing down the old back-to-back slums and building the whole new estate."

"There's no reason why they can't build the Project into their calculations, though, is there?"

"No reason at all if they just took the trouble to ask people what they want. You'd think they'd have learned from the mistakes we made building this estate in the first place. But no, they just carry on doing good by force and then act surprised when folk don't thank them for it." Seeing Joyce so dispirited was almost more than Laura could bear.

"I'll have another go at Ted Grant tomorrow and see if I can persuade him to take it all more seriously. But they've put him on the committee that's planning the whole thing now, so I'm not very hopeful."

"You could get that man of yours to take the drug problem more seriously too."

"I've tried that," Laura said. "He says it's in hand."

"I don't think Donna Maitland thinks it's in hand," Joyce said. "A child that age with alcohol poisoning? It could just as easily been summat worse."

"I know," Laura said, recalling Donna's stunned shock which they had been unable to alleviate at all. She wondered how she would cope with even more bad news from Kevin Mower.

"I'll talk to Ted again tomorrow about my story. And if he won't go for it, I'll contact the magazine in London I've written for before. The whole thing's getting big enough for it to go national, whatever Ted thinks."

"You're a good lass," Joyce said. "I don't know what went wrong between me and your dad, but you've more than made up for it, pet. You really have."

Laura hugged her grandmother impulsively.

"It'll be all right," she said. "I promise."

Chapter Eleven

"You don't want me to handle the case then?" DCI Michael Thackeray's question dropped into the silence in Superintendent Jack Longley's office like a stone into deep water. When there was no immediate reply Thackeray shrugged and moved over to the window from where he could see the rain beating down onto the umbrellas of hurrying passers-by in the puddled square below. His anxiety felt like a physical weight on his shoulders. Longley shifted his bulk uneasily in the chair which never seemed quite commodious enough for him and grunted.

"What I want," he said at length, and then paused again as if embarrassed. "What I always want is a bloody text-book murder investigation. And you just seem to have thrown the text-book away."

"A quiet chat was all it was," Thackeray said. "He was never a registered informant."

"But should have been," Longley said.

"You could argue." The hollow feeling which had invaded Thackeray's stomach some hours ago when he had been called to a suspicious death seemed to be affecting his breathing.

"I do bloody argue," Longley snapped back. "He should have been registered if he was worth anything. But you'd no call to be chatting up Foreman's staff behind his back without cause in the first place. And if you seriously thought Stanley Wilson had useful information you should have played it straight, taken someone with you, done it by the book. Now he's dead it'll all have to come out. You're out on a limb, Michael, and for what? He gave you nothing and was never likely to give you anything. And now he's dead and turns out to be a worse little scrote than we ever suspected."

"So bring someone else in if you think I'm compromised,"

Thackeray said, unable to keep his own anger, which was directed mainly at himself, under control any longer. "Appoint someone else senior investigating officer if you think it'll help. Get the computer crime people in. It looks as if we'll need them anyway. Sir." The last word was added as an afterthought and Longley flushed slightly in response. But for the moment he contented himself with drumming his fingers on the file in front of him and breathing heavily.

Thackeray's mind flashed back an hour to his first sight of the ligature around Stanley Wilson's neck, which had been pulled so tight that it had broken the skin and become caked in blood. Amos Atherton, sweating in his plastic coveralls, had glanced up at the DCI from his position crouched beside the dead man's body as Thackeray struggled to conceal the awful realisation that this was a noose he might have provided himself.

"Didn't mean to make any mistake about it, did he?" Atherton had asked, oblivious to the DCI's inner turmoil. "You don't get many men strangled. Gay, was he?"

Thackeray, shrouded in the same oversized white coveralls as the pathologist, had nodded slightly.

"Liked young boys," he said, his mouth dry. "Or youngish, anyway. We'd not managed to do him for it."

"Happen one got his own back then," Atherton said unsympathetically, glancing at the dead man's trousers and underpants which were rumpled round his ankles. "He's been dead a while, that I can tell you. Probably killed some time yesterday, at a guess. He's as stiff as a board. You'll be looking for a boyfriend, I'd say. Popped in yesterday for a bit of nookie and it all got out of hand. Into S & M was he? There's some odd marks on his arms."

"I've no bloody idea," Thackeray had said, although he was as certain as he could be that Wilson's violent end had more to do with his own intervention in his affairs than the dead man's sexual preferences. His mind sheered away from the thought that perhaps Wilson had been tortured before being killed, and that the information someone had been trying to extract had something to do with him.

"How was he found?" Atherton asked.

"Postman tried to deliver a packet and when he got no reply he looked through the window," Thackeray said shortly.

"Must have got a nasty shock seeing his bare bum in the air like that."

Atherton turned back to his examination of the body with a grim smile and Thackeray turned away. He had already glanced round the modestly furnished living room of the terraced house where Wilson had evidently eked out a pretty impecunious existence and wondered what Barry Foreman had paid him for his services. Not a lot, if the threadbare carpet and worn brown armchairs were anything to go by. Or perhaps Wilson had other uses for his money than interior décor.

He left Atherton to his examination and went upstairs where a different explanation for the impoverished appearance of Wilson's house soon presented itself. In one bedroom an unmade bed and a few sticks of furniture indicated where Wilson had spent his final night. But in the back bedroom, where thick curtains kept out the daylight and the floor was deeply carpeted, it became clear what Wilson had been spending his money on as soon as Thackeray switched on the light. The DCI found himself facing a bank of high-tech equipment only some of which he recognised. A computer, video recorders and a wall stacked high with tapes and CDs crowded the single padded black leather chair from which Wilson had evidently indulged a hobby which Thackeray guessed, knowing Wilson's tastes, would have seen him arrested without much ceremony had the law ever invaded his privacy here. And whatever he had earned, it was clear that a large proportion of it must have been spent on travel: the unlikely sight of Wilson clad in various unlikely combinations of swimming gear and sarongs smiled out from a wall of snapshots taken in exotic locations, young boys at his side. Even before examining a single tape Thackeray felt a shudder of revulsion go through him. This room alone, he thought, would launch an investigation which could last for years. He was thankful that the force had a special unit to deal with pornography and computer crime.

Without moving any further into the room he had looked around carefully, but the written records he sought were not in evidence. Everything, he thought, must be locked away in the computers, and to crack their passwords and codes he would need expert assistance. Quietly he left the room and closed the door behind him with a plastic gloved hand. It was possible, he thought, that Wilson's extra-curricular activities had brought down the vicious retribution which Atherton was examining in the livingroom below. But the sort of images Wilson had been downloading from the Internet, and quite possibly copying and circulating amongst his friends, were more likely to involve young children on the other side of the world than anywhere near at hand. So why had someone killed him?

Superintendent Longley must have been talking again for some time before the sound of his voice jolted Thackeray back to the present and his unenviable situation on the boss's carpet. He turned away from the window with a start.

"Are you bloody listening to me?" Longley asked irritably as his colour rose from pink to puce.

"Sir?"

"I was telling you why I'll let you handle this case, if you could do me the courtesy of paying attention," Longley snapped.

"Sorry," Thackeray said. "I was just wondering how many thousands of images that bastard has been distributing."

"Aye well, that's one of the things you'll have to find out, isn't it? And who he's been distributing them to. You can bet your life that the answer to his death's somewhere in that disgusting trade, if that's what he was into. We'll get some help on the computer side of things. But you can go ahead and look at his bank accounts and any other financial information you can find. And find out where he went on his jaunts abroad. He must have been coining it if the scale of the thing's as big as you say it is."

"I'll need to talk to Barry Foreman. He was his boss."

"Of course you will," Longley said. "And you'll do it by the book. Background on the dead man's what you're after, not fantasies about Foreman's affairs. Not unless and until they're relevant. Understood?"

"Right," Thackeray agreed without enthusiasm. "It's at least possible that someone told Foreman I'd been talking to Wilson," he said. "He wouldn't be best pleased."

"After your last chat with him he's already wondering if you're going off your rocker," Longley said. "'Stressed out' he thought you were, when I met him at the regeneration meeting. Finding out you've been wasting your time investigating him through Wilson'll confirm his worst suspicions."

"Nice to know I've got your support," Thackeray said. Longley looked at him for a moment, taking in the furrows of anxiety which seemed to have deepened around angry blue eyes since the previous day, and reckoned that Barry Foreman might have a point. He was more than usually aware that Thackeray had almost blown his career once and he wondered whether he was about to make the attempt again.

"You've got my support, Michael," he said more calmly than he felt. "Get the incident room set up. By the sound of it Stanley Wilson's not much loss to the world, but we need to know who put him down. They may not be so discriminating next time. Keep me on top of the investigation, will you? Oh, and by the way, what's the state of play on the Adams boy? Have we come up with anything to shut his father up?"

"It's run into the sand," Thackeray said shortly. "Just as I always thought it would. The kids won't say anything. But I think I've shut Grantley Adams up anyway, if that's all you're worried about. He's found out the hard way what we've known for years – that the law's an ass where soft drugs are concerned – and he'd much rather his precious Jeremy remained an innocent victim than got himself a criminal record for possession – or worse. I don't think we'll hear much more from Mr. Adams."

"He's raising his voice loud enough in the Gazette," Longley said doubtfully.

"Well, he's got what he wanted as far as the Carib Club's concerned. The place is closed. He'll have to be satisfied with that."

Laura Ackroyd drove back to the Project on the Heights that lunch-time out of a sense of obligation rather than with any enthusiasm. She had spent much of the morning trying to persuade Ted Grant to find some space in the paper for a feature on the drug problems of Wuthering but without much success. His attention, never long-lasting, had switched overnight to the threat that the flood defences – protecting low-lying parts of the town – were about to be overwhelmed by the rain which had been relentless for most of the winter. Reporters had been dispatched to talk to threatened householders, photographers sent out to snap the teetering walls of sandbags which were all that now protected some streets from inundation, page layouts had been sketched out and possible headlines tossed around the editorial meeting: Laura's argument that there was an equally serious crisis on the Heights met blank looks of incomprehension. In exasperation she had called the magazine editor in London for whom she had written before, but gained only an equivocal promise to think about the idea and let her know.

"Don't call us, we'll call you," she muttered as she heard the phone go down at the other end. "Thanks a bunch."

"First sign of madness, talking to yourself," Bob Baker had hissed in her ear as he passed behind her desk. "And by the way, I can't get anyone at police HQ to take your murdered druggie seriously. I should stick to knitting patterns if I were you, love. Leave crime to those who understand it."

Laura had swung round on her chair but Baker was already out of reach. Turning back to her computer screen angrily she wondered what would have happened if she had hit him. The sack did not seem too unpleasant a prospect today.

She parked as close as she could to the Project and wondered who owned the dark blue BMW which stood by the kerb on the other side of the road. She did not think much of its chances of survival, although the cluster of youths who habitually loitered around the flats appeared to be keeping well back in the shadows under the walkways on this occasion. She was aware of their hostile eyes following her progress across the muddy pathway to the doors of the Project.

Once inside she was surprised to find herself confronting a tall black man in designer jeans, expensive leather jacket and tigerish aspect.

"Yeah?" he asked.

"Sorry?" Laura said.

"Who are you?" the self-appointed gate-keeper demanded, barring Laura's way with a faint smile and unfriendly eyes.

"I'm looking for my grandmother. She works here," Laura said, attempting without success to sidle past her interrogator.

"Grandma?" The expression was incredulous now.

"Joyce," Laura insisted. "Can I come in please?"

"Oh, that grandma," the man said. "So you must be Laura?"

"If it's any business of yours," Laura said, feeling her temper, already reduced to the shortest of fuses by her morning in the office, flare again.

"You'd better go through then."

"Who are you anyway?" Laura insisted. "What business is it of yours?"

"You remember that old TV programme called *Minder*? That's what I am – a minder. Name's Pound. I'm with Barry Foreman who's paying your grandma and her friends a visit, as it goes. Dodgy area, this. You should know that, girl."

"Oh, sod off," Laura said, pushing her way past her tormentor. "I've had enough of bloody men for one day."

"So it's true what they say about redheads, then?"

Laura ignored the final jibe from behind her and, following the sound of voices, made her way across the refurbished, if still slightly scarred, reception area and into the main classroom where she found Joyce sitting at the teacher's desk with Kevin Mower at her shoulder. A smartly suited Barry Foreman sprawled across a table in front of them, listening to Joyce in full flow with a condescending smile on his face. He glanced at Laura without great surprise when she came in, before turning back to Joyce.

"It's much more important to get the local folk behind you themselves if you want to make any long-term difference to these families," Joyce was saying. "It's not the same if you just drop facilities in their lap. It has to be something they need and want. They have to be involved."

"We'll still be waiting for this lot to get involved come the next bloody millennium," Foreman said dismissively when she had finished. "Any road, there won't be so many of your precious deprived families up here when we've finished rebuilding the place. What the new community'll need is a purpose built college with all the trimmings."

"Which'll throw the most difficult kids out just like all the others have done," Kevin Mower said quietly.

"And you've turned these kids lives around, have you?" Foreman asked. "Sent 'em all off to the university and all that? Not what I hear."

"We've got half a dozen of them into rehab," Mower said. "That's worth the effort. And some of them are learning something for the first time in their lives. It's a slow process…"

"Too bloody slow," Foreman said. "You've not got the resources to make any serious difference. Nor the staff. What's a copper like you wasting his time up here for, any road? You're not a bloody teacher. You should be out chasing villains."

148

Laura saw Mower's expression harden and she wondered whether he had told Donna yet about his day job.

"We'll not agree, Mr. Foreman," Joyce said. "I dare say Councillor Spencer and his new cabinet will have to decide which way to go. But we'll make a strong case for a voluntary centre when we see him. You can be sure of that. Money's all very well, but it's not everything. People are important too."

"Aye, well, we'll see about that," Foreman said.

He slid off the desk and made his way to the classroom door.

"Don't hold your breath," he said as he went out and was joined by the tall figure of his bodyguard who had been lounging against the wall outside.

"That man is a bastard," Laura said, giving first Joyce and then Mower a fierce hug of consolation. "If he thinks he's running the town, what chance do ordinary people have?"

"The DCI doesn't trust him further than he can throw him," Mower said. "Yet he seems to have got onto some sort of inside track with the council. I don't understand it."

"Have you told Donna that you're in the Force?" Laura asked. "Because I don't give much for your chances there if you haven't. It'll be all round the estate shortly."

"I told her last night when I got back," Mower said. "She wasn't best pleased. She couldn't come in today because she's gone to fetch Emma home from the Infirmary, but it's maybe just as well. I don't think Donna and I are much of a team any more."

"I'm sorry," Laura said.

"You don't have to be. There was no future in it and I think we both knew that."

"Nothing seems to be going right up here," Laura said. "I came up to tell you that I can't persuade Ted Grant to do much about the problems on the estate. Floods are his top priority this week. Apparently the Beck's going to burst its banks, the Maze will back up and half the lower part of the town's going to be under water by the end of the week."

"The Beck?" Mower asked, looking blank.

"Ah, you can tell you're an off-cum-d'un," Joyce said, smiling.

"A what...?"

"A stranger, not a local, a bloody southerner," Laura explained with a grin. "What you probably don't realise is that there's a river runs right under the centre of Bradfield. Or a big stream, anyway. Comes down from the hills and joins the Maze at Eckersley. But some bright Victorian decided it got in the way of his regeneration scheme in about 1860 and shoved the whole thing into an underground culvert. Pushed up land values a treat, I dare say. Nothing changes, does it? Anyway according to the environment people, the culvert isn't going to take the strain when all the rain we've been having runs off the Pennines and no one knows quite what'll happen then. There'll be a lot of water sloshing about, anyway, and Ted Grant is issuing the troops with their Wellie boots, just in case."

"It flooded once back in the forties," Joyce said. "But they deepened the culvert and it was supposed to take anything after that."

"But not global warming," Laura said. "No one anticipated that."

"Aye, well, there's a lot to be said for living on a hill, even if it is Wuthering," Joyce said. "One thing we won't need up here is Noah's Ark."

No, Laura thought angrily, but you might need the cavalry before long.

Michael Thackeray and DC Val Ridley – acting sergeant in Kevin Mower's absence – sat in Barry Foreman's comfortable office later that afternoon listening to the security boss's dismissive description of an employee so incompetent that it seemed to Val Ridley a wonder that he had been employed at all. Foreman fingered through the buff file on his desk.

"I'd have sacked him but his dad did me a favour years

ago, lent me some money when I was setting up. I'm not generally a sentimental sort of bloke but I felt I owed Stanley. But I always thought there was summat a bit odd about him. Gay, of course. You'll know that, I expect?"

Thackeray nodded non-commitally.

"Good enough at his job, though, was he?" he asked.

"Good enough. It was only a bit of low level accounting he did. Clerking really. Seemed to be enough for him. He never complained. Of course he'd no family to support. He wouldn't have, would he, being that way inclined?"

"Was he liked in the office?"

"Give over," Foreman said. "They're not right politically correct, the sort of lads I employ. They put up with Stanley. Made his life a misery now and then with their shirt-lifter cracks. What d'you expect?"

"Protection?" Val Ridley said. "From his boss?" Foreman looked at her for a moment with contempt.

"He were lucky to have the job. He knew that, I knew that and everyone else in the bloody company knew that. He didn't ask for any favours and he didn't get any. Tell me the police are any different and I'll die laughing."

"And his pay? How much was that?" Thackeray asked.

"I'll get a computer print-out for you," Foreman said. "He did some overtime sometimes. Mind I did sometimes think he must be making a bit on the side somehow. Took some exotic holidays now and again, did Stanley. Thailand a couple of times. Goa. Odd, that."

"We'll need to talk to everyone he worked with," Thackeray said.

"And how long's that going to be carrying on?"

"Just as long as it takes," Thackeray snapped back. "He doesn't sound the most popular man on your payroll and he may have made enemies you don't know about." Or friends, he thought, wondering whether any of Foreman's other staff shared Wilson's interest in pornography.

"Right," Foreman said with evident lack of enthusiasm.

"But they work shifts, you know. You'll have to catch them when you can."

"So do we, Mr. Foreman," Val Ridley said. "If you give me a list of when your lads come in and clock off I'm sure we can match it."

Thackeray got to his feet slowly as Foreman relayed the police's requirements to someone in an outer office. He glanced up at the DCI.

"Is that all?"

"For now," Thackeray said. "Except I was still wondering if you ever heard anything more from Karen. Those babies of yours must be getting quite big now. Don't you feel the need to keep in touch?"

"If I thought they were mine I might," Foreman said. "As for Karen? Turned out a slag, didn't she? They're all the same." For a second Thackeray thought he saw real rage behind Foreman's usual bland expression but it vanished before he could be sure and was replaced by a smile which came across as more of a grimace.

"Still with that red-headed lass from the Gazette yourself, are you?" he asked. Val Ridley hesitated by the door and stood very still though Thackeray did not reply and the silence lengthened.

"I met her, remember, when we had that bit of trouble wi'Karen's brother?"

Thackeray nodded carefully, his heart thumping, knowing that there must be a reason for Foreman's questions and frantically trying to work out what it might be.

"Laura," he said at last.

"Aye, that's her. Laura. I saw her the other day up at Wuthering. She was with that sergeant of yours, the dark, good-looking lad, the one who came over all heroic with the little scrote with the shotgun that time. Pretty lass. Make a nice couple, those two. So I just wondered if she's buggered off and left you, an'all. A moment of fellow feeling, as you might say. Tarts!"

Thackeray did not reply. He spun on his heel and Val Ridley followed him out of Foreman's office aware only that the DCI's face appeared to have turned to stone.

Laura got home late, hair flying, carrier-bag full of food for the evening meal threatening to spill all over the floor as she struggled to close the front door of the flat behind her with one foot. She found Thackeray sitting in front of the television with an expression so frozen that even in her haste she could not fail but notice that he did not respond in any way to the scrambled kiss she offered the back of his neck. She dumped the shopping in the kitchen and slipped out of her jacket, flinging it onto the back of a chair.

"What?" she asked. "What is it?" Her mind skipped through the sorts of bad news which could have led to this reaction and her breath caught in her throat as panic threatened to overwhelm her. Her mind flew to her grandmother.

"Is it Joyce?"

Thackeray shrugged and turned the volume down with the remote control.

"Not Joyce," he said quickly.

"Then what? There was a murder today. I heard about it in the office...?"

"Not that," he said. He gazed at the flickering images on the screen for a moment as if unable to speak.

"It's you, I suppose," he said at last, not looking at her directly. She slid onto the sofa beside him, trying to control a wobble of relief and trepidation in her voice.

"And just what have I done this time?" she asked, as lightly as she dared. "Or is it the Gazette that's annoyed you again? I refuse to take the blame for the sins of Bob Baker."

"It's nothing to do with that."

"Then what, for God's sake? You sit here looking like a thunderstorm and won't tell me. What sort of a welcome is that when I come in after a hard day at the office."

"Was it, Laura? Was it really?" Thackeray snapped back.

"Was it what?"

"Was it a hard day at the office? Or did you find time to go and chat up Kevin Mower up at Wuthering? They make a nice couple, I was told. What's that all about? And why didn't you tell me you'd seen Kevin? That he was back in Bradfield? As far as I knew he was still in Eckersley trying to sort himself out at a clinic."

"Ah," Laura said more soberly. "That's what the fuss is all about, is it?"

"So it's true? You have been seeing him?"

"Michael Thackeray, I do believe you're jealous," Laura said wonderingly, a flicker of amusement in her green eyes.

"No," Thackeray said fiercely. "I didn't think I had anything to be jealous about. Until I discovered you'd been deceiving me."

"Deceiving! That's a bit strong, isn't it?"

"I don't know," Thackeray said. "People tell me he's an attractive lad, our Kevin. I think even you told me that once. And we both know he's not exactly restrained where women are concerned. So what am I to think when you apparently forget to tell me you've been meeting my sergeant behind my back."

"I knew it wasn't a good idea not to tell you," Laura groaned. "But he asked me not to."

"And of course you always do exactly what Kevin Mower asks?"

"Yes, I mean no, of course not," Laura said. "He had his reasons."

"And did you have your reasons too?"

"Oh, Michael, this is crazy. Yes, it's true, I have been seeing Kevin, as it goes, but not in the sense you mean. I bumped into him quite by chance when I went up to the Project that Joyce is working at on the Heights. He's helping out there too, working with the kids..."

"He's supposed to be in rehab," Thackeray objected.

"Well, I think it is a sort of rehab for Kevin," Laura said.

"He says he's off the booze, but I'm not sure he's convinced he wants to stay in the Force, which is hardly surprising after everything he's been through. That's why he asked me not to tell you what he was doing. He's trying to get his head together before he decides what to do next. And there – you've made me break all sorts of confidences now."

"And I suppose he's been egging you on to investigate what's going on up there too. You know how dangerous that is."

"Not really," Laura said. "No more than Joyce and Donna Maitland, anyway. They're all distraught about what's happening to the kids on the Heights. You know that."

Laura reached out to take Thackeray's hand but he shrugged her off and got up to stand by the window, gazing out at the shadowy garden where the bare branches made a faint tracery against the slate grey sky. Laura followed him and put an arm round his waist.

"I'm sorry," she said. "You know I wouldn't deceive you about anything important."

"To hear that from a bastard like Foreman…" Thackeray said quietly.

"Foreman," Laura said. "Of course, he was up there today, as if he owned the place."

"…it was like being kicked in the balls." Thackeray continued as if he had not heard her.

"He's a seriously unpleasant man."

"You don't begin to understand just how seriously unpleasant I think that man is. And I'm not even beginning to be able to prove it."

Thackeray leaned his head for a moment against the cold window-pane. Laura felt him shudder and tightened her grip.

"I'm sorry," she said. "You must know there's nothing going on between me and Kevin. He's found himself some female company up there anyway. You know what he's like. But he's as keen as I am to help sort the kids up there. It's getting completely out of hand."

"Leave it alone, Laura," Thackeray said turning and taking her in his arms. "It's too dangerous for anyone but the drug squad to be asking questions up there. Please, please leave it alone."

But Laura stiffened in his embrace.

"I have my job to do too," she said, her face obstinate. "It's not as if I'm chasing after dealers or anything stupid like that. I'm just describing the effects, what's happening to innocent people like Donna Maitland and the kids who've died. Someone has to do that, and if it's not the Gazette, who will?"

Thackeray suddenly pushed away from her and strode to the front door without looking back.

"I need some air," he said, before the front door slammed behind him, leaving Laura leaning against the window where he had been standing, too shocked to move.

"Oh, shit," she said softly to herself. "One of these days I'll blow this sky high, and then where will I be?"

Chapter Twelve

"So, do you want me to take you up there?" Laura asked her grandmother, trying to keep the tension she was feeling out of her voice. She was standing in the middle of Joyce's tiny living room on what seemed to be becoming her daily ritual of a lunch-time visit to the Heights. Joyce had rung to say she needed a lift to the Project but when Laura had let herself into the bungalow she had found her grandmother sitting stock still in her favourite armchair, a look of frozen anger pinching her usually cheerful features. In front of her on the coffee table was a list of names and phone numbers. Laura's two page feature, illustrated with photographs of the planners' models of the new development on the Heights, was spread on the floor beside her with crucial passages outlined firmly in fluorescent marker. The telephone cord extended tightly from the plug in the wall to the apparatus on Joyce's lap.

"I tried to get hold of you first thing," Joyce had complained bitterly as soon as Laura had walked through the door. "How can you be so certain the Project is for the chop? Who told you?"

"Dave Spencer wouldn't say yes or no," Laura admitted. "I was reading between the lines when I wrote that. But I'd put money on it. They're not interested in what the residents want. They want the whole thing wrapped up neatly so as not to frighten the yuppies they want to sell the new houses to. It stands to reason, Nan. You know what they're like. They don't want facilities for young junkies on the doorstep of the posh new executive homes."

"The regeneration committee met yesterday," Joyce said. "I did manage to find that out from Spencer's secretary – or PA, as she calls herself."

"Yes, I know, I heard that much in the office, but they didn't issue any statement afterwards. Apparently Spencer and some of his precious committee have gone to London for meetings today."

"The early flight," Joyce said scornfully. "In my day we were lucky to get a train trip third class. They've gone to meetings at the department of the environment, according to little Miss Snooty."

Laura could see the tears of frustration in her grandmother's eyes.

"Did you try anyone else?" she asked, glancing at the long list of names and numbers on Joyce's pad.

"I tried everyone I could think of," Joyce admitted, slumping back in her chair and letting the phone slide across her knees. Laura took it off her gently and put it back in its place on a side table. The defeated look in Joyce's eyes caught her breath.

"I'm too old, love, that's the problem," Joyce said. "All the folk I used to work with are long gone and no one else wants to know me. You can see why folk end up on the booze or drugs or on the rampage up here, can't you? No one wants to listen to a word anyone on the Heights says. Me? They've forgotten Councillor Ackroyd. Now I'm just that stroppy old baggage who doesn't want her bungalow knocked down. Standing in the way of progress, that's what I'm doing now. You'll see. Doesn't your editor say as much in his editorial? 'A great step forward for Bradfield'. I don't know how he works that out."

"It's not over yet," Laura said gently. "It's only just beginning. Remember, no one outside the town hall's seen the details of the plans till this morning. No one up here's going to like it when they see it spread out like that in black and white. They may want the flats down but they don't want to be thrown out of the area to make way for luxury housing. And there'll be lots of people who'll fight for the Project and what that's doing for the kids."

Laura knew that there had been a time when Joyce's writ had run the length and breadth of the long polished corridors of Bradfield town hall, and even a time, for some years after she had retired, when if she wanted information for any of her many campaigns, friends and acquaintances would have produced it for her within hours. But gradually the number of councillors and officials she remembered and who remembered her had dwindled, and what Joyce still regarded as the golden age of municipal socialism had become an embarrassment to the new, young councillors. They were far too busy creating cabinets and executives and scheming about the powers of an elected mayor and the opportunities opened up by public-private partnerships. The new modernised town hall, Laura thought, must seem to Joyce like a foreign country. She had, inexorably, become an exile in her own land.

"Come on," Laura said. "I'll run you up the hill. Donna will be wondering where you are."

Joyce tidied her papers on the table and folded the Gazette neatly into its original shape.

"She's a good lass, is Donna," she said as she got painfully to her feet. "We need a few more like her to stir this estate up. Most of them are so ground down with it all they'll let Councillor Dave Spencer walk rough-shod over the lot of us if we don't do summat dramatic."

"I think the taste for marching on town halls may have died out," Laura said carefully, as she helped the older woman manoeuvre her arms into her coat.

"We'll see about that," Joyce said. "At least we've got a reporter on our side, pet."

Laura nodded, but with a sinking heart. Joyce might believe she carried some weight at the Gazette, but if Ted Grant had made up his mind on the issue of the Heights – and his editorial comment had been about as enthusiastic as Ted ever got for anything municipal – she knew only too well that there was going to be very little that she could do about it. She helped her grandmother lock up the house carefully and tucked her into the passenger seat of the car. Joyce's increasing lack of mobility worried her more than she was prepared to admit to herself, and Joyce never admitted it at all, gritting her teeth against the pain of the arthritis which threatened to immobilise her completely. But Joyce, Laura reckoned, might have to give up the independence her small home afforded her even before the developers' bulldozers moved in. And that would certainly break her heart.

Donna Maitland was sitting at one of the Project's more up-to-date computers when Joyce and Laura arrived. She gave a small wave of greeting as the older woman hobbled in, took her walking stick off her granddaughter and kissed her on the cheek. Eventually Donna turned away from the Internet pages she had been studying with fierce concentration. She picked up a sheaf of papers from the desk beside her and waved them at Joyce.

"I must have written to fifty of the bastards, all local companies, and not one of them's even offered another clapped out computer for the kids to use," she said. "Half of them haven't even bothered to reply."

"And we need a lot more than that," Joyce said.

"I told them that when the redevelopment goes ahead we'll be appealing for funds to rebuild this place and equip it properly," Donna explained to Laura. "It's obvious the bloody council's going to do nowt for us, so I'm giving them plenty of warning that we hope local business will fill the gap. You can do us a bit of good an all, love, if you cover the story for us in t'Gazette."

"I'll do my best," Laura said feeling overwhelmed by the weight of expectation the two women were placing on her. "In the meantime I'm going to be late back. I'll see you later, Nan."

"The council hasn't actually said they won't rebuild the Project yet," Joyce said after the door had closed. She didn't dare mention Laura's conviction that Donna was right. But Donna shrugged, running a hand through blonde hair that had fallen across her eyes.

"Look at this one. Grantley Adams. Isn't he the bloke whose son nearly killed himself wi'drugs. 'It's not our policy to donate to organisations which are not long-established charities.' These beggars are screaming for computer literate staff and here we are trying to train some of them and all we get is a kick in the teeth. What's the matter with these people? They don't seem to see the connection. Is it because a lot of the kids are black or junkies or what?"

"Of course it is," Joyce said. "They're frightened of the Heights, a lot of them. Scared witless, always have been. You give a neighbourhood a bad name and it's impossible to get rid of."

"But they're going to regenerate the bloody place," Donna said. "It's just the bricks and mortar though, is it? No plans for regenerating the kids as well? No seeing what they can do, given a bit of help and encouragement? No chance they'll recognise that some of us are trying to live decent lives and do summat to help the rest? Just pull the place down and get rid of as many of us as they can, is that it?"

Joyce looked weary and could offer no reassuring counter to that analysis. Increasingly she believed it was true.

Donna flung the letters back onto the desk and turned back to the computer but within ten minutes she had to switch the machine off as the Project was invaded by half-a-dozen argumentative teenage girls who only gradually agreed to settle at the desks and switch on the collection of machines which Donna had already begged and borrowed from local businesses and families when she set up the Project. But, slowly, the raucous gibes and giggling gossip subsided as the two women persuaded the youngsters to concentrate on the elementary word-processing skills which were their objective, and for an hour a sort of peace reigned.

Just before lunch-time Dizzy B Sanderson put his head round the classroom door to whoops of delight from the girls, ready for any distraction now.

"Is Kevin around?" he asked.

"Should be in any time," Donna said.

"I'll wait out here," the DJ said, ducking back out of the door, to dramatic groans of disappointment from the class.

"Come on girls, finish off now. We all need a break," Donna said. But their concentration was broken and she had difficulty controlling their restlessness. But just before she gave in and dismissed them, there was a loud crash in the outer reception area and a muffled shout seconds before the door to the classroom burst open and several men in jeans and leather jackets burst in. Several of the girls squealed in alarm and Donna reached across her desk for a mobile phone which lay underneath some papers.

"Police," the evident leader of the group said loudly. "Everyone stay exactly where you are."

Joyce Ackroyd pushed herself painfully to her feet from the chair at the back of the room where she had been sitting next to one of the girls.

"Can we see your identity cards, please," she said firmly. The leading police officer glanced at her with something close to contempt and flashed a warrant card in her direction.

"And your name is?"

"DI Ray Walter, drugs squad," he said. "Now just sit down, Gran, we've a warrant to search these premises."

"Whatever for?" Joyce said, still standing.

"That's for us to know," the officer said. "For now I want all of you sitting exactly where you are while we look round. Then we'll want names and addresses."

The girl next to Joyce began to sob noisily as one of the officers picked up her bag and began to root through it. Joyce's lips tightened and she glanced at Donna who had gone pale and tense, one hand still grasping her mobile, until one of the men noticed it and took it roughly out of her hand. Outside they could hear Dizzy B Sanderson's voice raised in anger and then recede as if he had left, or been taken out of the building. Systematically the men began to open every cupboard, desk and drawer in the room and go through the contents. When they had finished with the classroom, one of them remained behind to watch the occupants while his colleagues moved on through the rest of the building. After ten minutes or so, DI Walter came back into the room and nodded at his colleague.

"Right," he said. "We want you all down at the station for questioning. Now."

With her arm round the girl whose sobs had now become hysterical Joyce stood up again.

"On what grounds?" she asked.

"On suspicion of handling Class A drugs, which were found on these premises," Walter said.

"Are you arresting us?"

"We'll deal with the formalities at the nick," the DI said.

"What drugs?" Donna asked, her face like a white mask gashed by her red lipstick. "There are no drugs here. I make sure of that."

"You telling me we don't know a kilo of heroin when we find it?" Walter sneered. "Get real. Now let's have you. All of you."

From his car parked some hundred yards away from the Project, Sergeant Kevin Mower watched in fascinated horror as a procession of girls, closely followed by Donna Maitland and Joyce Ackroyd, filed out of the building and into two police vans parked with several squad cars on the road outside. He had pulled up sharply on his way to meet his own students when he had seen Dizzy B, in handcuffs, being similarly ushered out and into custody and decided that on this occasion he would forego any fraternal greetings the colleagues doing the ushering might expect from him. He recognised Ray Walter from an abortive stint he had done with the drugs squad some years earlier. He had not liked the squad or the man then and he liked him even less when he saw just how Donna was being roughly "assisted" into custody.

"Hell and damnation," he said softly to himself as he pulled his mobile out of his pocket.

"Laura?" he asked as his call was answered. "Can you meet me at the Lamb? The shit seems to have hit the fan."

Grim-faced, DCI Michael Thackeray replaced the receiver on his desk and gazed at the two visitors who had just arrived in his office.

"They've been taken to Eckersley," he said. "Apparently the drug squad's running their operation from there. All done on a need to know basis and apparently I didn't need to know."

"I'll go to Eckersley then," Laura said angrily. "I'll get Victor Mendelson to go down and play hell with them about Joyce. But what about the rest of them? They won't have any big guns out on their side, will they?"

Thackeray swung round in his chair to face Kevin Mower, who was sitting as far away from his boss as he could manage and studiously avoiding catching his eye.

"What the hell have you been playing at, Kevin?" Thackeray demanded. "What was wrong with telling me what you were doing? It's not as if it's illegal. Or did you have some idea of what's been going on up there? That there was likely to be a kilo of heroin stashed away in the kitchen? Did you know that? It won't just be me asking when it becomes known you've been working there. They'll want you down at Eckersley too. Tell me you were playing some devious game of your own to find the pushers and I just might believe you, but Ray Walter won't. You can bank on that. He'll chew you up and spit you out. Is this how you want your career to end?"

Laura and Sergeant Mower's meeting at the Lamb had been brief. Five minutes discussion had presented them with only one course of action and they had walked across the centre of town to police headquarters together in gloomy silence to see Thackeray. The DCI had listened in increasing disbelief as Laura spelt out what little they knew before making the series of phone calls needed to discover where those arrested at the Project had been taken.

Mower gazed at his Timberlands without answering Thackeray's tirade. Then he shrugged wearily.

"Anyone could have stashed heroin at the Project. The estate's awash with the stuff. But I don't believe for a moment Donna Maitland knew anything about it. She's passionately against hard drugs. She lost her own nephew, for God's sake. But the kids who use the place? Who knows?"

"It's true," Laura said, willing Thackeray to believe her. "Donna couldn't have known. It's just not possible, any more than Joyce could have been involved. The whole thing's absurd."

"It's the drug squad you need to convince, not me," Thackeray said. "And you'll find they think they've heard all that before. If Donna's in charge of the premises she has a duty to make sure no one brings anything in they shouldn't. You know that, Kevin. People have gone to jail for less."

"You're joking," Laura said sharply. "Donna can't search them every time they come through the door. Any one of those kids could have brought something in."

"Brought," Mower said softly. "Or planted, maybe."

Laura glanced at him sharply.

"Someone who wanted the place closed down, perhaps?"

"You're going to need solid evidence, one way or another," Thackeray said sharply. "In the meantime Joyce and the others are in a lot of trouble. Laura, I suggest you get down to Eckersley with a lawyer and get Joyce out of there, at least."

"Right," Laura agreed, although she glanced at Mower anxiously before slipping on her jacket. "I'll keep you in touch with what's happening," she promised. The silence lengthened after she closed the office door behind her. Thackeray eventually stopped drumming his fingers on the desk and sighed.

"How long have you been working up there?" he asked.

"Three, four weeks," Mower said.

"And the booze?"

"I'm OK, guv," Mower said, very aware that Thackeray

would see through evasion on that score. "They were happy with me at the clinic. It was an aberration. When I sat down and sorted my head out I discovered I could leave it alone."

"I hope you're right," Thackeray said, recalling the dozens of times he had told his superior officers much the same and proved himself wrong within days. "You're going to need a clear head to get yourself out of this mess."

"So what happens next?" Mower asked, his face unusually pale beneath the beard.

"You talk to the drug squad, I talk to Jack Longley. But before I do that I want to know one thing."

"That I wasn't dealing heroin?" Mower asked with a crooked smile.

"I'll take that as read," Thackeray conceded. "I don't know your friend Donna Maitland but you and Joyce Ackroyd don't look much like candidates for Mr. Big up on the Heights to me. No, what I really want to know is whether or not you want your job back."

Mower shrugged again.

"It looks like I may not have the choice," he said.

"Stop playing games, Kevin," Thackeray said.

"Do you want me back?"

Thackeray's chilly gaze weighed up the younger man, bearded and dishevelled in his jeans and sweatshirt, and softened slightly.

"If you want me to fight your corner, I will," he said. "But I don't want to stick my neck out and then have you chop it off."

Mower rubbed a hand over his face with a faint rasping sound and attempted a smile.

"Rita wouldn't have wanted me to pack it in, would she?"

"I can't answer that, Kevin," Thackeray said. "What I need to know is what you want."

"It's another two weeks before I'm due back…"

"It's about two minutes before I have to see Jack Longley

and tell him what's been going on up at Wuthering. And I've a murder inquiry to run."

"Yeah, I heard." Mower got to his feet wearily and opened the door. He hesitated only for a moment.

"I don't know what I want, guv. I can't pretend I do. It's not that I'm not grateful..."

Thackeray shook his head impatiently.

"Get down to Eckersley and talk to Ray Walter. Give him whatever help he needs."

"Sir," Mower said and closed the office door behind him.

"Damnation," Thackeray said after he had gone.

Later that afternoon Mower drove furiously back up the hill to the Heights and pulled up with a screech of brakes outside the primary school where a cluster of gossiping mothers with pushchairs and an isolated father watched in astonishment as he got out of the car and began pacing the pavement anxiously. It was ten minutes or so before the children began to straggle out of the school door with coats half on and bags trailing behind them to find their parents.

Mower had spent the intervening hours since he had left Thackeray at Eckersley police station where the drug squad had taken their time over interviewing him and taking a statement about his involvement in the Project. Ray Walter had arrived personally to see him sign it, with a sneer on his face that told Mower as clearly as any words that the DI regarded him as compromised.

"Nice set-up they had going there," Walter said when Mower handed him the completed document. "Just a pity you didn't notice what was going on."

"What do you mean," Mower asked.

"Kids coming and going, in and out of the place all hours. No questions asked. No cash and goods changing hands on the street. Ideal. Just a pity you didn't suss it."

"There was nothing to suss," Mower said flatly.

"No?" Walter raised an eyebrow. "Never mind, Kevin. I

don't suppose they'll mind that you've lost your nose for an iffy set-up when you get kicked out of the job."

Mower had not responded to that, battening down his fury and concealing clenched fists in the pockets of his leather jacket.

"Have you released Joyce yet?" he asked.

"We've let the old girl out. Real spitfire she was, demanding her rights. She's got a record for civil disobedience as long as your arm. I expect she's into legalising cannabis now."

"Yeah, right," Mower said. "And Donna?"

"No way. I reckon she's ripe for aiding and abetting even if we can't pin the dealing on her. We'll keep her here for her full twenty-four, I reckon. And the iffy king of the turntables, Sanderson. One of them must have know what was going on."

"No way," Mower said. "Dizzy B's never been to Bradfield before this weekend as far as I know."

"As far as you know. All I can say is you've got some dodgy friends, Kevin. I should think about that, if I were you."

"There's nothing dodgy about Donna. She hates the drug scene."

"Maybe," Walter conceded. "Any road, your precious Donna gave me a message for you. Would you pick up her kid from school, she said. Got a little thing going there, have we, Kev? Be waiting for her when she gets out, will you?"

"Sod you," Mower had said. "Sir."

He waited another twenty minutes outside the primary school, watching the last stragglers crossing the playground, before he had to accept that Emma was not amongst them. His heart thumping, he hurried to the main door of the school and found a pleasant-looking woman putting files away in the school office.

"I've come to collect Emma Maitland," Mower said. "But she doesn't seem to have come out with the rest of the children."

"And you are?" the woman asked.

"A friend of Emma's mother. She's been unavoidably detained."

"I'm Pat Warren, the head here," the woman said. "I couldn't just let Emma go with someone I don't know, you know, without Donna letting me know herself. But in any case, you're too late. Emma's already been collected."

"Who by, for God's sake?" Mower's mouth suddenly felt dry. The head teacher's face softened slightly.

"I'm sorry," she said. "Social services came to pick her up. They had an emergency care order. There was nothing I could do about it and I had no idea where Donna was, so I couldn't call her. I got no reply when I tried the Project."

"Jesus wept," Mower said. "Donna will go completely spare. She worships that child."

"I know. I'm sorry, Mr...?"

But Mower had spun on his heel, his face pale and set, walking quickly across the now deserted playground where a couple of soft-drink cartons blew with the crisp packets in the sharp wind and out into the street where an alcopop bottle rolled in the gutter before he kicked it viciously across the street. It could not be coincidence, he thought. Just because you were paranoid did not mean they were not out to get you. And he was totally convinced that someone was out to get Donna Maitland and, through her, him.

Chapter Thirteen

"You could say that whoever garrotted him did us all a favour," DC "Omar" Sharif muttered loudly enough to be heard across the incident room at that morning's briefing on the investigation into the death of Stanley Wilson.

"You could say that," Michael Thackeray agreed. "But as far as I'm aware we haven't restricted the protection of the law to people we approve of – yet. Perhaps that's something you should think about, Omar. There's a lot of people in this town who might like to count you out. Now, can we get on and summarise exactly what we know so far, please. Val? Progress report?"

"Everyone's seen the post-mortem report, guv. He was strangled with a piece of electric flex. No sign of anything similar in the house. No evidence of sexual activity immediately prior to death, in spite of his state of undress. No sign of a struggle but some curious marks on his arms, under the shirt sleeves, which Mr Atherton thinks are fresh cigarette burns. There's no sign of a break-in and all the doors were locked so we have to assume Wilson let his killer, or killers, in and that he or they left by the front door, which has a Yale lock which would close automatically. No witnesses so far to anyone seen arriving or leaving the day before he was found."

"What about regular visitors?" Thackeray asked. "Have the neighbours seen anyone coming or going at other times. My guess is that Stanley hadn't given up his interest in young men, but it's possible he never invited them home, I suppose. We need to know whether he had a boyfriend. And then there's the computer stuff. How was he distributing that? Did people call to collect packets with videotapes in them? Or did he post stuff out? Try the local post office. See if he was a regular customer there."

"The house-to-house inquiries are continuing this morning,

guv," Val Ridley said. "We'll bear all that in mind. We're still waiting on the computer unit at county to come up with details on what was in that machine. According to Foreman Security he was being paid into an internet bank, so it will take some time to get hold of his records although some of them may be in the machine as well. And if he was distributing the pornography – and the rest of the equipment and the copies of tapes he had stacked away there certainly indicates that he was – then there must be names and addresses somewhere."

"If they come up with those sort of lists, you've been offered some help from the computer porn experts," Thackeray said. "There are international databases available."

"Some beggars get all the fun," someone muttered but a scowl from Thackeray quelled incipient laughter.

"There might be hundreds of customers on Wilson's list," Val Ridley said.

"There might," Thackeray conceded. "It's a line of inquiry we'll have to follow if the list exists and if it seems relevant to the killing. But in the meantime we'll stick to the local angles. What about fingerprints?"

"A few apart from Stanley's," Val Ridley said. "They're looking for a match with records."

"Right. And it's certainly worth chatting up the local gay scene. See if Stanley was known and who his contacts were. Whether there's a boyfriend, or ex-boyfriends around. I think it would be a good idea for Omar to follow that line of inquiry, don't you?" Thackeray glanced across the room at the young Asian DC who flushed in embarrassment as a ripple of laughter went round the assembled detectives.

"Nice one, guv," someone called out.

"By the book, Omar," Thackeray said.

"Sir", Sharif muttered, through gritted teeth.

Thackeray made his way back to his own office, feeling slightly ashamed of himself for baiting Sharif. But he could see no other way of impressing on him the fact that prejudice worked in all sorts of directions than by forcing him to confront the reality. In a town where tensions were high and seemed to be rising, young Mohammed Sharif uncurbed posed a risk the police could not afford to take.

He sat for a moment at his desk before turning to the pile of files which had proliferated since Stanley Wilson's body had been found. He had slept badly after a devastating evening spent bickering with Laura who had returned from her grandmother's house aflame with indignation at the behaviour of the drug squad, who had released Joyce without too much delay but had decided to keep Donna Maitland and David Sanderson at Eckersley overnight for further questioning.

"You must know who the dealers up there are," Laura had protested. "Donna's one of the few people who might actually be willing to give evidence against them, if she had any to give. Joyce too. And Dizzy B's an ex-copper and a mate of Kevin Mower's. What sort of impression are you putting across if you arrest the good guys and ignore the crooks?"

"Donna has a responsibility to keep the stuff out of the Project," Thackeray had said, toeing the official line. If he had misgivings about it, he did not think this was the moment to discuss them with an already outraged Laura. "Somebody took that heroin in there. Somebody must have seen something."

"Perhaps the police took it in. No one saw them find it, Joyce says. They simply announced that it was there."

"Come on, Laura," Thackeray had protested. "Your grandmother's view of the police hasn't changed much since she was manhandled out of Grosvenor Square in 1969, has it? Be honest. Times have changed. I've no more reason to think the drug squad's bent than I have to imagine you make up your stories as you go along. There's a few dodgy characters in any profession, but thankfully not a lot."

"Joyce said they were thugs, most of them."

"You don't get into the drug squad without being able to

handle yourself," Thackeray said. "They're hard as nails. They need to be."

"This was women and girls they were dealing with," Laura objected. "Not armed criminals."

"If there was heroin there, there might have been guns not far away. This is nasty, brutal, violent crime we're talking about, Laura, not a Sunday School outing. This is why I was so anxious when you went snooping around up there. Perhaps you'll believe me now when I say you're taking too many risks."

"And perhaps you'll believe me when I tell you that some of those kids on the Heights were murdered."

"Did you tell Ray Walter that?"

"I didn't tell Ray Walter anything. They wouldn't let me in to see Joyce. Victor went in and I sat kicking my heels for an hour till they both came out. Then I took her home and went back to the office where Ted Grant was doing his nut, of course, because I'd taken most of the afternoon off. I don't think I can put up with him much longer either."

"What do you mean, either?" Thackeray had asked quietly. Laura had looked at him for a long time before she answered.

"I feel, with you, sometimes, that there's a brick wall between us," she said at last. "I thought for a long time that we might be able to break it down. But now I'm not so sure. I think you've boxed yourself in there with your guilt for so long that you're never going to be able to break out. Aileen and the Pope between them have killed something in you, and nothing I do seems to bring it alive again for long. It's as if you're in a glass coffin. I can see you, and talk to you but I can't really touch you. Not in any way that really matters." And with that Laura had turned away and gone into the bedroom where Thackeray, frozen by her unexpected assault, listened to her sobbing to herself for a long time before he dared to follow her, only to find her sprawled across the double bed, her face stained with tears, fast asleep. He had gone to bed himself, much later, alone in the spare room.

Wrenching himself back to the present, Thackeray suddenly thumped the desk in frustration and instead of turning to his files picked up the phone.

"Amos?" he said when it was answered. "Did you get anywhere with that little query I left with you?"

"I did, as it happens," Amos Atherton said. "As you suspected, there was no match with the sample they provided from the putative father."

"So tests were done, then?"

"Oh, aye. They were done when the babies were two months old."

"But they weren't Foreman's kids and we don't know whose they were?"

"That's about it, unless they went elsewhere with a sample from another candidate, as it were."

"Right," Thackeray said. "I can think of one likely candidate but I don't think there's a cat in hell's chance of persuading him to take a blood test. It wouldn't do his case any good at all. Anyway, that's a great help. Thanks, Amos. I owe you one."

"A pint of Tetleys'll do nicely some time," Atherton said. Thackeray hung up with exaggerated care.

"I'll have you yet, Foreman," he said to himself. "If I can catch you out in one lie I'll catch you out in the rest."

For an hour he tried to concentrate on the work in front of him, but was not sorry when his door was flung open without ceremony and superintendent Jack Longley dropped yet another file onto his desk and eased his bulk into his visitor's chair.

"What the bloody hell's going on up at the Heights?" Longley asked. "I've had the ACC in charge of the drug squad bashing my ear for half an hour about out-of-control coppers and interfering reporters and general slackness and insubordination getting in the way of his operations."

"I told you Mower got involved more or less inadvertently," Thackeray said mildly. "He had no reason to think that

174

this Project they're running up there was anything more than it seemed. If indeed it is."

"Well, according to the ACC someone's been running round alleging that at least one of the kids who's died up there was murdered. Was that Mower?"

"Ah," said Thackeray carefully. "Laura certainly believes that some of the deaths may not be as straightforward as they seemed. She's talked to people… "

"Apparently Ray Walter thinks it's all a load of bollocks," Longley said. "And given that not a single person has suggested anything like that to us, he's most likely right."

"Laura's no fool," Thackeray said defensively.

"Look, I realise you're in a difficult position where the Gazette is concerned. But have a quiet word, will you Michael? The squad's got a man undercover up at Wuthering and they don't want a loose cannon mucking up the operation. He was the one who tipped them off about drugs at the Project, apparently. As for Mower, you can tell him to pack in this moonlighting he's been doing and keep away from ongoing operations or he'll have no bloody job to come back to. He's lucky they didn't arrest him yesterday, from what I hear."

"Right," Thackeray said wondering where an ultimatum like that would push an over-involved Mower and fearing that it might be over the edge. To his surprise, Longley remained perched on the edge of his seat.

"I had Grantley Adams on the phone this morning too," he said eventually. Thackeray said nothing, but his lips tightened.

"His lad's recovering well now," Longley said. "He was anxious to know how far your investigation's got on the Ecstasy front."

"I told Adams we'd want to talk to the boy again when he had recovered, but I don't expect to get any further. He and the girlfriend have closed up tighter than clams. Has the school taken any action against them?"

"Grantley's been throwing his weight about there too, I hear," Longley said. "I don't know to what effect."

"Well, I can't see there being any charges. The cannabis we found wasn't worth a fiver. Perhaps being booted out of their posh school is just about what they deserve. I didn't get the impression the head would worry too much about a little matter of evidence."

Longley smiled, though it was a mirthless effort.

"I thought you wanted to pin Grantley to the ground," he said.

"It crossed my mind," Thackeray said. "He's an arrogant bastard, but you can hardly blame kids for the sins of their parents, can you? Not when we all pay for them in so many other ways."

"Aye, well, I'd not know about that," Longley said. "Anyway, keep me in touch, will you. The brass are not happy bunnies right now. I don't want to give them owt else to fret about if I can help it."

Kevin Mower glanced at his watch with some anxiety. It was half-past-one and he had arranged to meet Donna Maitland at twelve-thirty in the Woolpack in the centre of town. Dizzy B sat across the table from him with both hands wrapped around a pint of Stella Artois looking as tired and gloomy as Mower himself.

"She not have a mobile, man?" he asked.

"No, she's mislaid it," Mower said shortly. "I can't understand it. She's arranged to be at social services at two o'clock to talk about Emma. She won't want to be late." He had already called the Project and Donna's flat and got no reply from either.

"They didn't waste any time grabbing the kid," Dizzy said.

"If I could get my hands on whoever tipped them off she'd been arrested…"

"The drug squad wouldn't give a monkey's how many

176

kids she had or what happened to them. You know they're a law unto themselves, that lot."

"But I don't see why they'd go out of their way to shop her to the council."

"Maybe," Dizzy said doubtfully. "Though if they thought it would bring extra pressure to bear…"

"I think I'm losing my grip," Mower said, running a hand across his beard. "Time was I wanted to be part of the bloody drug squad."

"You're too involved with this case. Unless you're going to pack the job in completely, you should keep your head down or DI Walter'll chop it off. He's still got me down as some sort of major dealer, even though there isn't a shred of evidence to link me to anyone on the Heights ever. I'd never even heard of the bloody estate till last week. At least he let Donna out last night. He kept me sweating till this morning when he bloody well had to let me go. His time was up."

"Don't worry. I've been officially warned off interfering on the Heights," Mower said. "If I want to keep my job, that is."

"And do you?"

Mower shrugged.

"I wish I knew," he said. He emptied his glass and glanced at his watch.

"I tell you something odd, though," Dizzy B said. "I saw Darryl at the Carib this morning. He's furious about the closure. In fact he thinks he might get out of Bradfield there's so much hassle here. He's had an offer for the place from some developers he thinks he might take."

"That figures," Mower said. "That whole area's being tarted up. But the Caribbean kids won't be pleased. It's the only place they can really call their own."

"Tell me about it," Dizzy said. "I tried to persuade him not to sell." But Mower had lost interest in the Carib. He looked at his watch anxiously again and sprang to his feet.

"Will you stay here, mate?" he asked. "Do us a favour? I'll go up the hill to see if I can find Donna. She was in a terrible state when she got home last night. She's going to be late for this appointment if she's not careful and that won't go down well with the nannies at social services. Bell me if she turns up?"

"Safe," Dizzy B said, curling his arms around his glass as if about to fall asleep over it.

By the time he had driven up the steep hill in the pouring rain to the Heights, Kevin Mower felt far from safe. He knew from what he had gleaned of the drug squad operation that there were likely to be eyes watching every move on the Heights, and what the drug squad saw Michael Thackeray might well hear of too. But the gnawing anxiety which had been growing while he had been waiting for Donna could not be denied.

He had been there to greet Donna at the flat the previous evening when she was eventually released on police bail and he had explained Emma's absence as gently as he could. She had reacted more calmly than he anticipated, turning pale and tight-lipped but holding back the tears and contacting social services by phone without any great show of emotion. She had arranged to see them the next afternoon at a case conference to discuss Emma's well-being. But Mower could see the tension quivering beneath the façade and had objected angrily when she had eventually asked him to leave at about nine o'clock.

"We'll get her back," he had said fiercely. "I promise you that. Let me stop over and I'll go to the meeting with you tomorrow."

"I'm OK, Kevin," she had insisted. "I haven't done anything wrong, whatever that bastard inspector Walter says. I need a decent night's sleep. I've got some pills. Then I'm going to see the kids at the Project as usual. And at two o'clock you can come with me to see social services. They're well out of order with what they've done and I'll have Emma back tomorrow if it's the last thing I do. I'll see you in the morning."

But she hadn't, because at nine that morning DCI Thackeray had called Mower in and told him to keep away from the Heights, an instruction it had only taken him a couple of hours to decide to ignore. He could see even from a distance as he got out of the car and buttoned his fleece against the downpour that the Project was in darkness and the doors closed, which was normal enough at this time of day. A couple of girls lingered outside, clutching thin jackets around themselves against the sharp wind and bone-numbing wet but they would not be allowed in until the adults returned to unlock the doors at two.

Leaving his car at the foot of Priestley House he made his way up the concrete stairs where the rain ran down in small waterfalls between the litter. He splashed through puddles along the walkway until he reached Donna 's door. There were no lights on inside the flat in spite of the gloom and when he tried the door he found that it was locked. He knocked again and again but there was no reply. Alarmed now, he called Dizzy B on his mobile.

"Anything?" he asked, but the answer was negative.

"Shit," Mower said to himself. Looking round to make sure that he was still alone on the walkway, he pulled a credit card from his wallet and slid it against the lock, which held for a moment and then slid open, allowing him to slip into the flat apparently unobserved. Inside, when he turned on the light everything appeared normal enough. The small living room was tidy, and in the kitchen the glasses and plates which he and Donna had used the previous evening had been washed and left to dry on the draining board. He glanced into Emma's small room where the bed had been neatly made and a Barbie doll leaned against the pillow, and then knocked lightly on the door of the main bedroom before opening it. There the double bed had evidently been slept in and the bedclothes left thrown back with a blue silky nightdress lying across the pillows. A bottle of pills stood on the bedside table and he glanced briefly at the pharmacist's label without surprise, recognising the tranquilliser she had evidently been prescribed, although he had never seen her take them while he had been at the flat. But of Donna herself there was no sign.

Only the bathroom was left and Mower turned the door handle with a growing sense of alarm. At first he could see very little but as his eyes adjusted, even before he tugged on the light-pull, he could see that the water Donna was lying in was dark and he knew instantly what that meant. She was lying with her head still above the water and her eyes half open but sightless, her arms floating gently and revealing deep gashes across both wrists.

"Oh, God, no," Mower said despairingly, leaning against the door as his knees threatened to give way beneath him. He fought back waves of nausea for a long time before he felt able to step across the damp floor and look down directly at the dead woman. He checked for a pulse in her neck but without any expectation of finding one. A single razor blade lay on the floor close to the side of the bath, he noticed. It was probably one of his own. Donna had been dead some time, the water in the bath was cool to the touch and her naked body felt cold. She must have been lying here, dying here per- haps, for hours, he thought bitterly. If only she had allowed him to stay the night as he had wanted. If only. He gently closed her eyes as if to allow her to rest in peace.

"Oh, Donna, why?" he whispered. "We were going to get her back. Why, oh why, did you give up on it now?" Desolation overwhelmed him, this new death reopening the still barely healed wound left by Rita Desai's violent death. It was as if he was fated to bring destruction to women he allowed himself to grow fond of, he thought, as if what he touched he destroyed.

It was not until some time later, sitting in Donna's living room, with tears drying on his face, that he realised that there were things he must do. He glanced at his watch. It was two thirty and the case conference Donna should have attended must have convened itself and dissolved itself by now. He called police HQ first and asked the duty officer to deal with what appeared to be a suicide, then he caught up with Dizzy B, still patiently waiting for news in the pub. Next he phoned social services and told them that Emma Maitland's mother was dead. They seemed less than anxious for Mower to see the child and he had not the heart to argue his case. Still dazed, he went into the kitchen and splashed his face with cold water and dried it on a tea-towel. Then he stood on the balcony outside the flat, taking deep gulps of rain-sodden air waiting for the patrol cars and the officers who would deal with the incident to arrive down below.

As the fresh air cleared his brain he finally began to consider his own position which, he thought, whichever way you looked at it was not a comfortable one. While Michael Thackeray might just concede that fear for Donna's safety was a reasonable excuse for ignoring his instruction to keep away from the Heights, he was sure that the drug squad would be less than impressed when they discovered his willingness to disobey orders, as inevitably they would now do. Worse, it was conceivable that they might read far more into his relationship with Donna and her death than was justified. If Donna had reached rock bottom during the night, Mower was sure it was the threat of losing her daughter which had reduced her to despair. Ray Walter might well see it differently, interpret her death as an admission of guilt and be even more anxious to link Mower and Dizzy B, and quite possibly even Joyce Ackroyd, to whatever he believed had been going on at the Project.

Drenched by a particularly gusty squall, and seeing no sign of blue lights flashing on the approach to the estate, Mower went back into the flat to wait. He knew better than to touch anything just in case this apparently not very suspicious death turned into something more sinister when the pathologist had examined Donna's body, but he wandered from room to room, partly for something to do and partly because he could not sit still. He knew that he had spent enough time in the flat over the last few weeks for forensic traces of his presence to be everywhere if it came to that.

He had hoped he and Donna had finally understood each other. She might have been keen to find a new father for Emma, but he had given her no reason to imagine that was how he saw a future for the three of them. He did not think he had deceived her. He did not think he had pushed her to this desperate solution. But he was no longer sure of anything, and he began to cast around the flat for a note or message of some kind, perhaps addressed to Emma rather than himself, but could find nothing. She had no answerphone on which she could have recorded a message. And as he searched, and the effects of shock began to dissipate and his mind cleared, he began to feel that what had happened could not be the whole story, not in the sense that he could not believe the evidence of his eyes and that Donna was not dead, but that the method and even more the timing of her death did not make any sort of sense for the woman he thought he had come to know well. She might have spent the previous night frantic with worry and far closer to desperation than she had anticipated when she had sent him away, but the one thing he was sure she would never have done was abandon her daughter. Her death might have all the hallmarks of a suicide, but somehow it did not ring true.

You're losing it, Mower told himself, as at last he heard the faint sound of approaching police cars. You're finally going round the twist. Seeing one girlfriend murdered might be regarded as an unfortunate. Suggesting another might have gone the same way was a sure means of being referred to the funny farm by over-solicitous trauma counsellors. When the knock on the door from his uniformed colleagues finally came Kevin Mower showed them in mutely and waved them towards the bathroom.

"I'd arranged to see her this lunch-time. She didn't turn up so I came looking," he said by way of explanation. "She's in there." And he let the investigation swing into gear around him as he sat slumped on Donna's sofa, his eyes glazed and his head whirling with disconnected thoughts, in a posture that he knew his colleagues would put down simply to shock. But the shock had passed, to be replaced by a bitter anger as Mower watched the uniformed officers go through their routines. He had not the slightest shred of evidence to support his conclusion but he was nevertheless sure that Donna's death was the climax of the campaign of violence on the Heights. He knew there was something profoundly wrong with the way Donna had died and by the time he left the flat, dismissed by the uniformed inspector in charge just as Amos Atherton lumbered in, gasping from the long climb up the stairs, he had convinced himself that she had been murdered.

For a long time he sat in his car outside the flats watching the rain stream down the windscreen and reluctant to do any of the things he knew he now had to do. Eventually he started the engine and eased the car into gear but only travelled the few hundred yards down the hill to the Project where, he thought, the worst of his obligations awaited him. The reception area was milling with youngsters when he arrived, some of them leaving Joyce Ackroyd's class for remedial readers and some of them arriving for Donna's three o'clock group of computer beginners which had evidently not been cancelled.

"Donna won't be here this afternoon," Mower shouted across the chatter of teenagers coming and going. "Sorry kids, the class is cancelled." Cheers and groans greeted that news in equal measure and within a couple of minutes the Project had fallen silent as its clients disappeared in to the damp gloom outside. In the classroom doorway Joyce Ackroyd stood with one supporting hand on the handle and the other on her walking stick.

"What's happened?" she asked sharply, evidently reading the expression in Mower's dark eyes. "It's not the drug squad messing us about again, is it?"

Mower shook his head silently and took her arm, leading

her to one of the battered armchairs, still stained with red paint.

"Sit down," he said gently. "This is bad news."

"The worst?"

"The worst," Mower said.

For a long time after he had told her what he had found at Donna's flat, the two of them sat quietly, Mower with his arm round Joyce's thin shoulders, Joyce clutching his hand as if to prevent herself drowning in grief.

"I can't believe it," she said quietly at last.

"That she's dead?"

"No not that. You don't have to reach my age these days to know death can come out of a clear blue sky. But I learnt early, any road, losing my man in the war. No, I mean I can't believe that she killed herself. I can't believe she'd ever do anything to hurt Emma, and what could hurt her worse that this?"

Mower nodded, relieved that someone else's reaction was the same as his own.

"She had nothing to do with the heroin, did she?" he asked carefully. "I haven't got that wrong?"

"Of course she didn't," Joyce said angrily. "She detested the drug dealers. She'd have done anything to clear them off the estate."

"Maybe that's it then," Mower said. "Maybe she's got too many powerful people annoyed with her campaigning, the Project, helping kids get clean. It's not what the drug dealers want, or the men behind them, bringing the stuff in."

"You want to look at that computer of hers in there," Joyce said. "She's been spending hours on that just lately, when the kids have gone home. Learning to use the Internet was what she said she was doing. Does that make sense?"

"It might," Mower said. "Which one does she use?"

"The big one on the teacher's desk in there," Joyce said, indicating the classroom behind them. "It's newer than most of them we've got, the cast-offs we've begged. We managed to get one new one by pestering the retailers in town. That's the one she's been on non-stop since all the fuss started about the redevelopment. When I asked her what she was doing she just said she was working on the campaign. But she was printing reams of stuff, I do know that. Kept it all in a drawer but when I tried it, looking for some Sellotape, it was locked."

"Show me," Mower said. But the drawer was no longer locked and apart from a few office sundries, it was empty.

"She had a lot of paperwork in there," Joyce said obstinately. "And those disc things. A box of those."

"Could the drug squad have taken them?"

"I didn't see them taking paperwork. Why would they be bothered about the campaign for the Project?"

Mower switched Donna's computer on briefly and gazed at icons on the desktop as if willing them to reveal their secrets. He glanced at his watch.

"I need to go into the nick," he said. "But there may be files in her machine that will tell me what she's been looking at. I don't think it's safe to leave it here. Donna may have taken her paperwork and hidden it somewhere, or it may have been stolen. If it's been stolen, someone's going to realise that the machine itself may have information in it."

"Take it with you, Kevin," Joyce said firmly. "Do whatever you have to do."

They loaded the computer into the boot of Mower's car and he drove Joyce back to her bungalow.

"Will you be OK?" he asked, as he helped her to the front door.

"I'll ring Laura to tell her what's happened," Joyce said. "I dare say she'll come round later."

"If Donna was killed, I'll have them," Mower said.

"Aye, I'm sure you will lad," Joyce agreed as she opened her door. "But it won't bring her back, will it? Nothing's going to do that."

Half an hour later Mower found himself back in Michael Thackeray's office for his third uncomfortable session with his boss in less than that number of days. This time Thackeray was not unsympathetic. He had already been told about Donna Maitland's apparent suicide when Mower arrived from making a statement about finding her body but he did not hide his scepticism when Mower began to question whether the cause of death was as obvious as it seemed to his colleagues and, apparently, to Amos Atherton.

"There'll be a post-mortem, of course there will," Thackeray said. "But off the record Amos says he can see no signs of foul play at this stage. It's a bloody difficult suicide to fake without signs of violence on the body. She'd have to be semi-conscious at least to allow herself to be dumped in the bath without a struggle. Were there signs of a struggle, blood stains anywhere else…"

"Nothing I could see," Mower said. "But she told me she was going to take something to help her sleep. She could have been semi-conscious… Has Amos any idea when she died?"

"He's only guessing," Thackeray said. "The water had gone cold but there's no way of knowing how hot it was to start with. Anyway, the body wouldn't cool at the normal rate."

"She could have been there hours," Mower said angrily. "Since last night, even. She had pills in the flat. If she'd wanted to kill herself why not just an overdose? Why cut your wrists if there are easier ways?"

"Kevin, you're letting your imagination run away with you. I know you must be shattered by this…"

"But don't go over the top again? Is that what you're saying?" Mower asked angrily. He got to his feet slowly, as if every limb was heavy.

"I've done everything I can officially, guv," he said. "I can see you think I've lost it. But there's something wrong with Donna's death. I'll let you know when I've found out what it is."

Chapter Fourteen

"Donna Maitland's just another of the losers up there, isn't she?" Ted Grant leaned back in his executive chair easily next morning and offered Laura Ackroyd what passed in his lexicon for a smile of sympathy. "You can't make a bloody heroine out of her now, Laura."

"But that's exactly what we did make her six months ago," Laura said, spreading a copy of her feature on the opening of the Project in front of the editor. "You even wrote an editorial about her saying she was just the sort of feisty, enterprising person the Heights needed to pull itself out of the mire. People ready to make an effort instead of waiting for the State to provide, don't you remember? Don't you think our readers deserve some sort of explanation now she's dead?"

"I don't suppose our readers will remember a word we said about her," Grant said airily. "Anyway, she's obviously run right off the rails since then." He spun his chair round sharply on its castors and projected himself with remarkable speed for a heavy man towards the door of his office.

"Bob!" he bellowed across the newsroom. "Spare us a minute, lad, will you?" Bob Baker appeared in the doorway at a velocity to rival the editor's.

"This Maitland woman," Grant said. "What's the score with the police?"

"Not looking for anyone else in connection with the death," Baker said. He glanced at Laura and smirked. "And you know what that means. Off the record, they seem pretty sure she'd been turning a blind eye to what some of the kids she was supposed to be setting on the straight and narrow were really up too. And she couldn't hack it when the drug squad fingered her. But I don't suppose we'll ever know the truth of it now she's topped herself."

"Who told you that?" Laura asked. "It's not the way I hear it."

Baker tapped his nose and grinned at the editor.

"Sources, my love, sources. Maybe mine are better than yours."

"According to Laura, she doesn't have any police sources," Grant said, his eyes sharp with malice. "Nowt so much as a comment on the state of the traffic on the Aysgarth Lane roundabout ever passes the Detective Chief Inspector's lips. Allegedly."

Baker shrugged.

"I'll let you know if anything new develops, boss," he said.

"So that's a no then, is it?" Laura asked the editor.

"Of course it's a bloody no," Grant said. "You can't pretend the woman was never arrested, and from what Bob says, was highly likely to be charged. Even if she wasn't into drugs herself she knew the sort of kids she was dealing with. It was down to her to keep tabs on the little beggars when they were on the premises, wasn't it? That's the law. I've told you before. Zero tolerance is what the Heights needs, and if that's what the drug squad is doling out now then that's fine by me, and by the readers, if the letters we get are owt to go by. Donna Maitland slipped up and couldn't face the consequences, which would likely have been a spell in jail. End of story."

Her face set, Laura folded up the paper, from which Donna Maitland's photograph smiled out with the optimism of six months before. Whatever demons had driven Donna to take the course she had taken, she thought, they had left little room for her reputation to be redeemed.

"Give us a couple of pars on what's likely to happen to the Project now she's gone," Ted Grant conceded unexpectedly as Laura got up to go. "As I hear it, it's not got much of a future once the redevelopment gets under way. Barry Foreman and Dave Spencer've got other plans for education and training up there. Summat a bit less amateur. You should be pleased about that."

"Barry Foreman's an expert on these things now, is he?" Laura snapped.

"He's not daft, isn't Barry," Grant said. "That business of his seems to be growing by leaps and bounds. He's got money to burn and he might as well put a bit of it back into summat useful. You and your lefty friends should approve of that."

"Me and my lefty friends might just be a tad suspicious where the money's coming from before accepting it," Laura shot back tartly. "You'd think there'd been enough dodgy donations to political projects recently to persuade even Dave Spencer to take care."

"Bright lad, that," Ted said. "The next Tony Blair, I should-n't wonder. He'll go far."

"One way or another," Laura said, under her breath, recall-ing her grandmother's fury at the council leader's equivoca-tions.

"Get a quote out of him, any road. But keep it short. I've not got space to spare for sob stories from the Heights just now. They want to think themselves lucky up there. At least they'll be keeping their feet dry. They've got flood warnings out at Lane End. If this rain doesn't stop soon we'll have half the town under water by the weekend. "

"Right," Laura said. She went back to her desk and binned the back copy of the Gazette she had culled from the archives to refresh her memory about the launch of the apparently now doomed Project. It had seemed to promise so much to the kids on the Heights, but after the events of the last few days she had no doubt that the efforts Donna and Joyce had been making to secure its financial future would run into the sand. No one would want to be associated with an enterprise tainted by violence and fingered by the drug squad. Her grandmother, she knew, would be heart-broken by the loss of Donna and what could well be her last effort on the Heights. She glanced out of the windows at the leaden skies and the relentless rain which was beating against the build-ing and threatening to engulf Bradfield's narrow valley. If the Project died with Donna, she thought, hope for the

Heights would likely die too. And Joyce would find that hard to bear.

On the rain-swept upper walkway of Priestley House, Kevin Mower pulled up his collar and banged hard on the door of the flat two doors along from Donna Maitland's. He had already tried the six doors before Donna's and raised only a whey-faced young mother clutching a screaming baby and a night-worker irate at being roused from his morning's rest. Neither had heard anything suspicious during the night, they had told Mower irritably. One slept the sleep of exhaustion and the other had been on the other side of town at work. Neither of them knew Donna except by sight. Neither evinced either interest or concern at their neighbour's death. Mower was beginning to think that he really was chasing ghosts of his own imagining, as Michael Thackeray had suggested, rather than anything more substantial. Except for the two small niggling facts which had been enough to launch him on his solo investigations that afternoon.

He had woken from a restless sleep very early and stood at the back window of his flat gazing down at the scruffy garden where his downstairs neighbour's German Shepherd dog was already snuffling along the muddy tracks he had worn around the boundary fence. Barely able to see the loping animal in the grey dawn light as it nosed around bushes beaten down by the rain and left its mark at regular intervals, he had gone over and over in his mind what he had observed when he had discovered Donna's body. He knew that there was something wrong with what he had found at the flat, but also recognised that he had been far too distraught to be thinking clearly or professionally at the time. There was a lot of sense in the police rule that officers should not work on cases where they had any personal involvement. Even so he did not think he was letting his imagination run away with him, as the DCI obviously believed. If anything the bitter anger which consumed him had sharpened up his brain. Something about

Donna's death rang false and it was not just his conviction that she would not have despaired that night – when there was still so much to fight for on Emma's behalf as well as her own - which convinced him that he had missed some vital piece of information when he had broken into the flat.

But he could not pinpoint whatever it was that disturbed him and several cups of strong coffee later he had decided that this was something he would have to pursue on his own, whatever Michael Thackeray said. By eight-thirty he was parking on the Heights and, head down against the driving rain, dodging through the hooded teenagers and mothers with push-chairs and small children in tow who were battling their way from the flats to schools and nurseries on the periphery of the estate. The third floor walkway was deserted when he reached it, slightly breathless from the climb, and the police tape which had been stretched across Donna's doorway flapped forlornly in the wind. He detached the other end and stuffed it into his jacket pocket before using his credit card as before to gain easy entrance to the flat. He leaned against the front door, wiping the rain from his face and out of his eyes and breathing heavily, trying to reconstruct in his mind exactly what he had done the day before when he had come looking for his lover.

As he made his way from room to room, he found that little had changed. If his colleagues had conducted any sort of a search it had not been a very thorough one. He glanced into some of the drawers and cupboards in the living room, but there was no sign of the files and computer discs Joyce said she had kept at the Project. Perhaps the police had found and taken those already, he thought.

In the bedroom, Donna's deep blue nightdress still lay where she had evidently tossed it onto the pillows at the top of the bed. He picked it up and held it against his cheek, smelling her perfume and remembering occasions when he had helped her slip out of it. One strap, he noticed, was held in place only by a thread, as if it had been pulled too hard to take some strain. Was that, he wondered, why Donna had apparently taken it off and walked to her death in the bathroom naked. Or could there be a more sinister explanation?

He stood for a long time in the bathroom doorway. The room was empty now, the bath-water drained away leaving only a brownish tide-mark and some dark stains on the cork-tiled floor. But he could still see Donna as she had lain almost afloat in the brimming tub, eyes half open, her face surprisingly peaceful for someone who surely must have known that her life-blood was draining inexorably away. Had she taken enough pills, he wondered, to make the whole procedure stress-free, a painless exit from a life which had suddenly splintered apart? Or had she taken enough pills to make it easy for someone else to take her from her bed and put her into the bath with the minimum resistance? Why, if she had walked alone from her bed to the bathroom had she discarded her nightdress? It seemed an unlikely thing for a woman who knew she was going to be found dead to do, to choose to be found naked rather than even lightly clothed. Was it simply the lack of dignity in her death which made him so uneasy? Or something else?

And then suddenly, he had it. He banged his fist on the door jamb in fury and turned the light off and then on again. It had been almost dark in the bathroom when he had arrived the previous day, he thought, even though it had been mid-day and he remembered now that he had pulled the lightswitch on without thinking. Again this morning he had found the room gloomy and had switched on the light automatically as he had gone in. But if Donna had died much earlier, as seemed likely, then this small airless room must have been pitch dark when she had got into the bath and slit her wrists if the light had not been switched on. That, Mower thought, was not just unlikely, it was almost impossible. Someone must have turned out the bathroom light after Donna died and before he arrived the next day to search for her. And that someone had more than likely killed her.

The wave of red hot anger which threatened to overwhelm him subsided gradually and he splashed his face with cold water at the bathroom basin and dried himself roughly on one of Donna's towels before going back into the living room and flinging himself into a chair. His first instinct was to call Michael Thackeray and insist that he launch a full scale murder inquiry. But a moment's thought told him that might be counter-productive. He needed more, he thought, to break through the scepticism with which his new certainty would be greeted at police HQ. His credibility was already minimal, he thought, blown away by his difficulties over the last few months. It would take more than a sudden intuition in an empty flat to convince Thackeray that what looked like a perfectly comprehensible suicide was anything more. Superintendent Longley and the drug squad would be even harder to shift. What he needed was more evidence, and that might be hard to come by.

He glanced at his watch and pulled out his mobile phone. Amos Atherton started work early but he caught him before he had moved into the lab.

"She's scheduled for eleven," Atherton said in response to Mower's inquiry about the post-mortem on Donna Maitland's body. "There's what's left of two lads who drove into a lorry last night I've to look over first. I thought the Maitland women was a routine suicide. There's nowt else I should know about, is there?"

Mower hesitated. He knew that whatever he said to Atherton would get back to Thackeray, probably sooner rather than later.

"Just a niggle," he said. "There were people who had it in for her. I want to be sure that no one helped her on her way. She told me she was going to take some sleeping pills and get an early night."

"Friend of yours, was she?" Atherton asked. "Close friend?"

"You could say."

"I'll take a close look, then, lad," Atherton said. "A blood test for the pills, any road. But the wrist wounds looked bad enough to have taken her out pretty quickly, I reckon, from a first glance yesterday. Down to the bone on her left wrist."

"Unusually deep? For a razor blade? That's all I found in the bathroom with her."

Mower heard Atherton's slight intake of breath at the other end followed by a long silence.

"I'll let you have the report a.s.a.p," he said at last.

"I'm not in the office," Mower said and was unsurprised when this piece of information was greeted by another silence.

"So you'll not see it there?"

"Can I call you?" Mower asked, knowing he was putting his head into a noose.

"At home," Atherton had said eventually, giving him a number and hanging up.

Mower's second call was to a mobile and was answered instantly.

"Yo," Dizzy B said when Mower had explained what he was doing. "Strikes me you're taking all sorts of chances here, bro."

"I need your help," Mower said. "Where are you? Can you come up to the Heights?"

It took five minutes hard talking to persuade Sanderson that it was a good idea to return to the scene of his arrest and in the end it was only Mower's conviction that Donna could have been murdered which overcame his reluctance.

By the time he had finished his calls, the fire in Mower's belly had turned to ice. He took one last look around the flat, let himself out of the front door, reattached the police tape and began his hunt for witnesses to anything untoward which might have happened along Donna's walkway, or anywhere else in the block, the night Donna died. He was halfway down the concrete staircase when he caught a glimpse of movement below and began to hurry down two steps at a time. In the entrance hall he caught up with a skinny youth in a hooded top, grabbed his shoulder, spun him round and slammed him hard against the graffiti-covered wall.

"What's your problem?" he whispered in the boy's ear. "Live here, do you?"

"Who wants to know?"

Mower tightened his grip on the boy's neck and forced his head back against the rough concrete until he knew the pressure was hurting.

"Live here, do you?" he asked again. This time the boy nodded, as he tried ineffectually to unlock Mower's grip.

"Craig Leaward. Top floor," he said.

"Were you out last night?"

"Around," the boy croaked. "Just around."

"Did you see anyone up on the third floor, where Donna Maitland lived? Late on, midnight maybe?" The boy's eyes flickered momentarily and Mower knew that he had struck gold, though extracting it might be impossible. He bunched his fist and the boy's eyes widened in fear.

"Who was here, Craig? I need to know."

"I can't tell you that, man," Craig whispered hoarsely, and Mower relaxed the pressure on his throat slightly in response. "You know I can't tell you that."

"Was it the man they call Ounce? Is he the main man up here when you want some gear?"

But Craig's eyes merely widened in terror and Mower knew that he could not break the vicious circle of intimidation and fear which controlled the estate so easily. He released the boy and turned away in disgust while Craig pulled his jacket straight and scuttled up the stairs without a backward glance.

Laura's frustrations had grown all day. With the office in turmoil all around her as the water levels in the Beck had threatened to spill over the concrete banks which protected the low-lying houses in the valley to the west of the town centre, she had found it difficult to contact Councillor Dave Spencer at the Town Hall. And when she finally tracked him down he seemed abstracted.

"Nothing's been decided in that sort of detail yet," he said dismissively when she asked him about the future of the Project. "We're waiting for government approval for the whole regeneration area. Not that I think there'll be any difficulties, but it's early days yet. Lots of detail to be sorted out, financial ends to tie up, the building consortium appointed. You can't get something as big as this off the ground overnight, you know."

"So no thoughts on what's happened to the Project over the last few days?"

"You know I can't comment on a police investigation," Spencer said. "If you want an off-the-record opinion, I'd be looking to get my grandma out of there sharpish. But from what I've heard about Joyce, I've no doubt the Ackroyds think they know their own business best."

Laura had hung up quickly before the angry comment which sprang to her lips escaped and did her career no favours.

"Shit," she said under her breath as she struggled to concoct the couple of paragraphs Ted Grant had asked for. But by the end of the afternoon Joyce had raised her anxiety levels to new heights in a single phone call.

"Can you come up, love?" Joyce asked and Laura knew immediately from the quaver in her voice that something was seriously wrong. "Some beggar's put a brick through the window," Joyce said, so quietly that Laura could barely hear her.

As soon as she could get away from the office she drove to the Heights, leaving a stream of irate drivers hooting in her wake as she cut corners and chanced her luck with changing traffic lights across the town centre and up the hill to Wuthering. She parked outside her grandmother's bungalow with a squeal of brakes and realised before she even got out of the car that Joyce had played down exactly what had happened. Not just one, but as far as Laura could see, every one of Joyce's windows had been systematically broken, and the walls daubed with red painted obscenities.

"Bastards, bastards, bastards," she said aloud as she pushed open the front door, where even that small glass pane had been splintered and crazed by a heavy blow. In the living room Joyce seemed a shrunken figure, sitting alone in her armchair by the gas fire, shivering and on the verge of tears.

Laura took her in her arms for a moment, trying to control her own seething anger as the tears began to flow down Joyce's cheeks.

"When did this happen?" Laura asked at last, glancing round at the shards of glass which lay strewn around the room.

"I went up to the Project just to fetch some books. I was going to help some of the lasses with their reading down here. I wasn't away more than half an hour," Joyce said.

"You shouldn't have walked so far," Laura said, knowing how much of a struggle the short trip must have been.

"I can't stop here all the time, pet," Joyce said, scrubbing her eyes dry with a tissue. "I'll go barmy. I need to see folk."

"Have you called the police?"

"The community bobby called in about ten minutes ago. He gave me the name of a glazier to get the windows boarded up till they can be mended properly. But I hadn't the heart."

"Give me the number. I'll sort it," Laura said. She went into the small kitchen and cleared glass splinters off the worktop so that she could make tea. The back door, out of sight of the street, had been kicked almost off its hinges, she discovered. While Joyce sipped her tea she called the emergency glazing company and arranged for them to board up the house.

"You're coming home with me," she said flatly when Joyce protested. "You can't stay here. If you'd been in the house you could have been killed with all this glass flying around. Even when the windows are mended there's no guarantee they won't be back for another go." Still consumed by anger, she went into her grandmother's bedroom and bundled as many of her possessions as she could into the suitcase which she knew she kept under her bed.

"What do you want to take from here?" she asked as she went back into the living room. Joyce looked at her with a sort of dazed fear which broke Laura's heart.

"My photographs," she said, nodding at the collection of framed family snapshots which she kept on her mantelpiece. "I'd not like them lost." Laura collected up the pictures of her parents, of the grandfather she had never known, and several of herself as a child and a young woman, and piled them into the case. This is what it must be like to be a refugee, suddenly forced by brute violence to shovel a lifetime into a suitcase and flee, she thought. That Joyce should be reduced to this filled her with horrified rage.

As she helped her grandmother on with her coat, a knock at the front door set her heart thumping but when she glanced out of the shattered window, where the rain had already soaked the curtains, she was relieved to see Kevin Mower and Dizzy B Sanderson on the doorstep. She let them in quickly.

"We saw your car," Mower said. "And then the rest." He glanced around the room angrily. "Who the hell did this?" he asked, glancing anxiously at Joyce who offered the faintest of smiles.

"I wish I knew," Laura said, clinging to Mower's arm for a moment.

"Seems to me you've got real trouble up here," Sanderson said. "Tearaways out of control."

"This isn't random," Laura said. "Someone's got it in for Joyce..." She stopped and wondered if maybe she too was part of the target. "I'm taking Joyce home with me until we can get this place cleared up," she said.

"The boss'll love that," Mower said, with a wry smile.

"I'll not stop long, pet," Joyce said with an attempt at her usual fierceness. "Just while they patch up the windows."

"Well, we'll have to see about that," Laura mumbled.

Outside they heard a heavy vehicle rumble to a stop. The men had arrived to make the bungalow safe, or as safe, Laura thought, as it was ever likely to be again which would not be safe enough. Though whether she could convince her grandmother of that, she very much doubted.

Chapter Fifteen

When Laura had driven Joyce away, the two men sat in Mower's car for a moment watching the men in overalls board up the windows of Joyce's tiny home. Along the row of old-people's dwellings, an occasional curtain twitched and a pale, frightened face peeped out.

"I'm not having this," Mower said suddenly, swinging himself out of the car again. Sanderson followed reluctantly. But when they began knocking at the doors of Joyce Ackroyd's neighbours they met the same frozen stares and shaken heads that they had already encountered on the walkways of Priestley House. It was as if mental doors had been slammed, bolted and barred, and nothing Mower suggested in the way of encouragement persuaded any of them to open again. The elderly neighbours had seen nothing, and he knew that even if they had they would not tell him. They were too afraid.

"Jesus wept," Mower said, banging his fists on the steering wheel and watching the rain run in rivers down the windscreen.

"You'll not crack this," Dizzy B offered. "I've seen it before. Usually, the dealers only need to threaten violence. Here it's got very real. If you're going to find anyone to tell you they even saw their auntie going to the shop to buy the evening paper or the milkman dropping off a pint on a neighbour's doorstep, you're going to have to offer protection, and on our own we've none to offer. Talk to your guv'nor. That's my advice. If all this stuff's really connected you need an army up here to sort it out."

"Perhaps you're right," Mower said. "But there's one more thing it might be worth checking out, if only because it's something only I know about. It was never reported officially. Come on, Dizzy. I need back-up here."

The DJ shrugged massively but followed Mower back out into the rain-lashed parking area to Priestley House. This time when Mower knocked on Kiley Hatherley's front door it opened quickly and a different girl peered out. She had the same blank frightened eyes as Kiley herself but mascara lined and she was dressed in a mini-skirt and sleeveless top which showed off barely budding breasts. Under the make-up Mower guessed there lurked a child not much older than Kiley herself, but dressed for a night out clubbing on the town.

"You must be Kiley's sister," Mower suggested. The girl looked at the two men speculatively before nodding faintly.

"I'm Sharon," she said shortly. "Are you the fuzz?"

"Sort of," he said.

"I wondered if you'd come back. Someone's done him in, haven't they? I saw it in t'paper."

"What?" Mower said sharply.

"The bloke that gave our Kiley t'booze. And that snotty little Emma Maitland."

"Can we come in, Sharon?" Mower asked, bemused by this apparently random stream of consciousness. Sharon looked up and down the walkway, her eyes narrow with suspicion, but evidently seeing nothing to cause her any alarm she nodded.

"Me mam and dad's gone to Leeds for t'day," the girl said. "I'm minding our Kiley after school. They won't be back till right late."

Mower and Sanderson followed her into the living room of the flat, a cluttered space littered with overflowing ashtrays and empty beer cans and several days' copies of the Bradfield Gazette. Kiley was curled on the sofa, her thumb in her mouth and her eyes glued to the television.

"How old are you Sharon?" Mower asked, knowing that he would not like the answer. Sharon's eyes flickered momentarily.

"Fourteen," she said firmly. Mower did not believe her but

he guessed she thought that was a safe age to be allowed to babysit.

"Last time I came your mother wouldn't let me talk to Kiley about the man at the shops who gave her and Emma alcopops. Do you think she'll mind now?"

"They didn't know who he were till I told them," Sharon said.

"And who was he?" Mower asked. Kiley still stared steadfastly at the TV.

"He were this bloke who's been murdered. I saw his picture in t'paper. I told you."

"Right," Mower said. "You're quite sure about that?"

"Course I am," Sharon said. "He were always hanging around, weren't he, when we went for us dinner up the chippie. And outside t' school sometimes. He never did owt. He weren't dangerous or owt like that. He were just there, sometimes, talking to t'bigger lads. And that day he were in't shop buying stuff and when he come out he just gave Kiley and Emma t'bottles."

"He didn't want anything in exchange? Didn't ask them to go with him?" Sanderson asked angrily.

"He never does. He just chats to folk, mostly the lads, not the girls. Any road, I were there. I were watching Kiley. I bought her t'chips and I were going to teck her back to school wi'me when it were time."

"What class are you in, Sharon?" Sanderson broke in again.

"Year Six..." The girl stopped, realising she had been tricked.

"She's eleven," Dizzy B said flatly. "You need help here, Kevin. Parents, social workers, your guv'nor, the whole shebang. We're up a creek without a paddle."

Mower shrugged tiredly.

"Never mind," he said. "At least we've found someone on this bloody estate who saw something sometime. The rest of the bastards go round like the three wise monkeys." He pulled out his mobile and called police HQ.

"We've got two young kids here on their own who need to talk to DCI Thackeray," he said. "Can you deal?"

Martin Harman had slipped into police hands almost by chance when he walked into the Devonshire Arms, Bradfield's only gay pub, at the precise moment that DC Mohammed Sharif was asking the barman about Stanley Wilson's friends and acquaintances.

"Here's the lad you want to talk to," the barman said, not bothering to disguise his relief. "Martin's a good mate of Stanley's. Best mate maybe."

Sharif turned towards the newcomer to the almost empty bar and smiled the smile of a hungry tiger. The young man who had just come in did not smile in response. Instead his already pasty face acquired a greenish tinge and his pale blue eyes flickered this way and that, like a small animal seeking some burrow down which to dive in the face of the predator which Sharif undoubtedly believed himself to be. Harman was a skinny youth, spotty as well as pale, with unfashionably long fair hair straggling down his back in greasy strands onto a scuffed leather jacket. He glanced at the warrant card which Sharif flashed in his direction and flashed the tip of his tongue over dry lips.

"Best mate, is it?" Sharif said, his dark gaze never leaving Harman's.

"Not really," Harman muttered, glancing wildly round for the barman who had taken himself to the far end of the bar where he was busy polishing glasses and avoiding anyone's eye.

"You know Stanley's dead, I take it?"

"Yeah, someone showed me his picture in t'evening paper," Harman said.

"But you didn't think we might want to talk to you?" Sharif asked.

"I didn't think," Harman said. "I ain't seen Stanley for weeks."

"Well, I have a boss who's been thinking a lot about you."

"How has he?" Harman said wildly. "He doesn't know I exist."

"Ah, but he guessed you might," Sharif said. "Stanley Wilson being what he was. My boss just guessed there might be someone like you we'd need to talk to. So if you'll just come down to police HQ with me you can meet my boss and he'll tell you everything he's been thinking since we found Stanley. That OK with you?"

And just in case it wasn't he took hold of Martin Harman's arm with just a little too fierce a grip and turned him on his heel and marched him towards the door.

"Thanks mate," he called over his shoulder to the barman, knowing this would cause him maximum embarrassment with the handful of other customers who had been watching the proceedings anxiously. Outside in the gusting rain he thrust Harman into the front seat of his car, wiped his hands ostentatiously on his trousers after he had slammed the door, got in the driver's side and opened all the windows in spite of the weather.

Harman glanced at him fearfully but said nothing.

"One of my clients must have left something unpleasant under the seat," Sharif said, face as frozen as an Egyptian god, as he crashed the car into gear and swung out of his parking space at a furious pace. "Left a nasty smell." By the time he pulled into the car park at police HQ Martin Harman was shaking, although not another word had been spoken.

Harman was still looking terrified when Michael Thackeray himself came into the interview room where Sharif and Val Ridley were facing him across the bare and scratched table.

"Mr. Harman," Thackeray said mildly. If there was going to be a good cop, bad cop routine here it was clear that Thackeray had been cast in the kindlier role. "I'm glad we traced you. And I'm pleased you agreed to come in and talk to us." Harman shrugged his thin shoulders and glanced at Sharif with undisguised hatred.

"I didn't have much of a choice, did I?"

"I understand you knew Stanley Wilson quite well?" Thackeray ignored the tension which made the air in the enclosed space tingle. "You must have expected that we'd want to talk to you. Now, tell me how you met him, would you? Where and when?"

"I met him at the Devonshire, the way you do," Harman said. "It were ages ago. I can't remember exactly when, can I?"

"Bought you a drink, did he?"

"Yeah, that's right."

"And the relationship developed from there?" Thackeray offered Harman a cigarette which he lit with trembling fingers. Given the contempt radiating from "Omar" Sharif he felt more sorry for Harman than he might normally have done. After all, there was no reason yet to suppose that Harman had strangled Wilson after some lovers' quarrel.

"I suppose," Harman said, his eyes shifting uneasily now.

"And it became physical?" Thackeray insisted.

"Well, yeah, it did, as it goes. Now and then. It weren't a great love affair or owt."

"But Stanley was quite a lot older than you, wasn't he?"

"A bit. A few years."

"So how old were you when you met him?" Thackeray guessed his Asian DC would not like the answer, at least if it was even marginally truthful. Harman glanced down at the table while Sharif simply glared.

"Sixteen," he said and Thackeray thought that was close enough not to argue with. He knew Wilson preferred young men but as far as he knew he had never been accused of being a paedophile, in Britain at least. He seemed to prefer to play on the very edge of legality claiming, as no doubt he would have claimed in this case, that his partners knew their own sexuality and were willing.

"So you became his boyfriend," Thackeray went on, carefully keeping his tone neutral although he could sense the young Muslim DC seething beside him. "How long ago was this? Months? Years?"

"Three, four years ago," Harman said. "I don't remember exactly. It's always been a bit on and off. Stanley weren't the faithful kind, if you know what I mean. He was always on the lookout for summat new."

"Did he pay you?" Sharif said suddenly, his voice thick with emotion. Thackeray glared at him and Harman flushed uncomfortably.

"No, he bloody didn't," Harman said passionately. "It weren't like that. I'm not a bloody rentboy."

"I take it you were a regular visitor to Stanley's house?" Thackeray asked, the question apparently as innocuous as the rest.

"Yeah, course," Harman said. "He couldn't come to mine, could he? I still live at 'ome, don't I?"

"With your parents?"

"My mam. My dad did a bunk years back."

"The reason it's important, Martin, is that your fingerprints will be around the place at Stanley's house so we'll need to eliminate you. You've no objection to us taking your prints, have you?" Thackeray's tone left no doubt that a negative reply was not an option. Harman shook his head miserably.

"When were you last there, do you reckon?" Thackeray pressed him.

"Last week," Harman muttered. "Thursday or Friday maybe."

"And not since?"

"I've not seen him since."

"Not quarrelled, have you?" Thackeray asked quickly and saw Harman flinch.

"No, he were busy, that's all," Harman said. He hesitated for a moment, glancing at all three officers in turn before evidently making up his mind to continue. "Well if you must know he were in a right funny mood. Excited, like."

"Any idea what he was excited about?"

"He didn't say much, but he had a lot of holiday brochures in t'front room so I guessed he were planning a trip. I thought maybe he'd come into a bit extra, like. Most o't'time he were skint, but now and again he'd be flush and that were when he went away to one of his exotic spots. Course I knew what he went for…"

"He didn't take you with him?" Thackeray asked.

Harman laughed thinly.

"Fat chance. It weren't me he were going to Thailand for, or wherever. Get real."

"But you didn't see him again?"

"Well, when I thought about it I reckoned maybe he were all worked up because he'd found someone new. I were going round there about a week ago and I saw this black lad coming out. Right good-looking, he were, nice gear an'all. I just knew Stanley would go for him if he got half a chance. So I thought I'd bugger off for a bit, didn't I? Chances were he'd not last long and then Stanley would come crawling back to me."

"That had happened before?" Thackeray pressed.

"One or twice, yes," Harman admitted. "I told you. He were always on the pull, was Stanley."

"But there were other reasons why men might call on Stanley, weren't there?" Sharif asked. "You knew he was carrying on some filthy pornographic trade there."

"If you've been crawling all over his house you must know he had a little business going," Harman said, apparently unperturbed. "It were nowt to do wi' me, that. I'm not into all that stuff, pictures of kids an' that. Nor were Stanley, as it goes, but he reckoned he could make a few bob out of them that were. He were good wi'computers, were Stanley. You must have seen all the stuff he had upstairs in the back room."

"Are you saying you didn't help him? Come on," Sharif sneered, with fierce scepticism.

"I never," Harman said. "I don't know owt about computers. I'm not into all that technology stuff."

"It must have cost him to set all that up, though," Thackeray observed. "How did he fund all that on his wages?"

"I don't know," Harman said. "He had some of it before I met him. He did once say that someone loaned him some money, but I've no idea who. It's not summat you could ask the bank for a loan for, is it?"

"And you didn't raise any objection to the nature of this … business?" Thackeray asked.

"It were nowt heavy," Harman said. "Just pictures of kids on beaches, in the park, family snaps, that sort of stuff. Not hardcore. At least that's what he said."

"And you believed him?" Sharif's intervention was scornful. "You expect us to believe that?"

"It's the truth. I had nowt to do wi'it."

"So we won't find your fingerprints all over the computers?" Thackeray asked.

"No, you won't," Harman said. "I told you, I know nowt about computers. Never learned. And Stanley used to say that the beauty of the thing was that nothing important ever came off those machines. It were all stashed away there with passwords and codes – what is it? Encryption? All his contacts, customers, everything was in there."

"But he copied videotapes. Surely you know that?"

"He had a few customers for tapes," Harman said. "But mostly it went out over the internet. He said that were much safer. He didn't like doing the tapes but a few customers who couldn't use a computer liked them. He said if he ever got caught they'd be the ones who got done because he had their addresses, road names an'that. A lot of the others he only had computer addresses and he said that were much safer. Anonymous, like."

"Anyone you know take the tapes?" Thackeray asked.

Harmon shrugged.

"Special customers, Stanley said. Did it as a favour. I got the feeling there was someone important though – the person who bankrolled him, maybe. He talked once about his insurance being in that machine."

"His insurance? What did he mean by that?" Thackeray asked sharply.

"I'm not sure," Harman said slowly. "But I reckon there was stuff in there someone didn't want let out."

"You think he was into blackmail?"

"He had plenty to go on, didn't he?" Harman said easily. "But I don't know who so it's no good asking. I took care to keep well out of Stanley's business affairs. Too clever by half, I reckoned he might be. I wanted nowt to do with it."

"So you say you haven't seen Stanley this week," Thackeray changed tack sharply. "So you can tell me where you were on Wednesday."

"What time Wednesday?" Harman asked sulkily. "I were at work most o't day, till six any road."

"And where's that?"

"Dale's Engineering up Manchester Road. I work in t'finishing shop."

"But not today?" Sharif asked. "Or was that your dinner-hour when you came into the bar?"

"That's right," Harman said. "I saw the Gazette earlier and bloody well needed a stiff drink."

"And later on Wednesday. What did you do after work?"

"Went home, had my tea, watched a bit of telly and went to bed," Harman said flatly. "If you think I killed Stanley you must be barmy. I were actually fond of the old bugger, though I sometimes wondered why."

Thackeray got home late and tired. They had let Harman go, as they had to, having no evidence at all to link him to Wilson on the day he died. He had been about to call it a day when the uniformed duty inspector had called him downstairs where he found Kevin Mower, Kiley and Sharon Hatherley and a social worker crowded into an interview room waiting for him.

"We couldn't find their parents," Mower said. "But I think

they've got something to tell you which might be useful to your murder investigation."

Thackeray had listened in astonishment as the girls repeated what they had already told Mower.

"How often did you see this man on the Heights," he asked when they had finished. "Every day? Once a week? Can you remember?"

"Not every day," Sharon said. "Once or twice a week maybe. He were usually talkin' to t'older lads. He took no notice of girls, did 'e?" Kiley nodded solemnly but suddenly the huge blue eyes which had been gazing guilelessly at the assembled adults lit up as a new thought struck her.

"He were always there Tuesday," Kiley said.

"How do you know that?" Thackeray asked, surprised.

"Because it's PE after us dinner on Tuesdays and when we go to t'chippie we have to hurry back. The day Emma got sick it should have been PE and I missed it 'cause Sharon an' me waited for her mam to come down from t'Project, didn't we? And I like PE."

"And once he gave us a lift back to school in his car, and that were a Tuesday an'all because Kiley were going on about getting changed for PE," Sharon said.

"You took a lift with this man?" Thackeray had said, glancing at Mower in scarcely veiled horror.

"You must never –" the social worker had begun, until Thackeray stopped her with a wave of his hand. He did not want the children distracted.

"Tell me about his car," he said. "Was it a big one?"

"It were red, not very big."

"Anything else you can remember about it?" The two girls shook blonde heads in unison: as far as they were concerned, a car was just a car and the main memory of that Tuesday was of sailing down the hill back to the primary school while most of their contemporaries trudged through the rain on foot.

"So when this man gave you and Emma a drink you

already knew him? He wasn't really a stranger?" Thackeray pressed the younger girl. Kiley nodded, frightened now.

"Did you tell Emma's mum who it was?"

Mower shook his head angrily at that.

"I went round there to ask," he said. "Their mother wouldn't let me talk to Kiley."

"My dad said to keep out of it," Sharon said on her younger sister's behalf. "Said if Emma wanted to get pissed it were nowt to do wi'us."

"Your parents and Mrs Maitland didn't get on?" Thackeray asked.

"My mam said Donna were a stuck up cow," Sharon said. "I'm sorry for Emma now, mind," she added quickly. "Now her mam's dead."

Thackeray had led Mower up to his office after the social worker had taken the two girls home to wait for their parents.

"Love thy neighbour?" Mower said angrily, flinging himself into a chair.

"Come on, Kevin, you know what it's like up there," Thackeray had said. He looked at the sergeant critically, taking in the still unshaven beard and dark circles under the eyes. If Mower was on the way back to normality he was disguising it well, he thought.

"If there are links between Wilson and what been going on up on the Heights you may get what you want after all," Thackeray said.

"Was he propositioning these lads he was talking to, or was he delivering something for someone?" Mower asked.

"Something else to talk to the drug squad about," Thackeray had said. "It's quite possible they know the answer." He looked at Mower again thoughtfully.

"Do you still think Donna Maitland's suicide was a fake?" he asked.

"Amos Atherton said…"

"You're pushing your luck, Kevin," Thackeray had interrupted angrily. "Amos shouldn't be saying anything to you."

"One of the slashes on her wrists was very deep," Mower said, his face closed and remote. "Too deep, maybe, more like a knife than a razor blade. There was no knife in that bathroom when I got there. He's waiting for the results on the toxicology tests."

"I'll have a close look at the PM report," Thackeray had conceded. "And I'll have to talk seriously to Ray Walter now. We can't make any major moves up there without them on board."

"If you ask me they've not got a clue what's going on," Mower said. "And if Donna did kill herself, it's bloody well down to them anyway. They were out of order raiding the Project like that."

When Thackeray had finally got home he found Laura and her grandmother eating risotto at the table in the window which overlooked the long luxuriant garden which as much as anything had persuaded Laura to buy the flat. But tonight the curtains were drawn tight against the gusting rain outside, and the softly lit room seemed like an oasis of warmth in a cruel world.

Thackeray kissed Laura on the cheek and put a hand lightly on Joyce's shoulder. She had barely touched her food, he noticed.

"I heard you'd been vandalised," he said. "I'm sorry. I'll ask Jack Longley to kick uniform into putting some extra effort into finding the little toe-rags."

"I don't want any special treatment," Joyce said tetchily. "I'm not the only one being bullied up there, you know."

"She needs to stay here for a bit," Laura said, looking up at Thackeray doubtfully.

"Of course she does," Thackeray said quickly.

"Not long, I don't," Joyce said. "I'll not be in your way long. I'm not giving the developers the satisfaction of finding my place empty. Or the vandals for that matter. I'm going home as soon as the repairs are done."

Laura raised her eyes skyward for a second and Thackeray allowed himself a faint smile.

"I see the famous Ackroyd bloody-mindedness hasn't been dented too badly," he said.

"Anyway, you must know I'm a major drug suspect these days," Joyce said with satisfaction. "I'm sure it's not good for your reputation to be living with the likes of me for long, Michael."

"If I told you I thought the drug squad was misguided, Joyce, I don't suppose you'd believe me, would you?" Thackeray said carefully.

"Aye, well, they turned out to be a sight too misguided for poor Donna," Joyce snapped back, for once letting her bitterness show.

"The whole situation on the Heights is turning into a bloody tragedy," Laura said suddenly, glaring at Thackeray. "It's time the left hand told the right hand what it's doing. The bad guys seem to be running rings round you all."

"Which is why I'd like you both to keep away from the place," Thackeray said.

"We all have our jobs to do," Joyce said sharply. "And now I'll get to bed, if you don't mind. It's been a long day."

When she had closed the door of the spare bedroom firmly behind her, Laura glanced at Thackeray, who had slumped into a chair and closed his eyes. She slipped onto the chair arm beside him and put an arm round him.

"This is getting to you," she said. "What is it? Have you been talking to Kevin Mower? Do you really think Donna was murdered?"

Thackeray shrugged wearily.

"I don't know. But yes, in general terms you're right. There's a reign of terror going on up there and the drug squad seems to be compounding it rather than making it any better."

"And then there's Karen and the missing babies," Laura said. "No progress there, I take it?"

"I've put their mother on the missing persons' list," Thackeray said. "Mother and babies, as it goes. And asked social security to find out if she's picking up her child benefit and if so, where. Jack Longley would go spare if he knew how I was wasting police time but I still think there's something deeply suspicious there. But no one I've mentioned it to has come up with anything concrete. She just went, without a word, and no one seems to think it even slightly odd."

"You don't sound very hopeful of finding them."

"I'm not really. I've never underestimated Barry Foreman's intelligence. What I got wrong was the ease with which he could take other people in, whether it's Karen's mum or the local establishment. He's going to end up running this town if someone doesn't stop him buying friends and influencing people."

Laura ran her fingers through Thackeray's hair gently.

"Don't you think you're maybe getting a bit obsessive about Foreman," she said carefully. "You've got enough problems without taking on the whole of Bradfield's great and good. You say he's a bastard, so perhaps his girlfriend just got fed up and bunked off with her twins. If he's as bad as you say, she'll have taken care he won't be able to find her, maybe."

"I thought this sort of thing was meat and drink to journalists," Thackeray teased her, although his heart was not in it.

"If he's getting involved in the regeneration scheme I think that's interesting. I'd dearly like to find out what Councillor Spencer and the rest of that committee are getting out of this project. They've even got Ted Grant on board now, and the only reason I can think of for inviting him in is to make sure the Gazette doesn't ask too many questions when the contracts are handed out."

"Jack Longley goes to those meetings too," Thackeray said gloomily. "He doesn't seem to have picked up anything dodgy and he's got a nose like a ferret."

"Well, I expect they'd make sure they kept anything dubious away from him. I get the feeling that some of that committee are in the know and others are there as window-dressing."

"Or could it just be that this is a pot and kettle job?" Thackeray asked. "You don't like Spencer any more than I like Foreman. Maybe we're both letting our emotions cloud our judgement."

"Maybe," Laura said, getting to her feet and stretching lazily. "Anyway, with the Beck about to flood the town and your murder case, plus the mayhem on the Heights, a little bit of council corruption'll have to go on the back burner for now, won't it? It's getting to the stage where Ted's going to have us in the office twenty-four-seven. I'm going to bed. I'm whacked."

A short time later, when Thackeray slipped into bed beside, as he thought, a sleeping Laura, she turned towards him and slid her arms around him, running her hands down to his hips and pressing her body into his, with predictable effects.

"Don't let all this stuff get between us," she murmured.

"It'd be difficult just now," he said, kissing her neck and ears. "I just want to keep you safe. You know that."

"Life's an unsafe enterprise, or else it's very, very dull."

"Keep Joyce here where we can keep an eye on her is all I'm saying," he said, cupping her left breast so that he could kiss that next. "And let's hope she sleeps soundly because this bloody bed creaks."

Chapter Sixteen

It only became clear the next day, after fire officers and police had begun to work their way through the smouldering rubble, and Bradfield Infirmary had patched up half a dozen young men sufficiently to allow detectives to talk to them, that the fire which gutted the Carib Club was the cause and not the result of the Chapel Street riot. Laura Ackroyd and Bob Baker arrived together at the scene of the previous night's disturbance, in unlikely partnership at the insistence of their editor who for once seemed almost overwhelmed by the pace of events. The irony of one section of the town threatened with inundation and another burning was not lost on Laura who gazed in dismay at the still smouldering ruin of the club, a couple of wrecked and gutted cars and a fire-engine, like a beached whale, with its tyres slashed.

"Didn't they have a lovely time?" Bill Baker said.

"It was an arson waiting to happen," Laura said, stepping cautiously over broken glass and half bricks scattered across the roadway where Jeremy Adams had been run down. "The last time I was here someone set a fire against the door. Leaving the place empty for a week or so was asking for trouble."

"Licensing a club like this so close to Aysgarth Lane was asking for trouble, actually," Baker said.

"You'd accept a no-go area, would you? Here? Or on the Heights, maybe? That's exactly what the drug gangs want," Laura said, but she did not wait for a response. On the other side of the police cordon she saw a dishevelled looking Darryl Redmond, one hand bandaged, being helped out of the remains of the entrance by Dizzy B Sanderson. Behind them she could see fire officers sifting through the blackened interior of the club.

"Look," she said to Baker. "I'll talk to the owner again, as

I've already interviewed him. Why don't you see what you can get from the fire service and the cops. There's Val Ridley over there looking as if she's not keen to get her hands dirty. You know Ted wanted a definitive piece for the front page an hour ago." And before Baker could object to this allocation of responsibilities, which she knew he would if he could think of a reason quickly enough, she waved at Redmond and Sanderson and picked her way across the rubble strewn street to meet them.

"I'm sorry," she said to the club owner. "What a mess."

"Ah, miz reporter," Redmond said. "I told you last time we needed more protection here from those mad Pakis raving on about girls in mini-skirts and satanic music. You'd think Asian kids never went to clubs or sold drugs, the way they talk. But the police don' seem to have paid any mind to me. They couldn't even get a fire engine close enough to make a difference. They might as well 'a'bin pissing on the fire for all the good they did." He waved an angry hand at the crippled appliance further down the street.

"By the time they got hose pipes up and running the fire was out of control," Sanderson said. "The little bastards pelted the first crew with stones and bottles. They couldn't get near. The place is a write-off."

"Six years of my life up in smoke," Redmond said gloomily.

"Weren't you insured?" Laura asked, and then wished she hadn't. Redmond looked at her pityingly.

"What good's that?" he said. "The building is 'structurally unsound', according to the firemen. It'll have to come down - so you lose the kids for months, p'raps years, while you put the place together again and expect them to come back when you reopen? No way. No chance. The Carib's dead, which is what the men in pyjamas wanted anyway. I reckon they were inciting the kids to cause trouble here."

Laura glanced at the blackened wall facing the street and at the only windows, gaping holes in the brickwork now, at second story level above them.

"It was a petrol bomb, was it?" she asked. "It must have been someone with ambitions to play cricket for Yorkshire to get one through those windows."

Redmond shrugged again.

"They got different theories," he said. Laura glanced at Dizzy B, for further explanation.

"I had a talk with one of the fire service investigators," he said. "It doesn't look as if it was a petrol bomb at all. The seat of the fire's at the back of the building."

"You mean it could have been an accident?" Laura asked, surprised. "An electrical fault or something?"

"Oh, no, not an accident," Dizzy B said. "But maybe not kids on the rampage either. One of the emergency doors at the back had been forced and some sort of accelerant chucked about, petrol probably. This was arson all right, but by someone who really intended to gut the place."

"I should have sold out when the developers made me an offer," Redmond said. "I'd have been laughin' then, floggin' a goin' concern over the odds. It won't be worth more than the value of the site now."

"I didn't know you'd had an offer to buy," Dizzy B said. "Who from, for God's sake?"

"Some development firm Barry Foreman knew about. Wanted to convert into flats with shops underneath – like they done further up the street. They probably won't be interested now."

"What's the company called?"

"City Properties? City Ventures? Somethin' like that. Barry said they were the people who are going to redevelop the Heights."

"Are they?" Laura said thoughtfully and saw the flicker of interest in Dizzy B's eyes.

"You thinking what I'm thinking," he asked. "Maybe someone wanting to force a sale they couldn't get any other way?" Darryl Redmond shrugged.

"What difference does it make now? Come with me down

the police station, Dizzy, to make this statement they want," the club owner said, his face weary under the scattering of ash which clung to his dark skin and hair like mould. "If I ain't careful I'll find myself banged up for firin' the place myself."

"Right," Sanderson said. "Though I don't think I'm persona grata down there. But Laura, let's get together, can we? I think we need to talk."

"Call me when you're free," Laura said. "You've got my mobile number." She watched the two men pick their way up the street to Sanderson's car and waited until Bob Baker emerged from the ruined building where he had been deep in conversation with Val Ridley.

"OK?" Laura asked.

"Right, I think I've got the gist," Baker said airily. "The usual stuff, Asian and black lads in a skirmish outside the club. The place gets a petrol bomb and most of them turn on the fire engine and police cars when they arrive. Small riot, not many hurt, one Caribbean club down the tubes. No tears in Little Asia."

"Right," Laura said demurely, knowing that Baker had got it wrong in one crucial respect. But she would wait to contradict him, she thought happily, until they were reporting back to Ted Grant in the office. She owed him that.

Michael Thackeray listened to DI Ray Walter silently although his face was grim. He and the drug squad inspector were gathered in Jack Longley's office and the superintendent was watching the two younger men warily as Walter outlined his night's work with evident satisfaction.

"Even though the catch was a bit disappointing, the whole exercise keeps the bastards jumpy. They never know where we're going to hit them next. And that's half the battle," Walter said.

"So how many searches did you make?" Thackeray asked.

"Six altogether. All on information from the lad I've got undercover up there."

"And how much illicit material did you find?"

Walter glanced at Longley as if for assistance but none was forthcoming. Longley appeared to be waiting with as much anticipation as Thackeray for Walter's answer.

"Not a lot," Walter admitted. "We've a couple of lads down Eckersley police station looking at charges of intent to supply. But what I'm hoping is that they can be persuaded to tell me who their supplier is, the next one up the chain. That's what we're really after, and we're not there yet."

"Sounds like a lot of resources for a small result," Longley said. "All that overtime. Uniform won't be happy."

"They can live with it," Walter said. "And from their point of view it keeps the neighbourhood happy if they think we're picking some of the dealers up. But when I've talked to the two we nicked last night, plus the people at the computer project we arrested the other day, I reckon we'll be getting a lot closer to the main man."

"Donna Maitland's dead," Thackeray objected mildly enough, although inwardly he seethed at Walter's casual certainty.

"And what does that tell you?" Walter asked. "Couldn't face the music, could she? Anyway, never mind her. The so-called DJ Sanderson's up to his neck in the supply chain, I reckon."

"But he's only been in the town two minutes," Thackeray objected.

"So he says," Walter shot back. "In any case, London's not so far away these days. This is an international trade we're talking about, not some local scam run from a back room. It's big business. Run by big businessmen. You've got to work your way up the chain to find the top dog. We'll get there. I've got my man well in up there. He's not come up with a lot yet but I'm optimistic."

"I'm glad someone is," Thackeray muttered but said no more as Jack Longley flashed him a warning glance.

"What really bugs me is that your man Mower's been up

there for weeks as well without a word to anyone," Walter said pointedly to Longley. "He must have picked up some intelligence that was worth reporting back with. Didn't you know he was there, for God's sake?"

"Not until you made arrests at the Project," Thackeray cut in. "He's on leave. He's had a rough time."

"He's a bloody loose cannon if you ask me," Walter said to Longley. "Gone native, I shouldn't wonder. Any road, keep him out of my hair from now on, would you, sir?"

"He'll be told," Longley said, glancing at Thackeray.

"Jack here tells me you think I can help you with something?" Walter turned to Thackeray without any sign of eagerness to assist his colleague. "What's all that about?"

"Stanley Wilson," Thackeray said. "Have you any indication that he was involved in the drugs scene? He was seen up on the Heights regularly chatting to some of the lads for no very good reason that I can discover."

"This is the gay bloke found with his knickers in a twist, is it?" Walter said. "I've not heard the name, but I'll have a word with the team. He may have cropped up in some report or other. But surely his boyfriend has to be prime suspect, doesn't he?"

"Well, he's certainly on the list," Thackeray said. "But Wilson seems to have had a finger in more than one bit of unpleasantness so it's not impossible that he was into drugs as well. He worked for Barry Foreman." Thackeray dropped the name into the conversation without meeting Longley's eye, but he got no reaction from the drug squad officer.

"If I hear anything I'll let you know soonest," Walter said. "In the meantime keep me in touch with anything you come across that might be relevant. I'd like to know who torched the Carib Club, for instance. Could well be drug inspired, that. Sanderson was involved down there as well."

"As a DJ," Thackeray said.

"Did you source the Ecstasy the grammar school kids had

taken the night of the accident?" Walter asked. "Are you sure they didn't get it at the Carib?"

"We haven't sourced it anywhere," Thackeray said. "The parents have drafted in some big legal guns and the kids have conveniently forgotten all about where they got their pills."

"Do you want me to have a go at them?" Walter asked. "I know it's your case, but I'd dearly like to pin Sanderson and his mates down, even if they're not part of the main scene."

Thackeray glanced at Longley who shook his head imperceptibly.

"Thanks but no thanks," Thackeray said. "Leave it with me. I'll let you know if anything of interest emerges, but I'm not hopeful. Chasing sources of Ecstasy's a bit like asking five year olds where they got their jelly babies, isn't it? They've had so many they don't remember."

"Don't let the Chief hear you talking like that," Walter said getting to his feet. "According to him the war on drugs is winnable, so don't you go spreading negative messages if you want to make superintendent."

"And is it?" Thackeray asked. Walter shrugged.

"It pays the mortgage," he said.

When he had gone Thackeray flung himself into Jack Longley's most comfortable chair and ran his hands through his unruly dark hair.

"As your crime manager I have to tell you that half the crime in this town would disappear overnight if there was no black market in drugs," he said.

"Noted," Longley said. "Now, let's get back to the real world. Do you have any evidence that the Adams lad got his pills at the Carib?"

"None at all," Thackeray said. "Why do you ask?"

"I had Grantley Adams bending my ear again this morning," Longley said. "Apparently he's persuaded the school to keep the two of them on to take their A Levels so he doesn't want any more repercussions from us. If there's no charges apparently they're prepared to accept that Jeremy and his lass were drunk, not high, and that's acceptable for a sixth-former, apparently."

"This is the man who wanted the dealers locked up and the key thrown away, is it?" Thackeray asked. "And the headmaster who was so worried about his school's reputation that he wouldn't let either of them back in to collect their sports kit? So what happened?"

"Knowing Grantley Adams I expect he's made a hefty donation to the school's building fund," Longley said. "Come on Michael, it's no good looking shocked. You know how these things work."

"That doesn't mean I have to like it," Thackeray said.

"You've nowt to charge them with. You've no evidence they were dealing. And what's the point of a caution for possession? The whole thing's a waste of police time. You've a murder case to deal with."

Thackeray sighed, knowing that it was not the fact that two teenagers who had committed a minor misdemeanour were being let off which riled him, but the fact that Adams would be left believing that throwing his weight about had brought about the desired result. He was surprised that the superintendent did not seem to recognise the implications of that.

"Are you making any progress with Stanley Wilson?" Longley asked, obviously keen to change the subject.

"We found the boyfriend and he gave us a couple of new leads," Thackeray said. "He reckons someone loaned Wilson the money to set up the computer porn business, so I've got Val Ridley going through his bank accounts to see if there were any unexplained payments. And Harman also reckons Stanley had a new attachment, a young black visitor, so we're getting him to look at some mug shots, on the off-chance it's someone known. The house-to-house has turned up a neighbour who's seen a black lad coming and going too, and thinks he saw him around the night Stanley was killed. And fingerprints have found at least half a dozen sets apart from Wilson's and Harman's. They're looking for matches but haven't come up with anything so far. And of course if we can lay hands on a suspect there's the possibility of DNA matching."

"Keep me in touch, Michael," Longley said, turning back to the files on his desk dismissively. Thackeray got up to go, although Longley had not quite finished.

"Keep your eye on the ball, and you might make superintendent yet," he said. Thackeray paused, with his hand on the door-handle.

"I don't think I could stand the politics, sir," he said.

"Then you're a bigger fool than I take you for," Longley snapped.

Kevin Mower's small living room was heavy with cigarette smoke and the smell of lager consumed from the dozen or so empty cans which stood in ranks on the coffee table. Mower himself sat at the dining table in the window tapping impatiently now and again at the computer keyboard in front of him. He had been drinking but was not drunk. In fact his head felt clearer than it had for months. Laura Ackroyd stood at his shoulder watching the flickering monitor and Dizzy B Sanderson lay slumped in an armchair, can in hand, eyes half closed, the tinny rhythm from his Walkman headphones the only other sound in the room.

At length Mower let out a long sigh.

"Why the hell didn't Donna tell me?" he said. Laura put a hand on his shoulder, feeling the tension through the thin cotton of his shirt.

"What should she have told you?"

"She's been browsing round the Internet looking at construction companies, including these City Ventures people who wanted to buy the Carib. No doubt she downloaded whatever she found and that's what was in the file that disappeared. She'd have been much safer storing it in the machine, but maybe she didn't know how to do that. But what the people who trashed the Project didn't realise was that the machine keeps a record of the Internet pages that have been visited anyway. So there we are, look. Let's have a look at it ourselves, shall we?"

Dizzy B got to his feet and came to look over Mower's other shoulder as he found the page he was looking for and a logo and a set of views of new housing and other developments in towns across the North of England spread themselves slowly across the screen.

"Looks like quite a major set-up," Dizzy said.

"And Foreman's involved in that?" Laura asked. "I've never heard anything about him going into construction. I'm sure Michael knows nothing about it."

Mower glanced at her.

"The boss is convinced he's making his money from drugs," he said. "But I don't think he's got much to go on. Perhaps it's a whole lot more innocent than that. Perhaps he's just working for these people, sussing out suitable properties like the Carib. Or maybe he's just diversified quite legitimately into the building trade."

"So why not say so, especially if it's a successful venture? He seems keen enough to impress in other ways," Laura said.

"Maybe he's using the building trade to launder his drug money," Dizzy B, who had taken off his headphones and was listening intently, suggested.

"Possible," Mower said. "But bloody difficult to prove."

"Does this tell us where this company's based?" Laura asked. Mower followed a few more directions on the screen and brought up an address in Leeds, with a photograph of an anonymous office building called Ventures House, and in small print at the bottom of the page a list of the company's directors.

"No one there we know," Dizzy B said dismissively. "Foreman's not a director."

"No, but his girlfriend is," Laura said quietly. "Look, there – Karen Bailey's listed. The only trouble with that is that she's disappeared. Or maybe she hasn't. Maybe she's just keeping a low profile so that no one connects Foreman with this company which Councillor Spencer says has a good chance of getting the contract to regenerate the Heights. I wonder if Spencer knows about the connection? Whichever, it's a bloody good story."

"Or a bloody dangerous story," Mower cut in. "Don't get too carried away, Laura. It's just possible that Donna was killed because she stumbled on this information."

"Killed?" Laura looked at Mower in stunned surprise. "I thought…"

"What you were supposed to think, maybe?" Mower said.

"You've got no evidence, Kevin," Dizzy B said. "Come on, man, she had her problems…"

"Yeah, yeah," Mower said. "She had her problems, but were they so bad she had to slit her wrists? I don't think so. In any case Amos Atherton is sure that the cuts on her wrist were made by a knife, not a razor blade. There was no knife in the bathroom when I found her. It can't have been suicide. I never really believed it was."

Laura felt her stomach tighten as she realised that perhaps Thackeray's concern for her safety was more justified than either of them could have realised.

"She always struck me as a fighter," Laura said quietly, her grip on Mower's shoulder tightening slightly. "Joyce thought so too."

"I need to have another look round her flat," Mower said, his voice urgent. "Perhaps she's got stuff hidden away there that I missed."

"Tell Michael what you've found," Laura said. "He'll have seen Atherton's report as well by now, won't he? And you know how much he distrusts Foreman. This is just the lead he needs."

"Yes, I'll talk to him later," Mower said, although Laura thought she caught a note of reluctance in his voice. "Come up to the Heights with me, Dizzy, will you. I may need back-up."

Laura glanced at her watch and pulled on her jacket.

"I need to get back to work. But I'll tackle Councillor Dave Spencer about this redevelopment company. Even Ted Grant won't be able to rubbish this story. It's all getting very smelly indeed."

Chapter Seventeen

Mower drove back to the Heights in silence with Dizzy B slumped in the passenger seat beside him, headphones turned up high. Neither man seemed willing to talk and Dizzy Sanderson glanced out of the car window with increasing anxiety as they approached the tall blocks of flats which were almost obscured by the driving rain. He put his Walkman away as Mower parked in the lee of Priestley House.

"This place is beginning to give me the creeps," he said. "I reckon you have to assume you're being watched up here – by both sides."

"Probably," Mower said. He glanced towards Joyce Ackroyd's bungalow where the glass in her windows had still not been replaced, boards facing the street blindly. "If I were the drug squad I'd have video cameras up here full time. But we're on the side of the angels, remember?"

"They might still believe you are, man, " Sanderson said. "But I reckon my credibility's all blown away."

Up on the walkway as they made their way towards Donna Maitland's flat, Mower glanced down. The whole estate seemed deserted, as the rain gusted in bitter squalls across the muddy grass and the puddled car parks while the concrete of the blocks above and below them turned dark and streaky with damp. But even a casual glance convinced Mower that Sanderson was right. There were eyes which watched: here and there a curtain twitched and behind some massive dustbins he caught a flicker of movement which could have been a hooded head. But before he could focus he was distracted by Sanderson who had reached Donna's doorway first, to find the lock broken open and the door hanging drunkenly on its hinges.

"Shit," Mower said angrily, shouldering his way past his

friend and into the living room, where a scene of devastation faced them. The television and video and anything else of value had gone, and the rest of the flat, from the bedrooms to the kitchen and bathroom, seemed have been systematically wrecked. Mower stood in the door to Emma Maitland's room, where soft toys had been ripped up and the pretty bed-cover torn and tossed on the floor, and felt tears prickle at his eyes.

"Bastards," he muttered as Sanderson came up behind him and put a hand on his shoulder as he peered at the wreckage of the child's room.

"Her friends or ours?" Dizzy asked quietly.

"I wouldn't be surprised if it wasn't both," Mower said, swallowing hard. "If the drug squad bust in here the neigh-bourhood toe-rags would be close behind to see what pick-ings they could find."

"Let's look for what we came for and then get out of here," Sanderson said. "Though if your colleagues have been through the place the chances are they'll have taken anything of interest." And as they picked through the remains of Donna's home Mower soon became convinced that Sanderson was right. No files, no computer discs, no paper-work of any kind, not so much as an electricity bill, did they find amongst Donna's scattered belongings.

"Zilch," Mower said at last. "It's all been cleaned out and I don't believe the toe-rags took her phone bills and address book any more than the drug squad took the TV and video."

"Let's go," Sanderson said, his anxiety showing. "You may be able to get away with this, but I'm out on a limb here."

"Right," Mower said, following the DJ to the door, but before they reached it they heard a tap on the cracked glass panel and a postman, water streaming off his red and blue jacket, put his head round the drunken door, raised an eye-brow at the chaos and held out a single letter.

"Mrs. Maitland live here?" he asked.

"I'll take it," Mower said. The postman shrugged and

moved on, leaving Mower in possession of an envelope which he ripped open without ceremony. Inside he was surprised to find a copy of a certificate from the Public Records Office in Southport. Why, he wondered, could Donna have possibly applied for a copy of Grantley Adams's marriage lines. With Sanderson displaying signs of increasing impatience he tucked the letter away in his jacket pocket and followed him out of Donna's wrecked home.

The two men made their way down the concrete staircase, which had been converted into a waterfall by leaks in the roof above. On the ground floor a woman stood by the glass doors, huddled into a thin mac and with a sodden scarf over her head, her face haggard and her eyes reddened with crying.

"I thought it were you," she said to Dizzy Sanderson. "I were looking out o't'window and saw you come over here." That was one set of watching eyes accounted for at least, Dizzy thought, not quite recognising the mother of Stevie, the young junkie he had only seen in semi-darkness a few days before.

"Mrs Maddison? Lorraine?" Sanderson asked. "How's Stevie?"

"That's it," the woman said, clutching his arm in a frantic grip. "I don't know. I don't know where he is. He's run off, hasn't he? When he heard that Donna Maitland were dead he got into a terrible state, crying, he were. I've not seen him cry since he were a little lad."

"He was fond of Donna," Sanderson said by way of explanation to Mower who was listening with some bemusement.

"She got him sorted, did Donna. He'd never have done it without her," Lorraine said. "But he were right scared when he heard the news. Said that if they could get Donna they could get him too."

"He thought she'd been killed?" Mower asked. "Why should he think that?"

"Don't you?" Lorraine Maddison snapped back, verging on hysteria now. "Stevie thought they'd be coming for him next because he saw too much that night Derek died. I reckon he saw someone he knew, though he'd never tell me who. So he's run and I reckon he'll be the next body they find. Can you help me find him? He trusted you, Mr. Sanderson. You're the first person he's talked to about that night. I could never get owt out of him, not a bloody word. I need someone to help me look."

"This is DS Kevin Mower from Bradfield police..." Sanderson began but the woman grabbed his arm and pulled him away from Mower.

"I want nowt to do wi't'police," she said. "I don't trust bloody police. Look what they did to Donna. They're either bloody fools or in wi't'dealers themselves. Donna Maitland were t'best thing that's happened for the kids on this estate for years, and now look where we are. I just want you to help me find Stevie, that's all. I don't want any trouble, just to know he's safe. I've not got him off junk to see him killed now."

Sanderson glanced at Mower, who shrugged.

"I'll wait outside," he said, and went out into the downpour without looking back.

Michael Thackeray lay back in his armchair with a sigh and closed his eyes as he listened to Laura clattering around the kitchen next door as she made coffee. There were times when he thought that the wall he had carefully constructed around himself over the years would prove impregnable against even Laura's best efforts to undermine it. And there were evenings when he slid imperceptibly into a contentment he had seldom known when he got home to find Laura watching the TV news or beginning to cook a meal. He had promised half-heartedly to hone his own rudimentary domestic skills and take a share of the cooking and chores when they had moved into the new flat, but deep down lurked an unreconstructed Yorkshireman who secretly believed that everything beyond the kitchen door was a woman's domain. Even watching his father struggle with domesticity as his mother became increasingly disabled had not convinced him that there was an obvious solution to the boredom engendered by endless meals out of cans or a frying pan slammed straight from the stove onto the table.

Tonight his appreciation of Laura's cooking skills had been muted by the anxiety he read in her expression as soon as he came through the door. He watched her with a finger of ice touching his stomach as she brought a steaming dish of pasta to the table and served in silence.

"Did Kevin Mower call you?" she asked eventually, carefully avoiding his eyes as she twirled spaghetti round her fork.

"Should he have done?" he countered.

"He said he would."

"You've seen him again, then? Any particular reason?"

"He asked me to look at Donna Maitland's computer files with him – and I've got a cracking story out of it, as it goes." For a moment their eyes locked across the table, challenge in hers, fear in his, before he nodded slightly.

"I should have called him. We need to talk," he said quietly. "Not for publication, but he turned out to be right about Donna's death. Amos Atherton doesn't think it was suicide."

Laura hoped that her surprise did not look as feigned as it felt.

"You think she was killed?"

"It looks likely," Thackeray said. "I've got a meeting with Jack Longley first thing to decide whether we launch a murder inquiry. If Kevin's up to his neck in her affairs I'll need to interview him as a witness. I can't get through to him on his mobile, I don't know why, I've left messages on his voice-mail, but this he'll have to co-operate with."

"You should know why Kevin's so distant," Laura said. "It's obvious, isn't it? When he lost Rita, I was at risk too, don't you remember? But you found me. You got me back. He'd never admit it, but that must crease him up."

"Laura, that's psychobabble," Thackeray protested, remembering the day when he had thought Laura might be dead. It obsessed him like a wound he dared not probe.

"Is it?" she asked. "Is it really? I've seen you watching Vicky Mendelson's kids. Don't tell me you don't resent the fact that you lost your son and she's got hers safe and well and growing into smashing boys. I can see it in your eyes. And I can see it in Kevin's too, when he sees us together and he doesn't think I'm looking."

Thackeray glanced away, unwilling to go any further down that road.

"I'll need to talk to Joyce too, as she worked with Donna," he said.

Laura glanced at her watch.

"I said I'd pick her up at nine," she said. "She couldn't bear to miss her governors' meeting, even though it is a hassle for her to get to the school from here. She persuaded someone to collect her by car and I said I'd fetch her."

"And is this cracking story anything to do with Donna Maitland?" Thackeray asked, hoping fervently for a negative response. Laura shook her head.

"No, except in the sense that she seems to have stumbled on it first. But it is about someone else you're interested in. Barry Foreman. It turns out his girlfriend is a director of one of the construction companies bidding to redevelop the Heights. And if that isn't fishy, I don't know what is."

"His girlfriend? You mean Karen Bailey, the one who's gone missing?"

"Unless it's someone else of the same name, which seems unlikely," Laura said smugly. It was not often that she reduced Thackeray to the state of astonishment which seemed to have overwhelmed him and she could not restrain a small smile of triumph.

"The firm's called City Ventures and they've got offices in Leeds. It all seems perfectly open and above board, pages on the web, lists of directors. I'm going to call them in the morning and get an address for Ms Bailey. If it is the same person, then I think your Mr Foreman has some explaining to do. And possibly Dave Spencer as well. Ted wasn't in the office this afternoon but I don't think he can turn me down on this one. It could turn into a major corruption story. I think he can spare me off flood watch for that."

"You're not thinking of interviewing Foreman are you?" Thackeray asked, trying to conceal his horror at the idea.

"Don't you think he does press interviews," Laura said, her eyes full of mischief.

"With his innocent businessman's hat on I'm sure he does," Thackeray said. "But if you start trying to trace his girlfriend then I think you would be taking a hell of a risk. You've already had Joyce threatened in her own home. You don't want the same thing to happen here, surely? The man is dangerous, I'm one hundred per cent certain of that. Don't go near him, Laura. Please."

"I must," she said. "If he and Spencer really are in cahoots over the redevelopment that's a major story. The Gazette can't ignore it. Do you really think Foreman's behind all the intimidation on the Heights? Is he under investigation for that?"

"Not directly," Thackeray said.

"He's not your prime suspect?"

"He was a prime suspect long before the business with the gunman who left his employment so conveniently before he began taking pot-shots at hospital patients. Foreman got away with that and I've still got nothing I can pin him down with, if that's what you mean. That doesn't mean my instincts are wrong, Laura, or that he's not dangerous. Simply that I can't prove anything. I'll have to talk to Jack Longley in the morning and see what he thinks about the Gazette butting into an on-going investigation. I think it's a complication we could do without and you certainly could."

"What the Gazette investigates is up to Ted," Laura said, polishing around her spaghetti dish with a piece of ciabatta carefully and avoiding Thackeray's anxious eyes. "But one thing's for sure. If he thinks you or Jack Longley are trying to cover something up, it'll make my job of convincing him to let me go ahead very much easier."

Thackeray finished his meal in silence. He knew that there was very little chance of persuading Laura to change her mind in her present mood. One day, he thought, their jobs would bring them into such a violent collision that their relationship might be terminally damaged. But he had not yet found any way of deflecting her from a course she considered to be right and doubted that he ever would. He watched her as she cleared away the dirty dishes and put her coat on. There would be no way they could continue the argument once Joyce returned to the flat.

"Do one thing for me at least," he said, catching her hand as she went to open the front door. She put her head on one side, a half-smile on her lips.

"I'd do anything for you," she said. "Almost."

"I'm serious, Laura. Keep me in touch with what you're doing."

"I know," she said, kissing him lightly on the cheek. "I'll tell you what Ted says about Foreman tomorrow, and what I'm going to do next. Will that do?"

"I suppose it will have to," Thackeray said. But when she had gone, and he had heard her start her car and drive away down the hill towards the special school where Joyce was a governor, he flung himself back into his armchair and closed his eyes with a sigh. Laura was like a brightly coloured bird, he thought, and he loved her for her energy and grace and fierce independence. But after losing so much in a previous life he desperately wanted to keep her safe. Yet caged birds, he knew, would only too often languish and die. He hoped that he was strong enough to resist the temptation to trap her and, perversely, that she was strong enough to remain free, even if it did mean that they were destined to live in this perpetual state of tension.

He switched the television on to catch the local news which

was dominated by the efforts of the water authority to keep the Beck within its bounds. A glum looking official, filmed standing at the point where the swollen waterway plunged underground on the edge of the town centre was complaining that the channel appeared to be accommodating less of the threatened flood waters that it had been designed to take, and that they would be starting a hunt tomorrow for an obstruction concealed under the buildings of the town's commercial heart. That, Thackeray thought with some satisfaction, might keep Ted Grant's troops far too occupied for them to find time to follow up hints of council corruption. He had no doubt that Laura had probably stumbled on something serious, but he fervently hoped that he would be able to forestall her inquiries with some of his own.

Chapter Eighteen

"What the hell is going on, Laura?" Ted Grant tipped back in his leather chair, paunch straining against his shirt and the top button of his trousers, eyes popping like blue marbles, as he scowled massively at Laura Ackroyd. Laura shrugged.

"What do you mean?" she asked. Behind them the newsroom was almost deserted, most of the Gazette's staff already rushing out and about in the town which was sandbagging itself against a now almost certain flood unless the rain, which had not eased now for seven days, suddenly ceased. The lowering grey clouds, which meant that the newspaper offices were fully lit in the middle of the morning, gave no indication that any such salvation was likely. And in any case the forecasters were sure that the water now pouring down every deep gorge and shallow depression between the town and the waterlogged moorland above would overwhelm the flood defences regardless. Houses on the west side of the town were already being evacuated and the water board had begun its investigation of the Beck's concrete culvert, into which several cellars in the business district gave access. Earlier that morning, in the controlled chaos which the newsroom had quickly become, Laura had been allotted the task of coordinating the "human interest" stories which would shortly start pouring in as schools were closed and householders moved out of their homes and into emergency rest centres with whatever belongings they could carry. She had not had the chance to raise her suspicions about Councillor Spencer and his regeneration committee colleagues with Ted Grant, who was in Montgomery of El Alamein mode. Now she thought, it looked as if that particular can of worms had been opened some other way.

"What do you mean?" she asked, at her most disingenuous.

"Why have I had Jack Longley bending my ear this morning about the risk of reporters interfering with ongoing police investigations?" Thank you, Michael, Laura thought to herself ruefully, although she should know by now that if Thackeray set himself on a course of action he was as difficult to divert as she was herself.

"What have you got on Barry Foreman?" Grant asked.

"He seems to have gone into the building trade, in a secretive sort of way," Laura said sweetly. "And as he's a member of your committee that's going to be involved in handing out hefty contracts for rebuilding The Heights, I thought we should be asking a few questions. Don't you?"

Grant sighed melodramatically.

"But not today, Laura, for God's sake. Not now. For one thing these floods are going to take up every inch of news space we can prise out of the management's sticky fingers. Nothing like this has ever happened in Bradfield since the 1940s. I can't give you the time to go chasing wild geese this week. And if what Jack Longley says is true, the police are onto Foreman anyway, so the whole thing may be put on ice if they charge him with anything. It'd be all so much wasted effort. Can't that boyfriend of yours give you a steer on this. He must know what's going on. In the meantime concentrate on putting the flood pages together. I'm hoping to run eight extra pages on this and so far I've got bugger all to put on them."

"Right," Laura said more sweetly than she imagined Grant had anticipated. She went back to her desk and used her mobile phone to call Kevin Mower.

"Remind me of the names of the directors of City Ventures," she said. Mower read out the list of names.

"I've discovered another connection," he said then. "Althea Simpson is Grantley Adams' wife. It's her maiden name and Donna had sussed that out by getting their marriage certificate."

"And I know for a fact that she used to be an accountant,"

Laura said. "Well, well, what are the ever-so-respectable Adamses doing in the company of Barry Foreman's girlfriend who, as I recall, was a lass from Benwell Lane, born and bred and effin' proud of it, as she might say."

"I'm going in to see the boss at two," Mower said. "He invited me in – no excuses accepted."

"Good," Laura said. "It's time you two got your act together."

"Fat chance," Mower said gloomily.

"Well, in the meantime I might call on Mrs. Adams in my lunch hour – to ask her about young Jeremy's progress, you understand? And if the subject of City Ventures just happens to come up I'll try to find out exactly who those other directors are, and when she last saw Karen Bailey."

"Be careful," Mower said.

"You sound like Michael," Laura said softly. "But Donna deserves someone to follow this up."

"Donna deserved a hell of a lot more than she got," Mower said, his voice tight. "But take care, Laura. There's some very nasty people out there."

Laura spent the rest of the morning conscientiously sifting through the incoming tales of teachers arriving at school that morning to find water running through their classrooms; householders rescued by boat as streams broke their banks, inundating everything in their path; and the distraught farmer who had been innocently over-wintering his ewes, which had miraculously escaped the foot and mouth epidemic, in a normally dry fold in the hills only to find them trapped and drowning in a quagmire created overnight by the relentless rain.

"If this is global warming I think I'll pass on the Pennine olive groves," Laura muttered to herself as she fitted together grim tales and grimmer pictures of an uniquely sodden winter into a kaleidoscope of local catastrophe.

By lunchtime the job was done and the Gazette building began to shudder slightly as the presses began to roll. Laura switched off her computer terminal, buttoned up her waterproof jacket and made the dash across the puddled car park to her Golf. The low-lying part of the town centre was now cordoned off by police and fire brigade and she had to make a lengthy detour to reach the Adams house in one of the leafy suburbs in the surrounding hills. Mrs. Adams push-buttoned her through the gate and the front door as easily as she had done the first time and waved her into the sitting room overlooking the dripping, dark mid-winter garden.

"You look as though you were expecting me," Laura said as her hostess brought in a tray with coffee cups and a percolator.

"I've been expecting someone," Althea Adams said. "I wasn't sure whether it would be the Press or the police."

"Because of Jeremy? How is he?" Mrs. Adams nodded with a wry smile as if she knew that the question was mere prevarication on Laura's part.

"He's going to be fine. And the school is taking him and Louise back."

"So what's the problem?" Laura asked.

"I suppose it's just that the Jeremy business meant that Grantley has been throwing his weight about even more than usual. I began to think it would only be a matter of time before someone took serious exception to Grantley. I thought it would be that policeman, what's his name? He seemed unlikely to be either conned or intimidated."

"DCI Thackeray?" Laura smiled faintly to herself.

"Him. I knew he'd be furious about what went on. I heard my husband on the phone to Superintendent Longley, to the Deputy Chief Constable, to anyone he thought had some influence. I knew he'd get up someone's nose and that might expose him in ways he really doesn't need."

"But I turned up instead," Laura said.

"I didn't really rate you, any more than Grantley did. You were young and a woman. Just shows how sexist you get when you live with someone like Grantley for all these years.

He'd not have seen you as any sort of a threat, any more than he would me. We're just women, after all, here to do as we're told and keep quiet about it."

"Do I take it that you're not so keen to do as you're told any more?" Laura asked, taken by surprise by the vehemence of Mrs. Adams's complaints. "Or to keep quiet?"

"I'm fed up to the back teeth with all the lies and deceit," Althea Adams said. "At first it was just cutting corners. I knew all about that even before I married him. I did work for him, after all."

"As an accountant? I remember you saying…?"

"I did his books when the firm was still quite small," she said. "He never missed the main chance, even then. But now…"

"You're a director of City Ventures, aren't you? Using your maiden name? Althea Simpson?"

"You worked that out, did you? Yes, it's all a cover of course, women standing in for their men. We don't actually do anything, you understand. Just meet now and again as a board to rubber stamp whatever the blokes have decided."

"Like Karen Bailey stands in for Barry Foreman?"

"And Jane Peace, Jim Baistow's married daughter. The men on the board are the apparatchiks – company secretary, finance director and so on, but we four women are there representing other people, though Karen wasn't at the last meeting we had. Nominees, I suppose you could call us. Grantley persuaded me it's not illegal – just a convenience, he said, so that things didn't get muddled."

"Muddled" was one way of putting it, Laura thought, as she looked at the list of City Ventures' directors that she and Kevin Mower had downloaded from the Internet. Muddled, she thought, was not the word she would have chosen to describe the links between the committee members planning the redevelopment of the Heights and the building company which looked likely to be selected to do the work.

"So who's Annie Costello?"

"Oh, she's Dave Spencer's girlfriend."

"Councillor Spencer?"

"The same," Althea Adams said. "Which is when I decided that I wanted out. You could end up in prison for less."

"I expect you could," Laura said.

"And it'd be no good pleading ignorance because we all knew bloody well what was going on. And who was going to get the contract to regenerate the Heights. That was it as far as I'm concerned. I'm not going to jail for that gang of crooks."

"So what will you do now?"

"I've had it up to here with Grantley and his schemes. I've had my bags packed for weeks just waiting for the moment to leave. Jeremy can stay here but I'll take the girls with me. I think the moment's come, don't you? What will the Gazette pay me for my story do you think? Or do I have to go to the Globe in London?"

"I'd make it DCI Thackeray first, if I were you," Laura said. "When you've given me chapter and verse for the Gazette, of course."

Michael Thackeray gazed at Kevin Mower, slumped in his office looking just as unkempt as the last time he had seen him, and wondered whether Superintendent Longley might not have been right to turn down flat his request for Mower to rejoin CID immediately. The sergeant inspired no confidence in his boss although Thackeray had tried to persuade Jack Longley that it would be preferable, now that it had been decided to treat Donna Maitland's death as suspicious, to have him back on board rather than careering around the Heights like a white knight looking for a dragon to slay.

"You know someone's trashed Donna's flat, don't you?" Mower asked angrily. "Looks like the drug squad went in there with an enforcer and the locals finished the place off. Your crime scene's as good as wrecked. We'll never get a result there now."

"I'll talk to Ray Walter about what they found," Thackeray said. "Amos is not one hundred per cent certain we're dealing with murder here. She could have cut her own wrist with a knife."

"A knife that dematerialised? There was no knife in that bathroom, guv," Mower said flatly. "No trail of blood from anywhere else. And the light was out. You don't slash your own wrists in the bath in the pitch dark. That's what bugged me at first – I switched the light on when I went in and didn't realise till later what I'd done. What about the toxicology? How many sleeping pills had she taken?"

"Amos says she must have been pretty heavily sedated," Thackeray said.

"So what more do you want? She didn't kill herself. I knew that from the very beginning."

"Kevin, you're too involved in this to make any sort of judgement…"

"Yeah, yeah," Mower said wearily. "I know you don't think I'm off the booze but I am, you know. That's all history."

"You'll be OK when you have your medical, then, won't you? But that isn't what's worrying Jack Longley anyway. You were emotionally involved with Donna Maitland. That's a good enough reason for keeping you off the case. We want you as a witness on this one, Kevin, not an investigating officer. So my advice to you is to use the couple of weeks you've got left on leave to get yourself fit so you sail through the medical…" Thackeray hesitated, aware of the anger in Mower's dark eyes. He did not want to provoke him into doing or saying anything terminally stupid.

"So no one can come up with any excuse not to take me back, you mean?"

"I don't think anyone's looking for excuses," he said. "But you need to show you can cope."

"And in the meantime, I sit on my backside while you decide how much energy to put into finding the toe-rag who killed Donna? Whatever the drug squad thinks, she was a good woman. She didn't deserve what was happening to her. Ask anyone on the Heights."

Thackeray suppressed the sudden spurt of anger which threatened to overwhelm him too.

"You know we'll put in exactly the same amount of effort into clearing up Donna's death as anyone else's." His voice crackled like ice and Mower knew he had overstepped the mark.

"I didn't mean..." He shrugged. "Sorry."

"In the meantime, there is some good news," Thackeray said, changing the subject abruptly. "It looks as if we may be able to pin something on that bastard Barry Foreman at last, with what you and Laura unearthed about his business dealings with the council, and some unexplained payments Val Ridley turned up on Stanley Wilson's bank records. Bonuses, in theory, but I reckon it's much more likely that Foreman's been bankrolling Wilson's porno empire. I think Foreman has access to far more cash than his legitimate activities could possibly support and he's been syphoning it off into other activities, legal and illegal. It may take months to track his dealings down, but at least we've got a lead now."

"Still no sign of our unexpected company director Karen Bailey, though?"

"No sign of Karen, no sign of her twins."

"It might be an idea to keep an eye on Foreman," Mower said carefully. "In my spare time, guv."

"What you do in your spare time, Kevin, is entirely up to you," Thackeray said, equally non-committal. "You're on leave, after all."

It was not until the sergeant had closed the door behind him that Thackeray relaxed and smiled quietly to himself, a small satisfied smile which broadened when he answered his phone a few seconds later to be told that Mrs. Althea Adams was in reception, anxious to make a statement about her husband's business affairs. But foremost in his mind was another question he wanted to ask her: just how long was it since

Mrs. Adams and her fellow directors of City Ventures had seen Karen Bailey. In spite of his gnawing anxieties about Laura, this was turning out to be a good day after all, he decided. And not before time.

The hair on the back of Dizzy B's neck prickled and his throat tightened. He was sitting in his car, parked on the main approach to the Heights, watching through a rainstreaked windscreen as a group of hooded boys and young men congregated under the shelter of the walkways close to the entrance to Priestley house. It was only seven-thirty in the evening but pitch dark as squalls of wind threw icy rain against the doors and the whole vehicle shuddered under the impact. The few streetlights which still worked lit the roadway and the grassy approach to the flats, but dimly. The car's lights were off and he was pretty sure that the gang would not see him. But only pretty sure. As they milled around and some appeared to look in his direction he slid down in his seat, making himself as invisible as possible. It would be ironic, he thought, if one of the sudden surges of destructive energy such groups were prone to fixed on an unwisely parked car and he found himself the focus of a random attack on his wheels. Unwary drivers on Wuthering regularly found their tyres slashed, windows shattered or their vehicles reduced to a heap of twisted and burnt metal if the mood took some of the local kids. But he suspected that the group he was watching had other things on their mind. They looked as if they were waiting for something or someone. He fingered his mobile phone, knowing he might need back-up and very aware that the little he could call on might not save him if things turned ugly.

Sanderson had driven up to the Heights in response to Lorraine Maddison's frantic appeal to him to help her find Stevie. He guessed that if anyone knew where the boy was hiding it had to be one or other of his friends in the neighbourhood. But he knew from bitter experience that tackling large groups of youths on an out-of-control estate was a risky enterprise even with a warrant card to back you up. Out of the Force, out on a limb, far from his own turf, it was not a risk he was prepared to take. Only if a single youth passed by would he take a chance and ask a few questions. In the meantime he was content to watch what was going on at Priestley House, just so long as he did not attract any attention.

He did not see the unlit car which passed him until it swooped into the pool of light from the single lamp outside the doors of Priestley. Slightly unnerved, he slid even further down in his seat and watched obliquely out of the side window as the youths outside the flats approached the new arrival with a caution that surprised him. A single figure got out of the parked vehicle and the youths gathered round at what appeared to be a respectful distance, providing a bizarre guard of honour for a tall slim figure who made his way quickly towards the entrance and went inside. After a few cautious glances around the now deserted and rainswept estate, the rest of the group followed him and the doors swung shut behind them.

Sanderson remained where he was for a moment and then started his own engine, letting the car roll quietly down the hill and slowing almost to a stop opposite the doors. With some difficulty, he deciphered the registration number of the dark-coloured BMW which had been left unattended outside the flats and wrote it in ball-point on his hand. Either the owner was very confident that no one would touch his wheels, or did not care whether they did or not – which seemed less likely. Respect, Sanderson muttered to himself as he let in the clutch and moved off down the hill. And there was generally only one way of gaining that on an estate like Wuthering.

He pulled up again outside the old people's bungalows which gave him an unrestricted view of the parked car and the entrance to Priestley House through his rear view mirror and called Kevin Mower on his mobile.

"I think I've got one of the main men up here as we speak," he said softly. "D'you want to come up and take a look?"

"Give me ten minutes," Mower said. "Where are you exactly?" Sanderson told him where he had parked, but before he could slide down in his seat again he noticed that the nearest bungalow, the one which he guessed from its boarded up windows belonged to Laura Ackroyd's grandmother, was showing just the faintest sliver of light beneath its door. Cautiously he slid across to the passenger door and out of the car, ducking low so that he could not be seen from the flats and dodging quickly into the deep shadow at the side of the small house. Further down the row he could hear the sound of television sets turned up high by residents too hard of hearing to be able to pick up any sound other than *Coronation Street*. Cautiously he worked his way round to the back of Joyce Ackroyd's house, narrowly missing the dustbin, which was lying on its side, its contents scattered and sodden across the paving. He pushed gently at the kitchen door and to his surprise it swung open at his touch. He hesitated for a moment but the decision whether to step inside or not was taken for him when a hard object was thrust into his back and a hefty shove propelled him over the threshold onto his knees in the dimly lit kitchen.

"Jesus," Dizzy B gasped, knowing his luck had run out and expecting with heart-stopping certainly that he was about to die. But instead of the shot or crushing blow he anticipated, there came only a whistling expulsion of breath and a surprisingly breathless shrill voice.

"Dizzy B, man. What you doing here? I fuckin' nearly shot you."

Dizzy turned slowly towards his attacker and sat back against the cool metal of Joyce's fridge and expelled a long breath himself. He could feel his heart fluttering like a bird against his ribs as he struggled to control his breathing enough to speak.

"Stevie, man," he said at last, his voice thick. "What the

fuck are you doing with a gun?" The boy was still pointing the weapon in Sanderson's general direction and Sanderson worried about the steadiness of his trigger finger.

"Put it down, man," Sanderson said quietly. "I'm not going to hurt you. Your mother's worried sick about you and asked me to come looking."

"I'm OK," Stevie said, letting the weapon fall slowly to his side.

"You don't look OK," Dizzy said, getting slowly to his feet so as not to startle the boy. "You'd better give me that or you'll be in a whole lot of trouble."

"No way," Stevie said, holding the gun behind his back. "It's insurance, isn't it? I'm looking for the bastard that killed Donna. I reckon it was Ounce. An' if it wasn't Ounce then he'll know who did it."

"Who's Ounce, for God's sake?"

"The main man, is Ounce. No one does owt up here without Ounce says so. I saw Ounce t'night Derek fell, an'all. He were one on'em on t'roof. He'll know about Donna, and if I've got the gun, he'll tell me, won't he?"

"That makes no sense. You'll be the one who ends up banged up. Or dead."

"It don't matter," the boy said. "I've been jabbing needles in misen so long I've probably got Aids any road."

Dizzy opened his mouth to offer comfort but the look in the boy's eyes was so bleak that he knew he would be wasting his time. He guessed that Stevie knew more about his own condition than he had admitted to his mother. Just as he seemed to know far more about the violence and death which had overwhelmed the estate. He let his breath out in a long sigh.

"Where did you get the gun, Stevie?" he asked.

"They're not hard to get," the boy said.

"Tell me about it," Dizzy said. "But who did you get this one from?"

"No one you know." Even as Sanderson saw Stevie's grip tighten again on the weapon which he had been holding loosely at his side, they both heard the sound of a car approaching outside, and then an engine cut out.

"Did you call t'fuckin' pigs?" Stevie asked, his voice becoming hysterical as he raised the gun and pointing it directly at Dizzy B again. "You're a shite, Dizzy, man." But as Dizzy tried to speak, his mouth as dry as ashes, Stevie turned and dodged out of the back door into the darkness of the night.

"Damnation," Dizzy muttered to himself knowing that he had no chance of catching the boy across the back gardens and alleyways of his home territory. Wearily he turned towards the front door where someone was tapping urgently on the single pane of unbroken glass.

"Yeah, yeah," Sanderson said. He peered out into the darkness. "Kevin, is that you?"

He opened the door to let a soaking wet Mower into the bungalow and made them both instant black coffee in what was left of Joyce's kitchen with hands which were still shaking slightly.

"Jesus wept," Mower said when Sanderson had filled him in on Stevie Maddison's near murderous arrival and equally precipitate departure. "We can't mess about with this one, mate. We need the cavalry if the kid's running around with a loaded weapon. I need to get my guv'nor out of bed at the very least. We can't handle this on our own."

"I don't think he'll use the gun," Sanderson said. "I don't even know if it was loaded. He's looking for someone called Ounce. That mean anything to you?"

"Yes," Mower said. "We need backup."

Sanderson groaned.

"I thought you didn't care about the job any more," he said. "You know what those trigger happy bastards from firearms are like. It's the kid who'll end up blown away."

"And it's me who'll end up out of a job if I cover for him," Mower said. "We can't take the risk, Dizzy. You know that, for God's sake."

"OK. Call your boss and summon up the armed response vehicles," Dizzy said wearily, rolling a spliff as he watched Mower pull out his mobile phone. "What's another dead kid on the Heights?"

"Let's get out of here," Mower said when he had finished his call. "You don't want to be around when they start searching for Stevie, and I don't think I do either."

As they walked back to their cars Sanderson glanced back up the hill towards the entrance to Priestley House, which now lay silent and deserted.

"Did you see the BMW?"

"I saw the driver too," Mower said. "He was just leaving as I came past. He's one of ours, Dizzy. I recognised him. He's the drug squad undercover man, best left strictly alone."

"Tall black dude, driving a Beamer? Very nice."

"If he's got himself in with the suppliers he could be driving a Roller."

"Check it out, Kevin," Dizzy said. "You know it stinks." Mower shrugged and made another call on his mobile, dictating the registration number Sanderson had written on his hand to someone at the other end.

"Right, thanks," he said eventually when he had evidently acquired the information he wanted. He glanced at his friend who was leaning against his own car still smoking.

"It's registered to Barry Foreman," Mower said. "And if I don't tell my guv'nor that, I'm as good as dead."

Chapter Nineteen

"I don't think my business affairs are anything to do with you or the Bradfield Gazette, Ms Ackroyd." Annie Costello, general manager of the Three Ridings Housing Association tapped an immaculately manicured scarlet fingernail insistently on her crescent shaped desk and glanced slightly impatiently at the screen saver on her computer which was twirling languidly in front of her. "But I can assure you that if I were to be appointed as a director of a company it would be on my own merits, not as the nominee of anybody else. I'm not married, not even divorced, and I can assure you that any career decisions I make are entirely my own. I should imagine you'd say the same."

Annie Costello raised a faintly amused eyebrow, disturbing for a moment the perfect symmetry of her near professionally made-up ivory and gold features. She was, Laura thought, a unnervingly attractive woman, dark-haired and blue eyed and with an elegance, impeccably set off by black suit, cream shirt and heels, which made Laura, in cords, boots and a heavy waterproof jacket suitable for flood watch, her damp hair clinging in copper strands to her forehead, feel terminally scruffy.

"So the fact that you're a director of a firm bidding for a contract which your partner is involved in awarding is entirely coincidental?" Laura said, rather more truculently than she intended.

"If you know that City Ventures has a bid in you know more than I do," Annie Costello said, her voice frigid with dislike. "As far as I am aware tenders haven't even been asked for yet. There's a long way to go."

"Councillor Spencer would keep you up to date on that, would he?"

"Dave Spencer and I are busy people pursuing careers that

are parallel but not linked. We don't waste the little time we spend together discussing the day's work, I can assure you. We've better things to do." Annie Costello's expression implied that she doubted very much whether Laura could be so blessed.

"Even when it might be to your financial advantage?" Laura pressed sweetly though she recognised a blank wall when she hit one, especially as it was not the first she had crashed her head against today. In the very short time she had persuaded Ted Grant to give her to investigate what she was convinced was a major case of corruption, Annie Costello had turned out to be her only hope of adding anything to what Althea Adams had told her the previous day. When she had called Barry Foreman inquiring after the whereabouts of Karen Bailey, she had been met with a spitting, obscene fury, all urbanity thrown aside, which frightened her. She would not, she had decided, tell Michael Thackeray just how offensive the security boss had been about her personally and her partner indirectly. The fact that he seemed to know far more than he should about their relationship terrified her and she knew it would infuriate Thackeray.

And to add to her woes, she had discovered quite easily that Jane Peace, the fourth member of the quartet of women directors at City Ventures and daughter of another of Bradfield's major wheelers and dealers, now lived in Southport and was in any case on holiday in the Bahamas. Annie Costello, cool, high-powered and contemptuously dismissive, remained her only hope.

"Isn't there a conflict of interest anyway, if you run a major housing association and play a major role in running a local construction company as well?" Laura asked. "Do City Ventures build houses for this company too?"

Just for a second Annie Costello's response was not immediate and she glanced away. Laura knew she had scored a hit, but the respite was brief and Costello came back, all guns blazing.

"You do realise that if you put any of these lurid fantasies into the Gazette the next place we'll meet will be the libel court?" she asked. "And believe me, the damages would not be small. Quite enough, I should think, to see your career washed down the plug-hole. I'm really quite surprised that Ted Grant lets you out on a so-called assignment like this without a nanny. You really do seem to be out of your depth. Now, if you'll excuse me, I have another appointment in fifteen minutes at the Town Hall. If I see Dave, I'll certainly tell him you were asking after him, shall I?"

Annie Costello rose to her not inconsiderable height and pressed a buzzer on her desk. When her assistant poked her head around the office door, she waved at Laura, her eyes flashing with suppressed anger.

"Ms Ackroyd is just leaving," she said. "Please see her out." The last thing Laura noticed out of the corner of her eye as she was escorted ignominiously out of the office was Ms Costello reaching for her phone and punching in a number with enough force to splinter the enamel on her nails.

Outside the Three Ridings building, Laura found the rain lashing down with its now customary fury. She glanced at her watch. What she really wanted to do was to talk to Michael Thackeray to discover if he had made any progress with his inquiries into City Ventures and its unexpectedly connected female directors, but she knew she was already overdue at the Gazette office, where Ted Grant was preparing for a campaign of World War Two proportions as the council finally issued evacuation plans for the areas of the town now imminently threatened with inundation. In any case, she thought as she pulled up the hood on her waterproof jacket and yanked the toggles tight under her chin, Michael would not appreciate her inquiries any more than Annie Costello had done. And she had, she thought, suffered enough humiliation for one morning.

Cautiously she negotiated her way across the town centre where the gutters had turned into torrents on the hilly shopping streets and water was beginning to form lakes across the town hall square. It was only the middle of the morning but the street lights flickered in indecision unsure how to respond to the dark clouds which hid the hills above the town and pressed down onto the gilded top of the town hall's Italianate tower. A bus lurched past sending a wave of dirty water over pedestrians who had strayed too close to the carriageway. The whole town, Laura thought, with its unexpected lakes and streams and inhabitants scurrying to find shelter from the relentless downpour, was beginning to take on an atmosphere of crisis. She had no doubt at all that Ted was bashing out his latest Churchillian editorial at that very moment.

She turned down Chapel Street, which offered a short cut back to the office, and glanced briefly at the blackened ruin of the Carib Club, propped up now by scaffolding, as she stepped into the roadway to avoid the hoarding which protected the ground floor of the building from intruders. There were no Asian youths loitering now and she had glanced behind her to check for approaching traffic but saw none. Nor, muffled up in her waterproof hood, did she hear anything behind her before she was struck a crushing blow across the head and shoulders and fell face down on the puddled roadway. Her last thought as blackness engulfed her was that the Carib was collapsing on top of her and that this was a supremely pointless way to die.

Michael Thackeray raced into the accident and emergency department at the Bradfield Infirmary as if pursued by all the hounds of hell. He had not bothered with a coat, and his hair and the shoulders of his jacket were sodden and his eyes wild. The sights and sounds and smells of the busy waiting area choked the breath out of his body as he hesitated close to reception and tried to steady himself on palsied arms against the desk. But before the harassed reception clerk could turn her attention to him, he caught a glimpse of a police uniform across the room, changed his mind and spun away through the crush in that direction, grabbing the startled officer's arm in a fierce grip.

"Did you come in with Laura Ackroyd? An accident in Chapel Street?"

"Sorry, sir. You are…? The young constable unwittingly put his career on the line as Thackeray's face suffused with fury.

"DCI Thackeray," he spat. "Where is she, for Christ's sake? She's my wife." It was not until he had followed the now red-faced officer along the row of emergency cubicles that Thackeray realised what he had said and groaned.

A young Asian doctor Thackeray recognised vaguely was coming out of the end cubicle as the two policemen approached. The constable nodded and turned on his heel without speaking.

"How is she?" Thackeray asked, his voice almost failing him now.

"She's fine," the doctor said brusquely. "Badly bruised but conscious now. No fractures, fortunately. But we'll keep her in overnight. Concussion, you know…" But Thackeray was no longer listening. He pushed past the doctor and pulled back the flimsy curtains round the cubicle to find Laura lying on a high bed, her red hair scraped back and partly confined under bandages, her face pale where it was not disfigured with multi-coloured bruises already darkening from red to black, and her eyes dull. He stood still for a moment, hardly able to breathe before walking the few steps to the bed and kissing her cheek and taking her hand in a grip so fierce that she thought he would crush her fingers.

"Jesus Christ," he said. "I thought you were dead."

"They'll have to try harder than that," Laura croaked, her eyes full of tears, as she gently extricated her hand from Thackeray's. Every bone in her body seemed to be complaining at once and the painkillers the doctor had prescribed had either not begun to kick in yet or were too mild to help.

"They? They told me it was a car...?" Thackeray said. Laura tried to shrug and winced instead, closing her eyes for a second or two until the pain subsided.

"I don't think cars kick you in the ribs," she said. "I've apparently got a nice clear boot print on my back. A pretty effective way of telling me to mind my own business, I suppose."

"Foreman?" Thackeray asked.

"I talked to him," Laura admitted faintly. "He wasn't very happy."

"I asked you..." Thackeray began and then shook his head helplessly, knowing that this was not the place and that in any case he was wasting his time.

"I'll have him," he said instead, as a nurse pulled back the curtains and came into the cubicle. "I'll have that bastard if it's the last thing I do." The nurse looked startled and glanced behind her as if seeking help.

"There's a bed for Laura in the ward now," she said. "The porters will be here in a minute to take her up."

"And the other thing," Laura said quickly, grabbing Thackeray's hand. "Take a look at Three Ridings Housing. I think City Ventures has been doing their building too. Annie Costello's effectively been commissioning herself."

"You never give up, do you? Forget all that for now," Thackeray said as a porter began to push a wheelchair alongside the bed. He leaned over Laura and took her bruised face in his hands, gentle now, as he kissed her cheek.

"Don't do this to me," he whispered, his voice hoarse. "Please, Laura. It was like...Well, never mind."

"I'm sorry," Laura whispered back, but Thackeray had already turned on his heel and marched back into the reception are where the uniformed constable was chatting to the young woman on the desk. When he saw Thackeray approaching he flushed again and stood to attention.

"Sir?" he said.

"Stay at her bedside till I tell you otherwise," Thackeray

said. "I'll clear it for you back at the nick. I'm treating this as a case of attempted murder."

* * *

Dusk came early that evening, like a wet grey blanket over the town, so dense that the streetlights, which had flickered into life in mid-afternoon, could barely penetrate the gloom. Kevin Mower, with Dizzy B beside him, parked unobtrusively in a small car park almost opposite the offices of Foreman Security Services and watched as the rain drummed on the car roof and poured down the windscreen, and the water level in the roadway swirled across the tarmac and began to lap over the kerbstones. Water company vans were parked at the far end of the street and through traffic had been diverted as officials worked their way from one tall stone Victorian building to the next, issuing evacuation notices to the businesses in each block. Gradually most of the employees had picked their way through the flood to higher ground while lorries arrived out-side some of the offices and people began moving out filing cabinets and boxes of documents, computers – even furniture. Mower had been listening to the local radio station, which was providing regular updates on the floods, and he knew that this particular street in the lower-lying part of the town, had been built directly over the subterranean channel of the Beck soon after it had been enclosed. Some of the cellars even had inspection manholes which the water company now feared would give way under the pressure of the water beneath, allowing water to gush upwards and in all likeli-hood weaken the foundations of the buildings above. If that happened all bets were off and Mower was not surprised that the threatened firms were making every effort to salvage what they could.

Barry Foreman's headquarters lay at the furthest end of the street and, by four o'clock, regular visits by the firms' own vehicles had taken away quantities of electronic equipment and paperwork. But some of the lights remained on inside the building and Mower knew that Foreman himself had not left the premises.

"Do we know where all that stuff's gone?" Dizzy B asked.

"The boss has got someone checking that out," Mower said. Outside the street was rapidly emptying, lights going out, doors being closed on the offices behind them, abandoning them to an uncertain fate. Soon only the streetlights and two remaining lights on the ground floor of Foreman's building were left to reflect on the water swirling about the roadway and beginning to lap at the stone steps which led up to the main doors of each block.

"Look," Dizzy said softly and Mower turned the radio right down and picked up his mobile phone. A Land Rover had entered the street from the end furthest away from the water board vans, creating a bow-wave through the flood, and pulled up outside the security services office.

"That's Foreman's four-by-four," Mower said. He pressed a number on his phone. "Guv?" he said quietly. "I think we may have something." He peered through the gloom. "It looks like our friend Jake from the drug squad's just arrived to pick Foreman up."

"Jake?" Sanderson asked when Mower had disconnected.

"You don't need to know," Mower said. "God knows what name he's working under anyway."

"He's bringing something out," Dizzy said. "Boxes of stuff. And he's a copper?" Mower quickly relayed that to Thackeray.

"Looks dodgy, guv," he said.

"Good," Thackeray said. "Dodgy's all I need to know to convince Jack Longley we need to act. I'm coming down there. If the building's going to be abandoned we need to get in there with a search team before it floods if we can. And I'll get traffic organised to stop the Land Rover and search it as soon as it comes out of the flood zone. There's only one route out."

"The water people seem to think eight o'clock tonight's

going to be the most dangerous time," Mower said. "They want the area cleared by six."

"A good enough reason to get an emergency warrant to search the place then," Thackeray said, and cut the connection.

"Is this official now?" Dizzy asked Mower. The sergeant shrugged.

"Looks like it," he said. "Though I'm not sure what the Super'll make of our little surveillance."

It was a couple of minutes later, as they sat watching Jake and Barry Foreman himself ferry more boxes and packages to the Land Rover, that Dizzy B took Mower's arm.

"We've got trouble," he whispered, pointing to the side of the building where it was just possible to see a slight figure crouching in the shadows watching events just as they were doing from the other side of the street. Jake and Foreman went back inside the building together, leaving the doors half open and casting a single beam of light into the storm.

"I've a very nasty feeling I know who that is," Dizzy said. "And last time I saw him, as you'll recall, he was in possession of a serious looking automatic."

"Stevie Maddison," Mower groaned. He called Thackeray again.

"I'm on foot three minutes away at the end of the street," the DCI said. "Don't do anything till I get to you." But his instruction was too late. While Mower had been distracted by his phone call Dizzy B had opened the car door and was already sprinting, dreadlocks flying, through the ankle deep water which now spread right up to the front steps of the office buildings on the other side of the street. Mower watched, horrified, as the boy in the shadows, instead of fleeing as he expected, turned towards Sanderson and fired. Sanderson swerved but did not appear to be hit as the boy turned and made for the open doors of Foreman Security Services and dodged inside, closely followed by the DJ.

"Where are they?" Michael Thackeray asked as he pulled

open one of the rear doors of Mower's car and dropped into the seat behind him, water dripping from his hair and jacket. "Where's Sanderson? I thought you said he was with you?"

"He is, he was, he's gone playing James Bond," Mower said. "Sorry, guv, I couldn't stop him. He's chasing after the kid with the gun and this whole operation's going pear-shaped."

"No way," Thackeray said. He used his own mobile phone this time to call headquarters and summon up armed officers and as many other reinforcements as could be mustered in the middle of a civil emergency. "If that bastard's Foreman's got a Land Rover full of drugs out there we'll hang him out to dry."

"Great," Mower said. "But at this precise moment he's also got Dizzy and a fourteen-year-old boy in there and at least one of them's armed."

But even that no longer seemed to be the case as Foreman himself came out of the building holding a coat over his head to protect himself from the driving rain, ran down the steps and jumped into the four by four and drove off, swerving wildly through the water as he accelerated.

"Don't worry, he won't get far," Thackeray said. "Come on, we'd better take a look." Procedure might have dictated waiting for reinforcements but Mower was not in a mood to argue. The two men waded across the flooded road and, as they approached the building carefully from one side, the door was flung wide open and they could see Dizzy B on the top step waving wildly in their direction.

"I couldn't stop him," he shouted. "I was too fucking late."

"Where's the gun?" Thackeray asked harshly.

"It doesn't matter now, does it?" Dizzy B replied, and it looked as if his cheeks were wet with tears rather than rain.

They followed him through the reception area into an office with several workstations and immediately saw why he was so distraught. Stevie Maddison lay where he had fallen in front of a desk, his gun still clutched in his hand and a single bullet wound to the side of the head matting his short fair hair with rapidly darkening blood. His blue eyes were still open, gazing sightlessly at the world with a faint look of surprise in them, his jeans and t-shirt, sodden from the rain, clinging to a skinny body which appeared heartbreakingly small to the men crowded above him. The man Mower knew as DS Jake Moody lay sprawled on the other side of the room, close to a doorway leading to the rear of the building, his white shirt soaked with blood, another gun at his feet. Mower crouched down and felt his neck for a pulse.

"He's just about alive," he said feeling a flicker beneath his fingers. "He's our undercover man," he said. "Drug squad. Name's Moody."

"So what's the fuck he doing shooting kids?" Dizzy screamed at Thackeray. "What the fuck's going on? And where's the other bastard who was here just now, the bastard who ran?"

"Taken care of," Thackeray said shortly, using his mobile to ask for an ambulance urgently. He glanced around the room.

"Did you see exactly what happened?" he asked.

Sanderson shook his head, looking dazed now as the full enormity of the situation sank in.

"I heard the first shot as I came through the door," he said, his voice husky now. "I kept down, man. I'm not kidding you. Over there, behind the reception desk. Then more shots and one guy ran out and after that nothing, silence." Thackeray nodded.

"This is a crime scene," Thackeray said pointedly to Dizzy B, glancing at Stevie Maddison's huddled body and wondering if it would ever be possible to establish who was assailant and who was victim here. "I want you to wait outside till the ambulance and the heavy mob turn up and tell them what's happened. Kevin and I have something we must do before this place floods and evidence gets washed away."

They had all been conscious since they had entered the building that there was a rushing noise coming from further inside. As Dizzy B turned away to go outside, shoulders slumped, Thackeray led Mower further back through the offices until they traced the noise to an open door leading to descending stone steps. The rushing sound became louder, drowning out coherent speech but Thackeray did not hesitate, leading the way down steps into a cellar where a single light-bulb still burned. The floor was dry except for a damp trail of footprints from the steps to the corner where a heavy metal plate had been lifted to reveal what Mower realised must be Bradfield's hidden waterway, rushing beneath them with terrifying force.

"Why?" Thackeray mouthed at Mower pointing at the trail of water. He hurried to the manhole and lay flat on the floor, his face, as he leaned into the cavity, splashed by the torrent, making it even harder to see anything at all. Reaching around as far as he could stretch, he realised that on the downward side of the icy cold flow there was something solid. He could make out the mesh of a thick wire cage of some kind, which had been attached to the roof of the culvert that for large parts of the year carried no more than a modest stream of water down to the River Maze.

Suddenly something pale bobbed into view and wedged itself against the mesh. Thackeray reached forward to catch it but it was not easy to estimate the distance in the near-darkness and, after a frantic second's scrabbling at the edge of the manhole trying to regain his balance, he pitched forward into the stream head first and the rushing water closed over his head.

Shouting incomprehensibly and uselessly against the noise of the water, Mower flung himself flat and leaned as far as he dared into the opening, sick with fear and not seriously expecting ever to see Thackeray alive again. But to his astonishment after a few seconds he found that he could just make out the DCI wedged against some sort of grille with his nose and mouth barely above the waterline. More often than not the swirling stream rose and hid him completely, but every time he emerged again, his head bent under the culvert's stone roof, fingers clinging grimly to the mesh behind him, coughing and choking but undoubtedly still alive. If the mesh gave way, Mower thought, he would be gone, carried helplessly for the mile or so it took the culvert to carry the torrent back into the open air of a rocky defile between the hills on the eastern side of the town, and no doubt drowned long before he reached the open air.

For a moment the two men's eyes locked and Mower seemed to hesitate. Thackeray knew why and, for a split second, as the water surged over his head again and he was left choking helplessly in his sliver of breathing space against the slimy stone of the roof, he saw the face of Rita Desai, her eyes as full of light and laughter as they had often been before he and Mower had last seen her sprawling lifeless in the dust of a haulier's yard.

Half drowned, his chest compressed by the sheer force of the rushing water so that breathing was almost impossible even when his nose and mouth were above the surface, Thackeray almost gave up only to see, when he had shaken the water out of his eyes one last time, that Mower was leaning down as far as he could and trying to reach him. With a desperation born of despair, Thackeray eased himself slowly towards Mower against the pressure of the stream until the two men could just clasp hands.

With his own body now spreadeagled right across the open manhole, one hand clutching the edge with desperate determination, Mower hauled Thackeray inch by inch towards him until he too could gain a purchase with icy fingers on the edge of the manhole and, between them, arms locked, they could begin to haul themselves out of the reach of the greedy, sucking black torrent below.

It took minutes, every one of which seemed like an hour, before Thackeray scrambled out to fling himself flat on the floor like a landed fish, choking and gasping, alongside Mower who had also rolled away from the manhole onto his back, utterly exhausted. It was Thackeray who finally found the strength to get back to his feet, shivering in his sodden clothes, to push the metal manhole cover back into place, hiding the deadly stream and reducing the noise to the point where conversation was just about possible. He held out a hand and pulled Mower upright.

"I owe you," he said, holding on to the sergeant's hand for a second.

"Think nothing of it, guv, " Mower said with an attempt at a smile. If it had been him who had gone into the water like that, he thought, he might not have made any particular effort to get out.

"There's a sort of cage down there which Foreman must have been using for storage," Thackeray said. "In normal times it wouldn't have interfered with the flow of water, so no one could have guessed. It's only recently the water company started complaining about the flow of the Beck not being right. I guess if Foreman's made off with his stash of heroin or cocaine or whatever, the water's running more smoothly tonight. They might not get quite the inundation they were expecting."

"Shall we get out of here, just in case," Mower said, glancing at the manhole cover which was rattling from the pressure below.

"I don't think it'll come up that way, but this place will certainly flood if the water in the street gets into the offices and pours into the cellars from above," Thackeray said. It was only then that Mower noticed that the DCI had reached inside his sodden jacket and was clutching something in his left hand.

"What's the fuck's that?" he asked, not sure that he wanted to know the answer.

Thackeray shook his head, his eyes unreadable in the gloom.

"I'm not sure," he said. "But I think it's a baby's skull."

"Oh, Jesus," Mower whispered with a long slow sigh.

Chapter Twenty

"You're not going to like this," Michael Thackeray said to superintendent Jack Longley as he brought him up to date with developments the next morning. Apart from the darker than normal circles under his eyes he gave no indication that he had come so close to death the previous day. Only his wrenched muscles, and throat and lungs which felt as if they had been scoured with sandpaper, reminded him of how close to the edge he had been. His whole being now was focused fiercely on Barry Foreman and making sure that this time the security boss did not slip through his fingers.

"Try me," Longley said.

"I want to interview DS Jake Moody under caution, as a suspect."

"The drug squad aren't going to like that," Longley said, although his own expression remained relatively unperturbed. "It's when you tell me you want to interview me under caution that I might get alarmed these days. Did you read about the number of senior officers being suspended? Why Moody, any road? I thought he was a victim, not a suspect."

"Maybe," Thackeray said. "Obviously I want his version of what happened when he was shot." He hesitated.

"But that's not all?" Longley prompted. "You think he went over to the other side? He wouldn't be the first undercover cop to do that."

"Ray Walter hinted he'd not been providing much intelligence. Why the hell not, I'd like to know," Thackeray said.

"You think he was taking back-handers from Foreman? Playing both sides against the middle?"

"Maybe worse than that," Thackeray said. "Now we've got Foreman's fingerprints they turn out to match some on the dirty videos at Stanley Wilson's place. And our own intelligence did come up with something interesting when they were trying to match the unknown prints from Wilson's house. They came up with a Brian Freeman, who did a long stretch when he was in his twenties. He was an enforcer for a gangland boss in Manchester. One of the things he enjoyed was stubbing out cigarettes on people. And guess who he shared a cell with in Strangeways."

"Stanley Wilson?" Longley hazarded.

"I guess Foreman was terrified Wilson had told me about his change of identity. That would really have scuppered him just at the point when he was ingratiating himself into the legitimate business community in Bradfield. I don't know if anyone else was with him at Wilson's place when he was killed but I'm sure Foreman was there himself. And I guess he enjoyed the violence just as much as he used to in the old days." Thackeray hesitated.

"I want Moody's prints taken," he said. "Wilson's long-time boyfriend, Harman, reckoned that Stanley Wilson had a new black boyfriend but it's just possible that if the person he saw was actually Moody, he was visiting Wilson for his boss and Harman jumped to the wrong conclusion. I want Moody's prints taken and I want to see if Harman can identify him. If he was there, I want to know why, and what he knows about Foreman's visits."

"Moody's not gay, is he?"

"That's not the point," Thackeray said impatiently. "Foreman has been to Wilson's place, the home of a man he says was nothing more than an insignificant clerk in his organisation. Foreman's been paying him over the odds – bonuses he says, set-up money for Wilson's porn business more likely, part of Foreman's money laundering operations, like the development company in Leeds and God knows what else when we've finished going through his books. But recently, according to Val Ridley, who's been trawling through Wilson's bank statements, Foreman's been paying Wilson £1000 a month, on top of his salary. That looks more like blackmail to me, and Foreman's not a man to put up with that for long."

"You think Foreman tortured him and killed him?" Longley asked.

"It's a distinct possibility. So far we've only charged him with possession of the consignment of drugs he had in the Land Rover when he was arrested, but there was enough there to remand him in custody while we get our act together on the rest. And we've got his prints and a DNA sample so the forensic people can get to work on those. But before I start questioning him about Wilson I want to get to grips with Moody and find out just how far his undercover activities took him. Even if he's clean he knows more about Foreman's movements over the last few months than anyone else. We've possibly linked Foreman to one murder now and there are three more suspicious deaths being investigated. Mower says that he found a lad who saw something near Donna Maitland's flat the night she died. That needs chasing up too. But I need Moody's evidence first, and I need it quickly, not in a couple of weeks when the drug squad have debriefed him and decided what they want to tell us and what they don't."

"Is he fit enough to talk?" Longley asked. Thackeray shrugged.

"He's regained consciousness but he's lost a lot of blood so it'll be a while before I can do a detailed interview. But as soon as the doctors give the OK, I want to be in there, getting whatever I can."

"And Foreman's girlfriend?" Longley asked.

Thackeray glanced bleakly out of the window where it was possible to see streaks of blue in the sky above the cherry trees in the town hall square, and a pale sunlight for the first time for months.

"The underwater search team are down there now," he said. "They'll be there, all three of them, Karen and the babies, I'm sure of that, but how the hell we'll ever prove that Foreman dumped them there I can't imagine. There won't be

266

much forensic evidence if they've been trapped in that torrent for a while, possibly not even a cause of death."

"They probably drowned anyway," Longley said, his face sombre. "Poor little beggars."

"You can just imagine what an imaginative defence lawyer would get out of that: Karen was so distraught when she and Foreman split up that she chucked the babies in the Beck and then herself; or else, any one of Foreman's employees could have known about the access to the water from his cellar and dumped them in for some reason of their own; or else, all three of them slipped into the water accidentally in one of the downpours we've been having and the bodies were washed as far as the obstruction..."

"Could they have become trapped in Foreman's cage arrangement if they'd gone in higher up?" Longley asked.

"It's just about possible, though it would be a bizarre coincidence if that's what happened. The upstream side of the hiding place was only constructed out of wire strands. A body could have got entangled there, and then taken the full force of the water as the flood rose. It only needs the babies' pushchair to turn up somewhere higher up the stream to get him off the hook." Thackeray shrugged dispiritedly.

"And we all believe in Santa Claus," Longley said. "Talk to the Crown Prosecution Service. You were right about Foreman and I was wrong and that's the one I'd really like to pin on the bastard if we pin a murder on him at all."

"Oh yes," Thackeray said. "Don't worry. If it's humanly possible to make a charge stick, I'll do it. I can promise you that."

They buried Stevie Maddison and his best mate Derek Whitby side by side in the municipal cemetery high on one of Bradfield's seven windswept hills, Derek's friends and relations muffled in dark coats and hats on one side of the double grave, Stevie's, fewer in number and more casual, shivering in insubstantial multicoloured jackets, on the other. As the commital prayers ended and the ritual handfuls of dirt rained down onto the two coffins a tall black woman, her pashmina streaming in the wind, began to sing 'Amazing Grace' in a voice so powerful that not even the bitter Pennine gusts could whip the sound away completely. Standing between a tired-looking Michael Thackeray and a newly clean-shaven Kevin Mower at the rear of the crowd of mourners, Laura Ackroyd, wearing a soft black velvet beret to conceal the bandage she still had round her head, shivered and felt the tears prickle.

"What a bloody waste it all is," she said. Thackeray put his arm around her protectively as the hymn ended, the mourners began to straggle away and the grave diggers moved forward with their shovels, anxious to complete their thankless task before the dark clouds on the horizon unleashed more rain.

"Come on," he said. "Some good came of it all in the end."

"Foreman, you mean?"

"So far we've only charged him with drug-dealing but that's open and shut, and he'll go away for a long time. The rest will take longer to unravel but I'll have him for at least one of the deaths in the end."

"Karen and the babies, surely," Laura said with a shudder but Thackeray shook his head.

"Now the water's gone down, most of the remains have been recovered," he said, his face grim and Laura knew better than to press him for more. "They were all there, all three of them, but it'll be a forensic nightmare to prove how they died, let alone who killed them."

"And Stevie and Derek?" Laura asked, glancing back at the cars in which the Maddison and Whitby families were embarking on the rest of their shattered lives. "They were only kids."

"All those forensic reports are in now and the CPS is looking at charges of murder. Foreman's claiming that Stevie and Jake Moody, our undercover man, both had guns and shot each other, which we might have believed from the circumstantial evidence, but someone wiped the second gun clean after the shooting and the only person who could have done that was Foreman, no doubt in a moment of panic. Moody certainly wasn't in a fit state to be worrying about fingerprints on triggers. Foreman's claiming he tried to stop Moody from killing the boy but I think it's more likely Moody tried to stop Foreman so Foreman shot him as well. They removed three bullets from Moody's body, two of which definitely came from Stevie's gun, the third is so badly damaged that it's difficult to tell. They're still working on it. He's lucky to be alive."

"What's Moody saying?" Laura asked. "Isn't he fit to talk yet?"

"Moody's saying a lot of things, none of which make much sense," Thackeray said.

"Jake Moody was as bent as a three pound note," Mower suddenly said. "He was lording it around the Heights in the Beamer as Mr. Pound, Foreman's minder. Why, if he wasn't involved in the drug trade? He was in it up to his neck. Why else didn't he call his guv'nor when Foreman decided to move all the gear from his cellar to avoid the flood? If he was undercover, what the hell was he undercover for if it wasn't to look for an opportunity like that, to nick them with a serious consignment in transit, no argument? As it was, it was pure chance Dizzy and I were there to see what was going on and make sure Foreman was stopped in the Land Rover. As far as I can see the only thing we've got to thank for pinning Foreman down at all was the bloody weather."

"The drug squad don't like that interpretation," Thackeray said.

"They wouldn't, would they?" Mower came back quickly.

"Moody's claiming he did everything an undercover cop could safely do in the circumstances. But don't worry, Kevin. We're looking very carefully at his story too."

"And pigs might fly," Mower muttered.

The three of them walked towards Thackeray's car which

he had parked behind the two families' funeral cars on the gravel pathway some hundred yards from the new graves. Behind them the other mourners beginning to scatter, shoulders hunched against the wind and the first spots of rain, but as Thackeray unlocked the driver's door, Laura took his arm.

"This looks like a delegation," she said softly. The mothers of the dead boys were approaching side-by-side, each of them red-eyed but with a determination that was not diminished by the chilly gusts which made Laura shiver and Mrs Whitby clutch firmly at her large black hat. Behind them some of the rest of the mourners turned and stood watching in silence, like an accusing chorus.

"Inspector Thackeray? I'm Dawn Whitby, Derek's mother..."

"I know," Thackeray said. "And can I say how sorry..."

"It's too late for that now, Inspector," Mrs. Whitby said firmly. "Too late for Derek and for Stevie. What happened to them has happened. But Mrs. Maddison and me, we've come to a decision. We want to tell you some things that we learned while this was going on, some things we heard, some things we seen with our own eyes. We want to make sure now that no other boys die like our boys died. So if you want evidence, we will give you evidence. It's the least we can do, the least I can do before I go home to Jamaica. And we think if we decide to talk to you then maybe some others will too."

"We want the man they call Ounce off the estate," Lorraine Maddison broke in. "He's a dealer and he's maybe a killer too. Stevie told me he saw him the night Derek died. He was there on the roof when Derek was pushed off Priestley House."

"And he was there when I was trying to get Derek clean," Dawn Whitby said. "He was brazen that one. He came to my home offering Derek cheap drugs. He was the one who wanted to keep him hooked."

"You didn't say you knew who the dealer was," Laura said softly, recalling her own interview with Dawn Whitby. Derek's mother glanced away and Laura guessed that even she had been too afraid to disclose everything she knew.

"Do you know who he is?" Thackeray asked carefully. "Is Ounce his real name? Can you identify him?"

"Ounce is what the kids call him. It's like a joke, I suppose. He's called Mr Pound," Dawn Whitby said. "You see him aroun'. He drives a big blue BMW. I've seen him, even at the Project I've seen him where you'd think Donna Maitland would have more sense than to let a dealer in." She glanced at Lorraine Maddison.

"We can identify him," she said.

Thackeray's eyes met Mower's for a second and he saw the triumph there.

"It's Moody," Mower mouthed. "I bloody knew he was bent."

"You'll make statements telling us everything you've learned about Mr. Pound?" Thackeray asked the two women, who had linked arms now against the bitter wind. They nodded.

"Gotcha," Mower said, and raised a clenched fist in the air.

Later that evening, when Thackeray brought a tray to Laura where she was sitting with her feet up on a sofa, eyes closed and bandaged head resting against a cushion, the fury which had threatened to consume him ever since he had been told she had been taken to hospital gradually eased.

"You're safe now," he said quietly, putting the tray down on the coffee table and kissing her bruised cheek gently. She opened her eyes and smiled.

"And you're learning to cook. I'll domesticate you yet."

"I wouldn't bank on it," he said, peering at the scrambled eggs and bacon he had prepared with a sceptical look before perching himself on the edge of the sofa beside her.

"Are you all right?" she asked. "Now you've got Foreman? Is that the end of it?"

Thackeray did not reply immediately. Had he, he wondered, really exorcised the obsession with Foreman.

"Foreman's saying absolutely nothing but Moody's

decided that he's on our side after all," he said slowly. "He's giving us chapter and verse on Foreman's drug business, saying he had to get seriously involved to gain Foreman's confidence. And there's enough to charge Foreman with Wilson's murder on Moody's evidence. He says he dropped Foreman off at his house that day – not an unusual event, apparently. Foreman used to go there personally to pick up his dirty videos. And forensics have come up with corroboration of Moody's version of what happened the night of the flood. One of the bullets they took out of his body came from the gun that killed Stevie. Only Foreman could have fired it."

"So you've got him for two murders."

"There's a lot of loose ends though," Thackeray said. "It'll take months to be sure what will stand up in court and what won't. Donna Maitland's death, that's the one which is exercising Kevin Mower, but the crime scene was so contaminated that we'll be unlikely to make a case against anyone there. And Derek, the boy on the roof: Moody denies he was anywhere near the Heights that night, and no one else has come forward in spite of Derek's mother's efforts."

"And Karen and the babies?"

"Moody says he knows nothing about any of that either."

"Do you believe him? He could be covering his own tracks," Laura suggested.

"He could, but if we want him to give evidence as a witness on the rest we may have to accept we'll never know the truth about some things. It's rough justice but maybe the best we can do."

"I thought you didn't make deals."

"We don't make deals," Thackeray said. "But the CPS assess how likely we are to get a conviction, you know that. And you know what that estate's like. There's not enough evidence to pin down anyone for Donna's death, or Derek's, nor likely to be."

"Or to catch whoever tried to kill me?" Laura said, turning

away, overtaken by the tearfulness which had dogged since she came out of hospital.

"Maybe not," Thackeray admitted. "We've not traced any witnesses."

Thackeray sat very still for a moment beside her before he took her hand in his.

"That day," he began hesitantly. "That day, I really thought I'd lost you. I thought history was repeating itself and I was going to be alone again." His grip on Laura's hand tightened. "And the thing that hurt most was that I might have missed my chance of asking you what I should have asked you long ago."

Laura reached forward and put a finger on his lips.

"For a man who asks questions for a living you've been remarkably slow with this one," she said. "But I'm not sure this is the moment to choose. Can you give me some time?"

Thackeray looked for a moment as if he had been struck across the face, but then he nodded and touched her bruised cheek gently.

"Sorry," he said. "As much time as you need."